I0565561

THE YEAR OF THE DOG

A SLEEPING DOGS THRILLER

By:
John Wayne Falbey

The Year Of The Dog is a work of fiction. Any references to names, characters, brands, media, incidents, historical events, real people, or real places are the product of the author's imagination or are used fictitiously. Any resemblance to actual events or places or persons, living or dead, business establishments, events, or locales is entirely coincidental. The publication or use of trademarked products referenced in this work of fiction is not authorized, associated with, or sponsored by the trademark owners.

Copyright © 2016 John Wayne Falbey.

All rights reserved. Except as permitted under U.S. Copyright Act of 1976, no part of this publication may be reproduced, distributed, or transmitted in any form or by any means (electronic, mechanical, photocopying, recording, or otherwise), or stored in a database or retrieval system, without the prior written permission of both the copyright owner and the publisher.

Copyright fuels creativity, encourages diverse voices, promotes free speech, and creates a vibrant culture. Thank you for buying an authorized edition of this book. You are supporting writers by complying with international copyright laws by not reproducing, scanning, or distributing any part of it in any form without permission.

ISBN: 978-0-9855187-8-3 Print Edition
ISBN: 078-0-9855187-6-9 Digital Edition
Cover Design: Tatiana Vila

✵ Created with Vellum

Dedication

You don't choose your family. They are God's gift to you, as you are to them.

—Desmond Tutu

My wife and I are so fortunate. What are the odds that all five of our kids would grow up to be citizen-patriots, industrious, civic-minded, and terrific parents in their own right? I'm sure my laissez-faire approach to parenting ("experience is the best teacher; let 'em learn the hard way") had little, if anything, to do with their successes. Credit for that goes to the person who made countless sacrifices, drew on boundless energy and love, and instilled in each of them by example what taking personal responsibility means. That person is Phyllis Ann, my "Annie", who continues to show me every day what unconditional love and patience truly are. Sweetheart, you are the prettiest, calmest, most well-adjusted person I've ever known. You really don't know how special you are. And that makes you even more special.

For Those Who Came Late

This is the third novel in the Sleeping Dogs series of thrillers that incorporates international espionage, geopolitical intrigue, and paramilitary action. Readers have compared the thrillers in the Sleeping Dogs series to those of the late Vince Flynn, Tom Clancy and Brad Taylor, among others. The books combine relentless action, crisp dialogue, fully drawn characters, and thought provoking plot twists. Squarely on the same page with books by Vince Flynn, David Baldacci, Brad Taylor, and other best-selling thriller writers.

The following is a brief summary of the action in the first two books in the series, *Sleeping Dogs: The Awakening* and *Endangered Species*.

Sleeping Dogs: The Awakening (A #1 international bestseller on Amazon)

The president of the United States has been targeted for assassination—by the leaders of his *own* party. The killing must appear as if those who oppose the administration are responsible. To prevent the crime, the opposition turns to the only force that can stop it this late in the game—a mysterious hunter-killer team known as the Sleeping Dogs. This deadliest of black ops units was formed to carry out America's wettest, most politically incorrect missions abroad. A subsequently elected U.S. president, fearing discovery of the unit's activities could spark an international crisis, ordered its members to be terminated with extreme prejudice. They escaped by faking their deaths in a plane crash, and went to ground. Now, several years later, they are asked to leave the safety of their anonymity and risk their lives for their country one more time.

A seemingly unconnected car crash rapidly escalates into a series of plot twists involving Russian agents, crooked politicians, Ukrainian gangsters, a billionaire international arbitrageur, a secret society of patriots in the military and intelligence communities, the CIA, a doggedly determined FBI agent, and the six most dangerous men on earth—the surviving members of the paramilitary unit known as the Sleeping Dogs. As the Dogs relentlessly pursue the would-be assassins and their handlers, they begin to uncover, layer by layer, a plot to bring America to her knees and impose a one-world government on the entire planet. The enemy is powerful, with access to unlimited funds and the ability to manipulate rogue nations. If it succeeds, the world will descend into chaos and anarchy; and time is running out. But the one asset the enemy doesn't have is the Sleeping Dogs.

Endangered Species, A Sleeping Dogs Thriller

The world is descending into chaos. America is like a rudderless ship—its elected government gridlocked and ineffective. Rogue governments spit on Old Glory and defy a weakening America to stop them. Religious fanatics are dedicated to butchering all the world's citizens who don't convert to their primitive, seventh-century dogma. And the worst is yet to come. From Russian aggression to worldwide jihadism, from China's designs on Southeast Asia and beyond to a morally and financially bankrupt European Union, from violent and expanding drug cartels to Iranian nuclear ambitions, the members of the Alliance for Global Unity—AGU are close to achieving their goal: the anarchy and chaos that will usher in a single world government with them ruling it.

But appearances can be deceiving. In America, a shadow government of old fashioned patriots is working to change the course of events. Armed with deep financial resources of their own and critical positions in the government, military, and intelligence communities, they just might succeed. The key to victory is the world's deadliest hunter-killer black ops unit—the Sleeping Dogs. But keeping the six Sleeping Dogs alive is challenging. An outstanding Presidential Decision Directive ordered these men to be terminated with extreme prejudice. A vengeful FBI agent, believing his wife had an affair with the unit's leader, Brendan Whelan, is pursuing him with homicide on his mind. A rogue Russian agent seeks revenge because his mission to assassinate the president of the United States was thwarted by the Dogs. And, most chillingly, a huge and mysterious brute named Maksym is systematically hunting the Dogs down individually. The fate of the free world hangs in the balance.

Cast of Characters

This novel is one of a series. Several characters recur throughout the series. Others from earlier books in the series may be referred to in subsequent books.

Brendan Whelan (WHEY-luhn) – by appearances, an innkeeper in Dingle, Ireland, but also the reluctant leader of the deadly hunter-killer black ops unit known as the Sleeping Dogs

The Sleeping Dogs – together with Brendan Whelan, the most lethal black ops unit in history; genetically evolved—Mother Nature's beta models for humans in future generations:

Sven Larsen – the "Man With No Neck," he is the most physically powerful of the Dogs and closest to Whelan

Marc Kirkland – the "Zen Warrior," he is completely dedicated to mastering every style of martial arts fighting and weapons techniques

Nick Stensen – the "Serial Killer," a loner and certifiably insane; his singular is hunting down and killing criminals who have escaped the punishment of the law

Quentin Thomas – the "Philosopher King," is the best pure athlete of the Dogs and a professor of Eastern philosophies

Rafe Almeida (RAIF al-MAY-duh)– the "Runt Of The Litter," is genetically gifted like the other Dogs, but an inveterate substance abuser and skirt-chaser

Liam (LEE-um) *Stone* – "Lime Stone," is an Aussie who also is genetically gifted like the other Dogs, but is a recent member recruited to the unit

Caitlin (KATE-lin) *Whelan* – Brendan's wife, partner, and mother of Sean and Declan, two young lads who appear to be chips off the old block

Cliff Levell (Luh-VELL) – former Recon Marine officer and CIA operative, now leader of the Society of Adam Smith. The SAS is a shadow government attempting to counter the elected government's destruction of American values and freedoms. Although confined to a wheelchair because of injuries incurred in an automobile accident, he is tougher than most able-bodied individuals

Mitch Christie – an agent of the FBI who originally pursued Whelan and the other Dogs. He experienced an epiphany and joined the SAS

Maksym (Mack-SEEM) *Kozak* – a ruthless killer and, like his brother Brendan Whelan and the other Sleeping Dogs, genetically advanced. He works for the highest bidder

Harland Fairchilde IV – fourth generation scion of an über wealthy family. Leader of the Alliance for Global Unity (AGU), a global organization of financiers and government finance officials seeking to impose a one-world governing structure on mankind for their own financial benefit

Kirill (Keer-REAL) *Federov* – a former Spetsnaz (Russian special ops) colonel serving in the SVR, Russia's external intelligence agency (*believed to be deceased*)

Andrei Ulyanin (An-DRAY Uhl-YAN-in) – former Spetsnaz colleague of Federov's, now pursuing his killers

Tom Murphy – Caitlin Whelan's father and a former member of the UK's SBS; currently *An Garda Síochána* (the Irish National Police force) District Superintendent for County Kerry, Ireland

Padraig (Paddy) Murphy – Caitlin's brother and the Sergeant in Charge of the *An Garda Síochána* station in Dingle, Ireland

Maureen Delaney - chief executive of one of the largest and most successful technology companies on the planet, and Levell's love interest

*Luiz Fernando (Nando) Correia (*Kor-RAY-ah) – Levell's personal assistant, driver, and bodyguard; a master, or specialist, in *Capoeira Regional* and Brazilian Jiu-Jitsu

The Mueller (MULE-er) *Brothers* (Alfred, Hermann, and Tomas) – billionaire industrialists and patriots who fund SAS operations and provided leading edge technological support

Camila Ramirez (Ra-MEER-ez)– a sheriff's deputy in Albuquerque, New Mexico and Mitch Christie's lady friend

Nadir (Nah-DEER) *Shah* – leader of the Holy Army of the Caliphate, a radical group establishing an Islamic state in the Middle East

Zheng Bao Xun (Zhing Bah-oh Zhun) - the minister of finance for the People's Republic of China

Turan (Ter-RAHN) *Salam* (SuH-LAHM)— a Pakistani Waziri teenager recruited to jihad by Bazir Haqqani, trained in the mountains of North Waziristan for an attack on the U.S. homeland

Carolina (Cah-row-LEEN-ah) *Avila* (Ah-VEE-la)—a teenage neighbor of Turan Salam's in Santa Fe. He's been smitten by her beauty, but she begins to suspect he may be something other than he seems

Bazir (Bah-ZEER) Haqqani (Hah-KAHN-ee)— a Waziri and former Taliban fighter who has pledged his allegiance to Nadir Shah and the Islamic Caliphate. He recruited Turan Salam

Fermin "Frank" Cuellar (KWAY-lar)—a major in the New Mexico State Police and commander of its Special Operations Bureau

David Hidalgo (Hee-DAHL-go) — U.S. Customs and Border Protection agent stationed at the Antelope Wells Border Patrol port of entry and forward operating base (FOB)

HAC—the Holy Army of the Caliphate, the largest and most successful terrorist organization yet. It has declared a caliphate across a large swath of the Middle East and Africa with inroads into Europe, Asia, and the New World.

Prince Bandar bin Nayif al Saud - head of Saudi general intelligence and a close friend of Levell's

PART ONE: IT'S A DOG-EAT-DOG WORLD

You have enemies? Good. That means you've stood up for something, sometime in your life.

Winston Churchill

Chapter 1
TAL AFAR, IRAQ

THE FLIGHT TIME from Beijing to the former Iraqi Air Force base at Tal Afar was approximately eight hours aboard the Chinese government's customized Airbus A321. Zheng Bao Xun, the minister of finance for the People's Republic of China, was pleased that he was traveling in the Airbus and not the long-awaited Comac 919 produced by the state-owned Commercial Aircraft Corporation of China. Production of the Comac was years behind schedule. Worse, the prototypes produced to date demonstrated poor fuel efficiency due to the heaviness of the aircraft. Equally annoying was the resulting limitations on range—barely twenty-five hundred miles. That meant at least one refueling stop before reaching Tal Afar. Short of a tornadic headwind, the A321 had a range of forty-six hundred miles. It could cover the almost thirty-nine hundred mile trip without stopping. Zheng was comforted by the thought that the Airbus had a proven track record of safe flying. Privately, he feared that the Comac was years away from achieving similar confidence in its aircraft.

Tal Afar had been a primary base for the Iraqi Air Force prior to Operation Iraqi Freedom. Coalition forces had captured it in March 2003 and almost immediately set about rebuilding its 10,000-foot runway and taxiways. After Coalition forces withdrew, the resulting vacuum had been filled by the forces of the Holy Army of the Caliphate, commanded by Nadir Shah. The base currently was being used as a training camp for HAC's Warriors of Allah battalion. The city of Tal Afar was approximately twelve kilometers north of the base. It's population was mostly Turkmen and had declined in recent years by two-thirds. Approximately fifty thousand of its former residents had been Shi'ite Muslims. Except for a few lucky ones who had fled in time, they had all been slaughtered by HAC's extremist Sunni forces.

This particular site had been chosen by Nadir Shah for Zheng's meeting with him and the top Irani Quds general, Ali Sayad Kazemzadeh. The location caused concern for Zheng. While it currently was held by Shah's forces and was only seventy-five kilometers from HAC's prize, the beleaguered, city of Mosul, it also was a mere sixty-five kilometers from the nearest Kurdish-held lands. With deadly efficiency, the Kurds had been advancing steadily against Shah's troops. Mosul no longer had a serviceable airfield and the city was surrounded by the Kurds, Iraqi military, and Shi'a militia. Inside the city, special operations snipers were picking off any of Shah's troops foolish enough to take to the streets. Shah's headquarters city, al-Raqqah, also was out of the question. It was under constant bombardment by Russian and Syrian planes. Its airfield at al-Tabqa had been destroyed in a recent push by Syrian troops loyal to Assad.

Zheng hadn't wanted to make the trip at all, but had little choice. Jiang Qui Xing, China's president and Zheng's superior, had sent him to this meeting as a thinly disguised diplomatic mission. As his plane neared its destination, he reflected on the conversation he'd had with Jiang.

Jiang was not only the President of the People's Republic of China, but also General Secretary of the Communist Party of China, and the Chairman of the Central Military Commission. Those were the three most powerful offices in China. He had moved quickly and ruthlessly to consolidate power upon taking office and was widely considered to be the most powerful Chinese leader since Mao. As Secretary General of the Communist Party, he also chaired the Standing Committee of the Central Political Bureau of the Communist Party of China (PSC), a seven- to nine-person body consisting of the top leadership of the Communist Party of China. Presently, there were eight members. Zheng Bao Xun, as minister of finance and a ranking member of the party, was one of them.

None of the PSC members, including Zheng, kidded themselves. The committee was a mere figurehead under Jiang. Their sole purpose was to rubberstamp anything he demanded. When Jiang had summoned him to his office a few days earlier, Zheng didn't know what to expect from the mercurial leader. Was he to be commended for something he had done that made the president look good; or, stripped of rank and privilege and summarily thrown in prison? Perhaps he was to be tasked with a special job? To his relief it turned out to be the last of those possibilities.

Jiang had greeted him warmly—always a good sign—and motioned Zheng to an overstuffed, tufted leather wing chair. Following wise protocol, Zheng perched straight-backed and attentive on the edge of his own seat. He wondered why Jiang had chosen the ceremonial office for this meeting instead of his usual working office.

The president took a seat behind his large, heavy wood desk and settled back in his chair. The desk had three books stacked on a front corner and a cup of pencils and three telephones. Two of the phones were red; the third was white. The red phones were only distributed to those leaders with a rank of vice minister and above. Otherwise, the desk was empty. A Chinese flag was positioned directly behind Jiang along with a photograph of the Great Wall. The walls of the office were lined with bookcases. In addition to books, there were six photographs, including one of the president and his late father, an associate of Mao Zedong, as well as a photo of Jiang and his daughter, and one of him kicking a soccer ball during a visit to Rio.

"It is good of you to come on such short notice, Minister Zheng. I am aware of your busy schedule and many responsibilities."

"I am your obedient servant, Mr. Chairman; available any time, day or night."

Jiang smiled benignly. "You are a good man Bao. I wish I had more like you."

Zheng affected a shy smile of his own. "Your praise overwhelms me, Mr. Chairman."

Jiang appeared to be in an expansive mood. "These are glorious times for China, Bao. The West is weaker than ever and shows no signs of recovering its backbone. Our thickheaded neighbors, the Russians, are focused on expanding into Western Europe, the Middle East and beyond; even into South America. These foolish plans are beyond their means to accomplish and again will bring them to financial collapse. In the meantime, we are engaged in joint maneuvers with their forces, allowing us to gain great insight into their military capabilities while misleading them regarding our own. Involvement in the endless conflicts in the Middle East further weakens Russia and the other major powers."

Zheng bowed respectfully. "You are a great leader, Chairman Jiang. How may I serve you?"

"You realize, of course, that your Uyghur ethnicity and Muslim upbringing can be of great value to us in our dealings with the Islamists. It will enable you to develop a measure of trust with them, and that will facilitate our efforts to guide them in their war against the nations of the West. It is critical that they succeed in order for China to be able—at the appropriate moment—to exert our economic might across the entire globe."

Zheng nodded politely. "Is there a problem with the Islamists?"

A scowl swept across the president's face. "There may be one in the making. We need them to be the head of the spear that causes the West to focus its assets and energies on war and defense, providing China with an unchallenged ascension to dominant global economic power. Yet the Islamists' efforts to establish their so-called caliphate are failing, and the lands they'd previously conquered are shrinking rapidly. This troubles me."

"What would you like me to do, Mr. Chairman?"

"In our efforts to help Nadir Shah and his Holy Army of the Caliphate, our liaison in Turkey has managed to successfully persuade the Turks to focus much of their war effort on the Kurds. It's those damn Kurds who are kicking the jihadis' asses." Jiang sighed. "But we must do more. I want you to meet with Shah and learn how we may further assist his efforts."

"Just to be clear, you want me to go to the Middle East?" Zheng swallowed hard.

"Yes. And I want you to also meet with the top Iranian commander who is on the ground with Shah's soldiers. He would know better how we might assist them."

Zheng bowed slightly toward Jiang. "Please pardon my ignorance, Mr. Chairman, but I thought the Iranians were fighting the caliphate."

Jiang laughed jovially. "Yes, of course you do. The whole world believes they are enemies. In truth, the Iranian president has confided in me that his government secretly supports the caliphate in an effort to sustain the conflict and draw down the fighting forces on all sides except their own. Their goal is to be the sole power remaining in the Middle East."

"And we want them to realize this ambition?"

"Yes, of course. That will bring stability to the region which will benefit China's commercial efforts."

Zheng nodded his head slowly, as if in thought. "How soon am I to leave?"

"Today. And remember, China must not be associated with any of this. You are a master at transferring funds internationally in ways that cannot be traced back to us. But, in addition, all arms and materiels we supply must have been manufactured anywhere but in China. Understand?"

"Absolutely," Zheng said solemnly.

Chapter 2
DINGLE, IRELAND

Soothing New-Age music wafted softly from the massage suite's hidden speakers, filling the room with relaxing sounds of acoustic flute, sitar, tabla, and tamboura. The air was redolent with the scents of lavender, eucalyptus, and jasmine oils. They almost smothered the odor of the disinfectants used to sterilize the facilities every night. The experienced hands of the masseuse moved in perfect rhythm with the music, stroking smooth, hot river stones along the thick ridges of muscle flanking Brendan Whelan's spine. He breathed slowly and deeply, feeling more relaxed than he had in recent memory. Or as relaxed as a man gripping a fully loaded, chambered SIG 226 could feel.

If Whelan's weapon or the presence of a heavily armed man just outside the massage room alarmed the two masseuses, they gave no sign of it. They and the other employees at the *Sláinte Mhaith* resort and spa knew Whelan and his wife Caitlin well. They were regular customers of the spa. Its name in Irish Gaelic meant "Good Health." It was located on the eastern edge of Dingle Harbour less than three hundred meters from the Whelans' bed and breakfast, the Fianna House. Like everyone else on the Dingle Peninsula, the spa's staff had heard the rumors that several men had recently broken into the B&B

and tried to kill the Whelans. The rumors also had it that those men all had met violent, bloody deaths.

Whelan had purposely turned the massage table to face the closed door to the room. He lay on the table on his stomach, gun in his right hand, eyes closed, breathing slowly, calmly. But his ears were tuned to every sound in the room and beyond. With Maksym still at large, Caitlin and their sons were not safe. For years, Whelan had believed, as his late parents had, that his brother Conall (the "powerful one" in Gaelic), older by two years, had been kidnapped and killed when Brendan was only two years old. His parents had gone to their graves still believing that was true. But Whelan had learned recently that Conall, who now called himself Maksym Kozak, was alive. Worse, the man wanted to kill Whelan, his family members, and all of the remaining members of his old special ops unit, the Sleeping Dogs.

To Whelan's deep sorrow, his brother was not a good and decent man. Maksym—he preferred the name given him by the Ukrainian circus owner to whom his Roma, or Gypsie, abductors had sold him— had Whelan's same genetic gifts of strength and speed. But Maksym chose to use these gifts in the employ of the highest bidder. These men invariably were criminals, misanthropes, dictators, and far worse. The one thing they had in common, besides their inherent evil, was the financial ability to secure Maksym's services. One of these men had been the billionaire arbitrager Chaim Laski. Laski had served the interests of the Russian president, who was an unknowing pawn in the one-world plans of a global organization of bankers and financiers known as the Alliance for Global Unity or AGU.

One of Laski's tasks had been to arrange the assassination of the sitting American president. He had failed, but just barely. Whelan and the five surviving members of the Sleeping Dogs had foiled the attempt and killed Laski in the process. Maksym, as head of Laski's security, considered Laski's death an unacceptable failure on his part, and vowed to find Whelan and the other Dogs and kill them and their family members. He almost had succeeded. And Whelan knew he wasn't going to give up. Hence the weapon in Whelan's hand and the armed man outside the door to the massage room.

Brendan Whelan had long ago lost count of the number of men he'd killed. First it had been in the service of the country that had adopted him, the United States. He had been a member of the deadliest black ops unit in history, the Sleeping Dogs. The stuff of myth and legend, they were the most feared hunter-killers on the planet. To threaten America was to 'wake the Dogs,' and undertakers would begin working overtime. A subsequently elected U.S. president, concerned that, if uncovered, their activities could cause an international incident, had ordered that they be terminated with extreme prejudice. They managed to fake their deaths in a plane crash, and went to ground for several years. But with America now in the greatest danger in its history, a shadow government known as the Society of Adam Smith called them back into service. The leader of the SAS, Cliff Levell, was Whelan's mentor, more like a second father.

While Whelan was Irish-born, he had grown up in America and had no direct family in Ireland. But the family of his wife, Caitlin, had resided on the Dingle Peninsula for countless generations. Ever since the break-in, her extensive family together with friends and neighbors had organized round-the-clock protection for the Whelans. It didn't hurt that Caitlin's father, Tom, was the District Superintendent of *An Garda Síochána* (the Irish National Police force) for County Kerry. Her brother, Pádraig, was the Sergeant in Charge of the Garda station in Dingle. The protection would continue until Whelan succeeded in finding and killing the one man responsible for the continuing threat, his brother Maksym.

Everyone in Dingle and the lands surrounding it on the peninsula knew of Brendan Whelan. His freakish strength, speed, and intelligence were the stuff of legends. Some of the locals believed the ancient Celtic gods might have sent him, the reincarnation of the mythical hunter/warrior Fionn mac Cumhaill. Others believed the popular legend that Fionn never died, but had been asleep for centuries in a cave, surrounded by the loyal members of the Fianna, the fierce band of warriors that Fionn led. Legend had it that Fionn and his warriors one day would awake and defend Ireland in her hour of greatest need. At one point following the break-in at the bed and breakfast, five other men had come from America and stayed for a while with the Whelans at the Fianna House. These men also had Whelan's inexplicable strength and quickness. Some of the locals had wondered if Fionn and his warriors indeed had awakened from their long slumber and that Ireland, and perhaps the world, faced some dire catastrophe.

Chapter 3

TAL AFAR, IRAQ

WHEN ZHENG SAW HIS RIDE, his misgivings about this meeting deepened. It was a small, badly dented Saipa Tiba, a no-frills four-door sedan made in Iran. It looked like it had an inch of dust and grime clinging to its entire surface area. The windshield on the driver's side was the only area that had been cleared, otherwise, it was dark and gloomy in its filthy interior. Zheng hesitated for several moments before reluctantly and daintily climbing inside.

On the ride from the Tal Afar airfield to the meeting site near the intersection of Iraq's Highway 47 and the road from the airport, Zheng further reflected on the meeting with Jiang. He detested the man. To make matters worse, he had to kowtow—all but genuflect—in his presence. The fool's goal was so limited—weaken the West economically so that China could be the Big Dog on the world stage. *The hell with economic dominance; total world dominance was within reach.* While he certainly was on board with Jiang's plans to weaken the West by drawing down its substance in fighting foreign wars and domestic terrorists, he, Zheng, wanted it all.

On the surface, he had been working diligently to accommodate Jiang's plans; yet here the fool was, rattling sabers in the South China Sea and again threatening Taiwan. Such activity could precipitate a war with the West before the terrorists had sufficiently weakened it internally. It was making it harder for Zheng to effectuate his own plans, which were designed to cause short-term economic chaos at home sufficient to lead to Jiang's downfall, ultimately to be replaced by Zheng. Toward that end, Zheng had purposely misled Jiang by suggesting economic policies that looked good on the surface, but were designed to fail. He knew that Jiang's immense ego would cause him to take personal credit for the measures. And he had, forcing the other members of the PSC to endorse domestic stimulus programs, such as forcing state-owned firms to invest more in manufacturing even though private sector firms had relocated to other areas of Southeast Asian where labor costs were significantly lower.

Private companies accounted for three-fifths of China's economy and four-fifths of its workforce. Driving private equity out of the game, would result in surging inflation and high unemployment. Already China's economy had experienced several years of slowing growth and intermittent deflation. Under Zheng's subtle coaching, Jiang had twice cut the amount its banks were required to hold in reserve. The ensuing turmoil had caused China's currency, the yuan, to slide, thus prompting a huge outflow of foreign capital. If Zheng could persuade Jiang to call for an interest rate cut as a means of stimulating economic growth, the yuan would become even less attractive, fueling further outflows. Ultimately, these Jiang-driven policies would fail, severely damaging China's economy in the process. A desperate PSC with the backing of the military would eliminate Jiang and turn to the only person who could rescue the economy and make them look good in doing so. Zheng Bao Xun.

Chapter 4

DINGLE, IRELAND

CAITLIN AND WHELAN returned to the Fianna House feeling thoroughly relaxed from the effects of their massages. Whelan silently assessed the armed men guarding the dwelling. No one was unaccounted for. As he and Caitlin entered the premises, Whelan heard a muffled noise coming from the inn's kitchen. It was the sound of the refrigerator door being closed softly. Their sons, Sean and Declan, were in school. He gently but quickly nudged Caitlin into a small alcove. With the SIG 226 in his right hand, a round chambered and hammer cocked, he glided silently toward the kitchen area. Whoever the intruder was, he had to be among the best, because none of the armed men patrolling the area had been harmed or alerted.

As he eased up to the entrance to the kitchen, he heard someone say, "You wouldn't shoot a guy in the middle of his lunch, would you?"

Sitting at the kitchen table with his back to the doorway was Marc Kirkland. He had made a sandwich and was washing it down with a cold bottle of O'Hara's Celtic Stout. He turned, smiled at Whelan, and raised the bottle in salute.

Whelan smiled knowingly and shook his head. "Should have figured it was you. Or Stensen."

"Marc," Caitlin said as she entered the kitchen. "How were you able to get in here? There are armed men protecting the Fianna. You could have been killed!"

"Piece of cake," Kirkland said. "It's what Brendan and I and the others were trained by Cliff Levell to do."

"Did you hurt anyone?" There was a strong element of concern in her voice. "These people are family and close friends. If anyone was harmed...."

Kirkland smiled sheepishly. "Everyone's fine and none the wiser. I'm sure they're doing the best they can, but the truth is there's nothing that can keep us out, not humans, animals, electronics. Nothing."

Whelan laughed and grabbed two more bottles of stout from the refrigerator. He snapped the caps off with a thumbnail. They weren't twist-off caps. He took a glass from a cupboard and poured one of the stouts into it, handing it to Caitlin. "What Marc says is true."

"But if he can do it, so can that damned Maksym. He's the same as you are. Genetically."

"I'm sure Maksym's good, but he wasn't trained by Cliff Levell and his team. We were," Whelan said reassuringly. "It does make a difference."

Kirkland nodded.

Caitlin shuddered. "Not to be a poor hostess, but I think this just undid all the benefits of the massage." She took a small sip of the stout and sat down at the table across from Kirkland.

Whelan took another chair between them. The aroma of Caitlin's fresh baked Irish brown bread still lingered from earlier in the day. It was homey and comforting. "I'm sure you didn't just happen to be in the neighborhood, Marc. What's up?"

"I'm headed to the Middle East and thought I'd stop off. Spend an evening with two of my favorite people."

"Lot of shit happening in that part of the world. Which hot spot has your attention?"

"Qatar."

"Why Qatar?"

Kirkland smiled enigmatically. "I'm working on a personal project."

"I'm sure the news media will eventually fill us in, although your name will never be associated with it."

"Not if I do my job right."

The three of them sat quietly for a while, working on their beers. It had begun to rain. The soft, steady rhythm of the falling drops encouraged a welcome, if temporary, sense that all was clean, fresh, and right in the world. After several minutes, Kirkland went to the refrigerator and started to remove three more stouts.

Caitlin covered the top of her glass with her hand. "I'm good, Marc."

With a beer in each hand, Kirkland walked back to the table. He also popped the caps off with his thumbnails. He put one down in front of Whelan and slid back into his chair. "Remember the last time we were together?"

"Yeah, Cliff's place in Georgetown. When he got shot."

"You talk to him since then?"

"Right after I got back. He was just home from the hospital. With the pain of the gunshot wound and the death of Slash, he was in a nasty mood. But, despite being in his seventies, he'll recover just fine."

"Probably back at work already," Kirkland said and laughed. "He's easily the toughest Norm I've ever known, seventies or not." He used the term 'Norm.' It was what he, Whelan, and the other members of their old black ops unit called those who didn't share their rare genetic makeup.

"I'm sure the old bastard hasn't missed a day since he convinced the medics to release him. In fact, I'm surprised he hasn't contacted me yet."

"With some new high-paying, higher-risk challenge?" Kirkland said with a raised eyebrow.

"And the expectation that I'll agree to reassemble the unit." Whelan looked at his wife.

Caitlin's eyes were slightly narrowed. Her head was moving slowly from side to side in disapproval.

As if on cue, Whelan's cell phone pinged. He fished it out of a pants pocket and looked at the screen. It was a text message from Levell: "I need to speak with you and Kirkland. Call me. Now."

Whelan showed it to Kirkland, who said, "I swear that old bastard's psychic. How could he know I'm here? No one ever knows where I am."

Whelan laughed and shook his head. "Probably had tracers planted in us when we were sleeping."

Now it was Kirkland who shook his head. "Nothing he does would surprise me. But the question is, what do we do about it?"

Caitlin answered the question. "Call him and get it over with. There's nothing to be gained by delaying it. Find out what he wants and tell him 'no'." She paused momentarily, then added, "Firmly."

Chapter 5
TAL AFAR, IRAQ

THE MEETING with Nadir Shah and General Kazemzadeh was being held in a square, two-story, concrete block building about nine and one-half kilometers from the airfield. It was clear from its appearance that it was, or had been, an office building. A badly faded sign in Arabic proclaimed it to be the headquarters of a local pharmaceutical distributor. It also was clear from its bullet-pocked walls that the building was, or recently had been, in a war zone. Shah and Kazemzadeh, the Iranian Quds Force general, were waiting for Zheng in an upstairs corner office. There were two walls of dirt-smeared windows, some of which had been shattered by bullets and boarded up.

Kazemzadeh seemed pleasant. He shook Zheng's hand firmly and smiled. Shah, on the other hand was icy and aloof. He kept his arms crossed over the front of his black combat fatigues.

Does this fool not realize he can't survive without our aide? No wonder he's getting his ass handed to him by the Kurds and the ragtag Syrians. Zheng took a chair on the other side of the table from the one Shah had indicated with a dismissive wave of his hand. Zheng wanted his back to the wall where he could observe both the door to the room and the windows. *As Confucius said, the cautious seldom err.*

Because of the diversity of native languages of the three men, they were forced to conduct their discussion in English, except for Shah. Although he was knowledgeable in that language, he had brought an interpreter with him and insisted on using Arabic. "I will not defile my tongue with the language of Satan."

Kazemzadeh seemed amused. He smiled at Zheng and said, "The caliph means well; he's just not having a good day." He said the word "caliph" with a slight undertone of derision. "I hope the esteemed minister of finance of the Peoples' Republic of China is not offended."

Zheng shrugged. "I am here to help." He paused then added, "But it has been a long trip and I am hoping we can conduct our business swiftly and pleasantly so that I can return to my duties at home as soon as possible."

"Of course," Kazemzadeh said, looking at Shah.

Through the interpreter, Shah said, "I too am a busy and important man. In the interests of getting through this very quickly, I will get right to the point. We need munitions, and we need them immediately. Yesterday."

Nodding solemnly, Zheng said, "You will have them tomorrow if General Kazemzadeh's people act timely. Tomorrow morning four of my country's new Y-20 transport planes will land at Doshan Tapeh Air Base, near Tehran. Each carries close to two hundred tons of weapons, including 130 mm field guns, RPGs, ammunition, surface-to-air missiles, AK-47s, Dragunov sniper rifles, and of special interest, several BMP-2 infantry fighting vehicles." He turned to Kazemzadeh. "Your people are prepared to transport them to the caliph's soldiers?"

The general smiled and nodded.

Shah was silent for a long time. The other two men watched him, neither seemed in any hurry to speak. Finally, Shah said, "This is helpful. For a start. But more is needed."

"And you shall have it," Zheng said.

Shah's eyes narrowed. "And why is it that the Chinese are so eager to help the caliphate? They are infidels."

Zheng straightened his shoulders and said' "I am Uyghur. My people are devout Sunnis. We have prevailed upon the nation of China to support your worthy cause."

Shah seemed confused by the answer and looked back and forth from his interpreter to Zheng. "You are Muslim?"

Zheng nodded affirmatively.

"But China itself is not Muslim?"

"No, not the majority of Chinese."

"Then why is China helping us?"

Zheng glanced quickly at Kazemzadeh. "We do not believe a strong Russian influence in this part of the world is in our best interests. We support the caliphate as a check against that influence. It would stabilize the region."

Shah looked at Kazemzadeh and scowled. "I am not stupid. I am aware that the Iranian Shi'a secretly aid us while openly allied with the Russians who support Assad's regime. Clearly they are playing both ends against the middle. They play footsie with the Russian infidels, hoping to draw the Saudis, Jordanians, and Emirati into a war they can't win in Syria. Then the Iranis will conquer their lands. On the other hand, they also work with us and you Chinese to be able to counter the Russian influence when the time is right. Yes?"

Zheng said nothing. His face was expressionless. The inscrutable Oriental.

The Quds Force general smiled disarmingly. "You are right about the Russians. We appear to support them purposely to keep a close eye on their own ambitions in the Middle East. And, as you say, when the time is appropriate, we will eliminate their presence. There is plenty of room for the caliphate to coexist peacefully with Iran and our vested interests in this part of the world. Enough oil and wealth to go around."

The meeting lasted for another hour while Shah made clear his expectations of Iran and China, and Zheng gave concise instructions how money and materiels would be delivered. When it ended, Kazemzadeh walked Zheng out to the same dirty, battered Saipa Tiba that would drive him back to the airport.

The large Iranian slipped an arm around the diminutive Chinese, and leaning his head close to him said, "We both understand that Shah is crazy, and that the day will come when we—Iran and China, will need to eliminate him and his fantasy of a caliphate. That day will probably come sooner rather than later." He laughed at his own comment and said, "Working together, we Persians and Chinese will soon be the only two powers on this planet."

Zheng didn't reply. He nodded slightly and shook the general's hand then climbed into the vehicle and rode off toward the airport.

Kazemzadeh walked back into the battered office building and found Shah standing just inside the doorway watching him.

The Iranian smiled broadly and winked. "It's just as I told you it would be. The Chinese are easy to manipulate. They will provide unlimited resources to insure the success of the Caliphate. Ultimately, working together we will obstruct their aims on world economic dominance. Meanwhile, we Persians will sabotage the presence of Assad's benefactors, the Russians, so that they can be eliminated in due time." He paused and laughed heartily. "Life is good, my friend."

AS HIS PLANE bored into the gathering darkness on its return to Beijing, Zheng sat alone in the huge, luxuriously appointed cabin, sipping a cup of *Silver Tips Imperial tea* from Makaibari tea estates. Even at a cost close to $30 per ounce, it was plentifully stocked on the government plane. Nothing was too good for the privileged autocrats who led the Peoples' Republic.

As Zheng finished his tea, he smiled. It had been a good meeting. Things were going as planned. The caliphate was doomed, but phoenix-like, a well-placed number of its fanatics would arise from the carcass and continue to plague the West. But they were scattered and autonomous enough to be highly effective. And those fools, the Iranians with their delusions of a theocratic Persian empire once again stretching across the Middle East, were plunging headlong into the trap the Chinese were laying. *The price of such hubris ultimately is destruction.*

Chapter 6
DINGLE, IRELAND

FORTY MINUTES later Whelan reached Cliff Levell by special satellite communication. The phone was a product of a special lab owned by a series of international straw corporations ultimately controlled by the three billionaire Mueller brothers, Alfred, Hermann, and Tomas. It enjoyed intellectual contributions from the top tech people in the NSA, CIA, FBI, military intelligence, and two of the five deputy directors of National Intelligence, all of whom also were members of Levell's Society of Adam Smith, or SAS.

The lab developed communications gear for the American government's top security agencies. But what the government got wasn't the latest cutting-edge encryption technology. The pre-beta stuff went to Levell and a carefully chosen few members of the SAS. Whelan, as Levell's special ops golden boy, always had access to the latest equipment. Levell assured him that their encryption methodology stayed ahead of the curve at all times. In this particular instance, the communications traveled via satellites that were built and operated commercially by a Mueller brothers' enterprise. But the satellites also harbored highly encrypted communications equipment accessible only by persons specifically designated by the Muellers. To the rest of the world, the satellites broadcast music for commercial radio operations.

But digitally encrypted into the streams of music were the messages transmitted between Levell and the chosen few. The system utilized a newly developed 4096-bit asymmetric encryption that would require hundreds of billions of MIPS-years to crack it. MIPS is one million instructions per second.

Whelan and Kirkland were in the tiny office just off the B&B's kitchen. The satellite phone was set on speaker mode. After a few rings, Levell picked up on the other end.

"What the hell part of 'now' don't you understand?" His voice had its usual raspiness, aggravated by his obvious irritation.

Whelan and Kirkland looked at each other and grinned. Same old Levell.

"We were finishing a couple of cold ones," Whelan said.

"Must be all that humidity in Ireland. Your sense of priorities is fucked up. Both of you."

"Enough of the pleasantries, Cliff. How's the arm?"

"How the fuck do you think it is? I got shot. It hurts like hell."

"Yeah, but there must be some satisfaction in knowing you killed Federov in the exchange."

"That son of a bitch. I owed him that for Buster."

Kirkland said, "I'm sorry about Slash too. He was a good man."

"The best," Levell said.

"Found anyone to replace him yet?" Whelan said.

"Yeah, I hired a guy named Nando. It looks like he's going to work out. Now, if you two are through wasting my time, shall we get down to the reason for this call?"

Levell's voice reminded Whelan of boulders moving through a rock crusher. He smiled at the old Marine's irascibility. It was vintage Levell. "It's your dime, Cliff."

"Something's coming up, and we need you two and your colleagues to stop it."

"The recent loss of blood must have addled your memory, Cliff. Did you forget that the Dogs went their separate ways after the last mission?"

"Kirkland's there with you. That's a start."

"No, I'm just passing through," Kirkland said quickly. "I've got things to do."

There were a few moments of silence before Levell said, "Is there anything more important than the country that fed you, nourished you, gave you access to more opportunities than you ever would have gotten anywhere else?" After a brief moment, Levell added, "That goes for you, too, Whelan."

"I believe we've all more than repaid that debt over the years," Whelan said. There was an edge in his voice. Kirkland grunted in agreement.

"That's not the point," Levell said snappishly. "Are all of you so selfish that you think you can quit once you get what you want? What about the other three hundred and thirty million Americans? Don't they deserve a safe and free environment to pursue their dreams, too?"

Whelan and Kirkland looked at each other and smiled. Levell was famous for his efforts to manipulate other people on behalf of SAS.

"Why is that our concern?" Kirkland said.

"Because," Levell practically shouted, "globally, society is on the verge of collapsing into anarchy, chaos, and terror, and you six are the only ones who might be able to make a difference at this point."

"Because we're genetically different."

"Yes!"

"What exactly is it you think we can do, Cliff, that the SEALs, Green Berets, Deltas, Recon Marines, or Rangers can't do?"

"For one thing, this country's Marxist-jihadist friendly administration won't commit those forces. That wouldn't comport with its handlers' efforts to crush nation-states and replace them with a self-serving one-world government. Even if that weren't the case, things have reached the stage where we can't chance the fate of the free world on the frailties of normal human beings. Consider the state of the military after all the firings, forced retirements, and RIFs involving experienced personnel. Then there are the cuts to defense spending. Things have gotten so fucking bad that the US military is so desperate to acquire spare parts that it has soldiers, sailors, airmen, and Marines combing thru bone yards of discarded equipment trying to find useable parts for the aircraft, tanks, and more that are currently inoperable. Does that scare the crap out of you as much as it does me?

"The six of you move faster, think faster than normal humans can comprehend. You communicate silently and instantly, like a wolf pack. And, when you're focused on a target, you're the most ruthless, efficient killing machine this world has ever known."

Whelan looked at Kirkland and shook his head. Kirkland shrugged. Turning back to the sat phone, Whelan said, "Look, Cliff, even if I was of a mind to get involved, I have no idea where the other four are."

"I do," Levell said sharply.

"So you're asking me—and Marc—to put the unit back together?"

"Yes."

"For what purpose?"

Levell's voice was low and measured. "There's an attack on the homeland coming soon. We need you to stop it."

"Who's behind this threat?" Whelan said.

"The worker bees are Islamic terrorists, mostly HAC, the Holy Army of the Caliphate. But the guiding force behind it is China."

Chapter 7
THE LODGE

THE BLUE-GREY HYUNDAI SANTA FE cruised down Virginia State Highway 218, also known as Caledon Road, toward the town of Fairview Beach nestled on a wide bend in the Potomac. But the driver didn't take the turnoff to the town. Instead he continued on to a point about one and a half miles beyond a T-intersection marked on maps as the unincorporated community of Osso. Here an unmarked dirt road snaked off to the left into dense woods, twisting northerly in the general direction of the river. The driver had a trained eye for such things and didn't miss the cameras and sophisticated surveillance devices carefully camouflaged in the trees. He assumed there also were sensors buried throughout the property. Even the unsophisticated wouldn't help but notice the large signs with warnings posted in five languages. The first sign advised that this harbored both a private club and a consulate of a foreign country. Only members or persons who had been specifically invited were welcome; all others would be prosecuted. The second and final sign warned that all traffic was being monitored and non-members were about to be apprehended by armed security personnel.

The road accessed a three hundred twenty-acre tract that had been assembled quietly over the past several years by straw corporations with untraceable lineages. It was rugged terrain, thickly wooded and hilly. In the middle of the tract, a huge log structure sat on the peak of a ridgeline. Behind it was a second, slightly smaller, building. Because of the forest, none of this was visible to the driver yet. He wound around another of the countless twists in the road and came upon a gate and a manned guardhouse. There were three security personnel that he could see, but he suspected others probably were close by. One man was in the guardhouse. The other two stood behind waist-high concrete structures ten yards on either side of the road. The security personnel appeared relaxed, but their weapons were unmistakably at the ready.

The driver came to a halt and pressed a button on the armrest, lowering his window. The man in the gatehouse emerged and the driver leaned out and handed a plastic card to him. The guard took it, went back inside, and ran it through a reader. Satisfied with the results, he handed it back and said, "Welcome to the Lodge Mr. Christie. Enjoy your stay."

THE LODGE WAS A FIFTEEN-THOUSAND-SQUARE-FOOT, two-story building that looked like it belonged in the wilds of Montana. Its exterior was made of large logs. There was a brick chimney at either end of the building. In addition to the guards posted at the gate and elsewhere on the estate, an ultra-sophisticated electronic and video system provided twenty-four-hour surveillance of the entire tract. All the devices, including infrared cameras and ground sensors, were monitored by additional security staff. Nothing moved in the three hundred twenty acres that wasn't instantly detected. If that happened, a staff of professional, highly trained and well-armed security personnel would respond immediately. All of them were former Special Ops warriors.

The exterior of the structure clearly had been built to convey a rustic, masculine simplicity. But, in keeping with the Muellers' and SAS's insistence on absolute privacy, behind the façade the place was something else entirely. The walls, ceilings, and floors had been lined with materials that blocked penetration by infrared, ultrasound, and all other surveillance methods. Its technology and communications facilities had been designed by the best minds of patriots in the CIA, NSA, and the private sector, working on their own time. The facilities were upgraded continually in order to remain superior to anything available to the planet's top security agencies.

The interior was comfortably decorated and furnished in the style of a luxurious western ranch. The Lodge had eleven separate bedrooms and bathrooms, a state of the art operations center, a large dining hall, an ultra-modern, professional-grade and staffed kitchen, an extensive library, a fully equipped gymnasium, and a boardroom. A slightly smaller second facility, connected to the main building by a tunnel, housed some members of the staff, sheltered motor vehicles, and provided a few spare bedrooms and bathrooms for occasions when the main building was fully occupied.

One of the rooms in the Lodge was a solarium with an exterior wall made extensively of glass. It was designed to provide a bright, airy environment for relaxing and reading. It currently was occupied by a tall, lean, wiry-looking man with short iron-grey hair. Despite his ramrod bearing, he was seated in a wheelchair, poring over a thick stack of documents. He didn't seem inconvenienced by the fact that his left arm was in a sling.

There was another man in the room—medium build, olive complexion, and long, straight black hair. He stood, relaxed and silent, in an area where he could see the man in the wheelchair, the rest of the solarium, and the area beyond the windows. And he listened—to the sounds in the room, as well as those from the outside, and from the rest of the Lodge. The smart phone in the man's pocket vibrated.

He fished it out with smooth, cat-like grace. "Yes?" He listened for a moment then put the phone back in his pocket. Approaching the man in the wheelchair, he said, "Mr. Levell, your guest is here." He spoke with a slight accent. An experienced ear might have recognized it as Portuguese.

Levell placed the stack of documents on a desk and said, "Thank you, Nando. Let's go and greet him."

Nando pushed the wheelchair down the long, Mexican-tiled

hallway to the Lodge's library, a darkly wooded room with floor-to-ceiling stacks of leather bound tomes. He removed a chair from the library table and guided the wheelchair into the open space. A few minutes later, one of the security people ushered Mitch Christie in and closed the door behind him.

Christie shook hands with Levell, who waved him to a seat. He chose a chair opposite Levell. The newcomer glanced at Nando, then back at Levell with a questioning look.

"Mitch, this is Luiz Fernando Correia, my assistant. Call him Nando."

Christie sized the other man up with the experienced eye of a life-long cop. "Correia? Brazilian?"

Levell smiled and nodded. "Very good, Mitch."

"I'm going to make a wild guess that Nando is, among other things, an experienced practitioner of Capoeira."

"More than a practitioner, a master; or as Brazilians like to call them, a specialist. And Brazilian Jiu-Jitsu as well."

Assistant, my ass, Christie thought, *I know hired muscle when I see it.* "I'm sure replacing Mr. Rhee was difficult," he said in reference to Levell's late assistant/driver/bodyguard/major domo, who Levell had affectionately called "Slash" for obvious reasons. Only a month earlier, Rhee had been killed while trying to protect his employer from a rogue FBI agent, a former colleague of Christie's. "But Nando looks like he's up to the task."

All the while, the object of the comments stood with his back to a bookshelf, his face showing no emotion. Watching, listening. On the surface he seemed completely detached from his surroundings, but Christie had no doubts the man was prepared for virtually anything.

"How's the arm?" Christie said, looking at Levell's cast.

"Still hurts like hell at times, but it's coming along. A man reaches a certain age, and he no longer heals as quickly." Levell chuckled. "Ah, for the sweet days of youth."

Christie glanced at his watch. "Not to hurry you, but I'm sure you have a lot on your plate. What is it you wanted to see me about?"

A smile creased Levell's craggy, leathery face. "Once a Bureau man, always a Bureau man; just want to get to the facts."

"No, that's not what I…"

"It's alright," Levell said, making a dismissive gesture with his right hand. "We're both busy. Do you have an idea why I asked you to meet with me?"

"Because of what happened at your house. With Whelan."

"That's right. As I recall, you had the drop on Brendan, but gave him your weapon and told him you 'wanted in.' Is that right?"

"Yes."

"Do you know what 'in' is?"

"I think so. It's your organization, the Society of Adam Smith."

"Yes, the SAS. Do you know what we're about?"

Christie looked at Levell for a few moments, as if thinking over his answer. "My impression is that you're patriots who believe this country is in the process of being destroyed. Beyond that, I'm not real sure about the who or the how."

"Under the current ineffective leadership in Washington—and that includes both parties, this nation is highly polarized, Mitch. That makes it difficult, if not impossible, to reestablish a functioning government. Because of the administration's policies, the country has been economically and militarily weakened. It's no match for the machinations of our foreign enemies." Levell's jaw muscles tightened visibly and his raspy voice took on a harder edge. "Under these circumstances, the Society is compelled to take action. That includes diplomacy, but also—when diplomacy fails—espionage, sabotage, even assassinations; whatever it takes to protect the people of this nation. Including those fools who think everything is just fine."

Levell's tone softened. "I…we've vetted you very carefully, Mitch, and believe you can be trusted." He sat back in his wheelchair. "Put simply, the SAS is a group of patriots who are very highly placed in the government and military. We also have major business leaders in our ranks. It helps with finances."

"Including the Mueller brothers," Christie said.

"Yes, and they are very generous with capital, personnel, and facilities." He paused and made a sweeping motion with his good hand. "They have provided this Lodge, among other things. You spent a lot of time trying to gather intel on it during the Harold Case investigation, didn't you?"

Christie nodded. "I didn't get very far before someone at a higher pay grade pulled me up on a short leash. The SAS has a lot of power and influence. In fact, what I did learn about the Lodge is that it's frequented by military top brass and major political and governmental figures, but none from the current administration, its party members, or members of the 'moderate' wing of the opposition party. I also learned that the place is impervious to electronic surveillance of any kind. Even satellites' and drones' probes are jammed. And transmissions emanating from here are scrambled and encrypted beyond anything we have that could decipher them." He threw his hands up in a gesture of frustration. "I even tried to get a warrant to search the premises."

With a smile that would have done the Cheshire Cat proud, Levell said, "In the process you must have discovered that this is a consulate for a foreign nation, one in which the Muellers have made very generous investments."

"Yeah, and under Article 31 of the Vienna Convention on Consular Relations, the host nation may not enter the consular premises. Very clever, I'll give you that."

"And you want to become a part of this organization? Why?"

"Simple. I completely agree with you that this country's clearly on the wrong track, and it's picking up speed every day. I want to do whatever I can to reverse things—if it's not too late."

"It may be," Levell said grimly. "But if a person loves basic freedoms and is willing to risk everything to protect them, then the right path is clear."

Christie leaned forward in his chair, the muscles in his jaw standing out. "Tell me, *is* it too late?"

"Maybe. The fact is that our government is under the control of a group of international financial barons who call themselves the Alliance for Global Unity, or AGU. Their efforts have been underway for the past hundred years."

"Starting with the founding of the Federal Reserve, right?"

Levell nodded. "And they wisely gained control of one of this country's major political parties, proselytizing bleeding-heart liberals in academia, the media, and entertainment and using them to brainwash our countrymen with misleading narratives and outright lies. They created the welfare or entitlement mindset and spread it far and wide. Now, everyone's afraid they'll have to give up their 'free' shit if they don't support 'progressive' candidates. And those candidates get their marching orders from the AGU."

Christie looked at Nando. The man's stoicism was so profound, he didn't even appear to waste motion on something as simple as breathing.

"Agent Christie," Levell said, snapping the Bureau man's attention back to the discussion. "Can you recall a time when America was in this much danger globally? When the old orders were universally crumbling and frightening new ones were emerging?"

"No, I can't."

"You have a son and a daughter. Can you imagine the horrors of the world they will inherit? What are their chances for survival, let alone for the quality of life you've experienced?"

Christie stared down at his clenched fists resting on the tabletop and shook his head.

"But you've come to us because you want to do something about that."

"If there's anything that can be done."

"There's always hope," Levell said. "We'd be fools and cowards to just give up."

Christie raised his head and locked eyes with Levell. "Tell me how I can help. I'm ready to quit the Bureau and join with Whelan and the others to fight these bastards."

Levell held his gaze and looked at Christie thoughtfully. "I appreciate your sincerity and passion, Mitch. Pardon the pun, but Whelan and the other Dogs are a special breed of animal. They're not like us. They have skills and talents that enable them to survive situations that would cost us Norms, as they call us, our lives. Make no mistake; you aren't like them, and never will be.

"They seem to have an innate sense of right. They appear to tolerate us Norms because they find us amusing in our comparative weakness and frailty. And just maybe they're cursed with a sense of responsibility to look out for lesser beings."

"They seem to have an absence of fear too. Why is that?"

"Perhaps it's because they're intelligent enough to have no expectations of immortality. Plus, they know they're unusual and that the human aging process and longevity probably don't apply to them in the same way they do to us, so they tend to live life one day at a time. With the exception of Whelan; he has a family, and that makes a difference."

Christie smiled wryly. "Like the old saw: live fast, die young, and leave a good-looking corpse?"

"Possibly, but I don't envy their situation. They're alone in a sea of lesser beings."

"Yeah, I know," Christie said with a sigh. "I've had conversations with the geneticist, Dr. Nishioki. I know those guys are freaks genetically. I didn't really understand his explanation, but I've seen them in action, and they *are* different."

"Bill Nishioki is a brilliant scientist, as was his late colleague Jake Horowitz. Even though I helped to identify, recruit, and train the Dogs, until recently I wasn't sure I understood what it was that caused them to be what they are. Mother Nature playing a practical joke? The Deity preparing a species of mankind to survive a global holocaust? A giant leap forward in human evolution? Whatever it was, they're the best assets we have. And that still may not be enough."

"You said 'until recently' you didn't understand. Has something changed your perspective?"

"Dr. Nishioki and I have discussed a possible new theory. Are you familiar with the evolution of hominins, Mitch?"

"Hominids?"

"No, only the human element of hominids, properly known as hominins."

"What about them?"

"The genus *Homo* has spawned at least seventeen branches of which Homo Sapiens is the sole survivor. To the extent that any of the other branches overlapped with the arrival of our forebears, they were killed off or failed to adapt to changing conditions."

"Are you suggesting that Whelan and the others are a new...superior branch of the human tree?"

"Yes."

Christie stared at Levell, a look of puzzlement on his face. "So looking down the line what does that mean? Will we become extinct too?"

"Probably, replaced by the descendants of Whelan and the others who are like him." Levell saw the look of concern of Christie's face. "It's probably centuries away, Mitch. Hell, the Neanderthals coexisted with our ancestors for thousands of years, even interbred to some extent."

"But eventually they'll kill us off?"

Levell had a thoughtful look on his face. "Probably not. We'll do that all on our own by an inability to adapt to substantial changes in the environment, as well as our unfortunate penchant for killing each other."

"Not to piss on the parade, Cliff, but I thought there'd been a falling out and the Dogs had gone their separate ways."

Levell momentarily broke eye contact with Christie. "Yes and no. Are you familiar with the behavior of a pack of wolves, Mitch?"

"A little."

"When they're working together as a cohesive unit, they perform seamlessly. Each one does exactly what he should do with little to no verbal communication between them." Levell sighed. "But, again, these guys are not like us. Each is a unique individual with a distinctly different personality. Truth is they have very little in common with each other except the obvious genetic gifts of superior strength, quickness, and intelligence. Hell, there are times when they don't even like *each* other. This is one of those times."

Christie raised his hands palms up in a questioning gesture. "So, what are you telling me? Are they back together as a team? And, if so, how does that involve me?"

"Unfortunately, as you said, they've gone their separate ways...at least for the time being. But I've known these guys for many years. To reunite them, I need two things—a unifying cause and the right recruiter." Levell's leathery face crinkled into a wicked smile. "I think I've got both."

Christie thought about that for a moment. "Who's the recruiter?"

"There's only one man who could pull that unruly, dangerous bunch of bastards back together."

"Whelan?"

Levell nodded.

"He must be very persuasive."

"Shit, you've no idea."

"And the 'cause?'"

"In general, it's the threat to civilization posed by the coming AGU-sponsored anarchy. It has to be stopped. If it can be. But in particular, it's something I'm sure you've heard rumors of in the bowels of the FBI."

"A closer to home threat to the U.S.?"

Levell nodded again, slowly. "I'm delighted that you want to serve your country by working with us. We'll talk more tonight. There's a meeting that concerns the extent of the threat to the homeland. I promise it'll scare the shit out of you."

Chapter 8

LONG ISLAND

THE LIMO CLIMBED the long driveway from Cedar Swamp Road, winding through a thick copse of trees. It stopped in the estate's expansive motor court. A gruff looking, muscular man climbed gingerly from the cab's backseat, as if nursing an injury. As the limo pulled away, the man slowly looked around. The motor court was enormous, the largest he had ever seen. No less than seven individual garage doors lined the court to his left. In front of him, the manor house rose three stories into the night sky, looming over the motor court like an enthroned royal. Its stony vastness spread far to either side of the massive double oak entry doors that topped a series of marble steps. He had never seen anything quite like it.

The man had lived a rough life. Raised in poverty in one of Moscow's worst slums, he'd escaped to a career as a member of the Spetsnaz, the Soviet Union's dreaded special forces units. He'd joined near the end of the ten-year war in Afghanistan. He later saw considerable combat in the civil war in Tajikistan, the Chechen Wars, and the Russo-Georgian War, rising to the rank of captain. His valor and fighting skills had gained him entry into Vympel, an elite Russian Spetsnaz group formed from the merger of two FSB (Federal Security Service) units.

In time, General Gennady Vasilyev had handpicked him for the Sluzhba Vneshney Razvedki, or SVR. Vasilyev had been the director of SVR, Russia's external intelligence agency. Unlike the FSB, the SVR had primary responsibility for intelligence and espionage activities external to the Russian Federation. Similar to the CIA's Special Activities Division, the unit was responsible for the most secret and sensitive covert activities, as well as counter-terrorist and counter-sabotage operations. The position was so sensitive that Vasilyev reported directly to Russia's president.

Eventually, the man standing in the motor court had become disillusioned with his future prospects in the SVR. When he was offered an opportunity to earn ten times his former pay by training Muslim jihadis in Iraq and Syria, he took it. The move had left him on Vasilyev's and, by extension, the Russian president's shit list. Given his gritty background, the man didn't care whose shit list he was on as long as the money was good and kept coming. He even recruited Vasilyev's former protégé to join him in the Middle East. That man, Kirill Federov, had been in line to succeed Vasilyev. But a crucial assignment in the United States—assassinating the American president—had gone south and Federov had been held partially responsible.

Federov had been a brilliant and savage fighter with an Olympic marksman's aim. They'd been in many dangerous, even life-threatening situations together, and the man considered Federov to be a friend and colleague. Unfortunately, Federov had been burdened with a violent temper. He typically blamed everyone else for his own shortcomings, held grudges forever, and never stopped seeking revenge against those he believed had wronged him—whether the offenses were real or imagined. It was that flaw that ultimately led to Federov's apparent death. And that, in turn, had led the man here to this palatial estate in Long Island's most privileged community.

With a slight limp, the man climbed the half dozen steps to the massive front doors. There was a large ornate iron knocker mounted on each of the two doors midway between the astragal and their respective side casings. The man assumed they were for appearance sake and pressed the small, LED illuminated doorbell button to the right of the casing. Several moments later a butler in livery opened the door. The man handed the butler a card that the master of the home had sent him previously. The servant examined it carefully, inserted it into a small reader just inside the doors. Satisfied with the result, he pocketed it and beckoned for the man to follow him.

The man stepped inside and stopped in his tracks. He had never seen luxury carried to this point. Of course, he'd never been inside the buildings in the Kremlin or any of the czarist treasures in his native Russia, but still, it would be hard to imagine anything to rival the display of opulence surrounding him.

His reverie of astonishment was broken by the sound of the butler clearing his throat. The domestic gave the poorly dressed stranger the fisheye and motioned with his head for the man to follow him. He was led to a small antechamber off the immense two-story atrium that formed the entry to the dwelling. The butler indicated an ornate, over-stuffed chair. When the man had seated himself, the servant turned and left. He returned a few minutes later and again beckoned to the man to follow him. This time he was led across the vast atrium and down a wide hall to a large room lined from floor to ceiling with expensive-looking wooden bookshelves. Each shelf had been carefully filled with leather-bound books. The carpeting was thicker than anything the Russian had ever experienced. The room's furnishings and accessories quietly reeked of affluence.

When the man entered the room, the butler closed the door behind him and departed. There was another man sitting at the table in the middle of the room, staring at the newcomer. Whatever he was think-ing, his expression didn't betray it. The two men looked at each other momentarily, then the seated man motioned to a chair at the table. "A pleasure to meet you, Captain Ulyanin; or may I call you Andrei?" he said with a smile.

"Call me anything you want," Ulyanin said in almost perfect English, "as long as you pay me well."

"A man after my own heart. As you no doubt gathered, I'm Harland Fairchilde, and I assure you that you will be very well paid for your services. "

Fairchilde leaned back in his chair, crossed his legs and said, "I believe I detected a slight limp when you entered. Is there a problem I should know about?"

Ulyanin shrugged noncommittally. "It is nothing."

"The result of a recent injury?"

Ulyanin nodded.

"Would you mind telling me what happened?"

Ulyanin shifted slightly in his seat. "I was shot."

"I can see you're a man of few words, Andrei. I admire that. But please give me some details."

Ulyanin again shifted uncomfortably in his chair. He didn't like to talk about himself, especially to strangers. Fairchilde was his new employer, but still very much an unknown entity. "Near Mosul. I was leading a group of incompetent ragheads on a training exercise when Kurdish Peshmerga ambushed us. The vaunted HAC cowards fled at the first shot. I fought my way out. The leg is a reminder of the close call, but it is healing."

Fairchilde stared at Ulyanin pensively for a few moments. "In your previous capacity, you trained Nadir Shah's fighters in his Holy Army of the Caliphate. And you've seen the capabilities of the Peshmerga at close hand. What is your assessment of the two?"

"If you are to believe your own news media, the HAC is all but invincible. Its fighters overwhelm the Iraqi forces at every opportunity."

"Yes, that's the impression the media give. But what does your personal experience tell you?"

Ulyanin sneered. "Most of the HAC fighters are a joke. If the opponent was anyone but Iraqi conscripts, they would have been annihilated by now. The only thing they are able to do effectively is blow themselves up. I admit terrorism does work in a limited environment. But, in addition to the Israelis, the real fighters in the Middle East are the Peshmerga. Look what they are able to do to the HAC's otherwise-unemployable camel jockeys. With little to no meaningful air support from your country, light weaponry that is at least three generations old, and the Turks and Russians attacking them on a second front, they are kicking the shit out of the jihadis. The so-called caliphate's territory has shrunk to a few beleaguered outposts."

"Yes," Fairchilde said with a rueful smile. "The Kurds seem to be quite effective at killing the enemy without having to blow themselves up to do it."

"Imagine how effective they would be if the Western nations provided them with modern weapons, artillery, armor."

"I'm sure," Fairchilde said, "but that runs contrary to what my colleagues and I are trying to accomplish."

"What is it you are trying to accomplish, and who are these 'colleagues'?"

Fairchilde made a dismissive motion with his right hand. "All in good time, Andrei. All in good time. But first tell me more about yourself."

"No," Ulyanin said firmly. "First *you* tell me about you and these 'colleagues' of yours."

Fairchilde stared at the Russian for several moments, as if debating whether, and how, to respond to the insolence. Finally, he said, "Very well, Captain. We'll do it your way…this time." He paused and stared pointedly at the Russian. "In my day job," he smiled at his own use of term, "I am the chairman of one of the most successful investment banking firms in the world. But it is my other pursuit that requires the unique services of someone such as yourself."

"What is this 'other pursuit'?"

"I have the distinct pleasure of chairing another organization, the Alliance for Global Unity or AGU. It is a global organization of financiers such as myself as well as the finance officials of various governments. Our common goal is the creation of a one-world governing structure."

Ulyanin glanced around the expensively appointed room. "Despite your obvious wealth, I doubt this goal of yours is a charitable venture. What's in it for you?"

Fairchilde's eyes narrowed and his thin lips stretched into a slight smile. "Whoever controls such a government, controls all of the wealth in the world."

Ulyanin nodded his head slowly. "It's good to know that greed and the lust for power are alive and well, as they were in Soviet Russia."

"It's more than greed. Far more. It means global peace, social justice, equality for all."

"Pardon my skepticism, but nothing is so simple. The world, particularly the fools in the West, will easily accept this scheme of yours. What have you left out?"

Fairchilde spread the fingers of both hands and brought the tips of them together, forming a steeple. "Our organization has been at this for decades. The governments of most of the Western powers officially or unofficially adopted socialism years ago. As a result, they are politically, economically, and militarily weak. The United States is the final domino, and, if I may mix metaphors, it is ripe for the picking. Through a major political party that we've controlled for years, we've managed to gut this country's military and intelligence communities, coopt its news media and system of education, and polarize groups within its society."

"And there is no opposition to your efforts?"

"Well, yes, there is opposition. Principally, there's an organization that calls itself the Society of Adam Smith..."

Ulyanin interrupted. "Adam Smith...the Father of Capitalism?"

"Yes. Quite appropriate, isn't it? They are something of a pain in the ass, but I plan to meet soon with their leader to see if they can be bought off in some fashion. If not, then I will require your services to eliminate him. Without this man, it's highly unlikely that they'll continue to be effective. You, of course, would be highly compensated."

Now it was Ulyanin's turn to smile. "Then I hope your meeting with this man fails."

"Now, let's talk about you, Captain. You speak English quite well. How did you manage that?"

"For a time, in the old Soviet Union, I was trained to be a plant in your country, what you call a mole. I was to pass myself off as an American, become employed in sensitive positions where I could report classified information back to Moscow, be prepared as a saboteur in the event of armed conflict with my country. Eventually, the authorities determined that I was more valuable in the Spetsnaz, our special forces."

"Interesting. Is that how you met the late Colonel Federov?"

Ulyanin gave Fairchilde a strange look. "We were part of a very elite force. We served together in several combat theaters. I considered him a close friend and comrade."

"Then I imagine that you took his death very hard…that you're distraught and seeking vengeance."

Ulyanin did not have Federov's hair-trigger temper, but he felt his anger rising. "Distraught is a strong word. Angry is better. But if you are suggesting that Kirill and I are faggots, you are very wrong," he said menacingly.

Fairchilde cringed at Ulyanin's politically incorrect slur. "I believe your interests would be better served with the use of the term 'gay.' And no, I wasn't suggesting you were homosexuals."

"What then?" Ulyanin's demeanor was guarded.

Fairchilde smiled disarmingly. "I have certain missions in mind for a man of your proven abilities, and simply want to fathom your motivations."

"Money. Money motivates me," Ulyanin said without hesitation. "And if these 'missions' offer an opportunity to make those responsible for what happened to Kirill pay for their actions, I will consider it a bonus."

"Excellent. I'm sure Colonel Federov would be pleased."

After a few moment's hesitation, Ulyanin said, "You appear to be certain that Federov is dead."

"Quite."

"You saw his body?"

"Of course not. What would I, the scion of a blue-blooded family and head of the most powerful investment firm on Wall Street—or anywhere for that matter—be doing viewing the body of an alleged criminal?"

"How is it then that you know he is dead?"

Fairchilde laughed. "My dear Andrei, you've no idea the resources available at my command. I have no doubt that the late Kirill Federov has departed this world."

"Where is his body?"

"His remains were shipped back to Russia."

"You are wrong about that. I have excellent connections in my home country. By way of DNA testing, they have confirmed that the remains sent to Russia definitely were not those of Kirill Federov."

Fairchilde tried to hide his stunned expression. "Are you suggesting he's alive?"

Chapter 9
WANA, SOUTH WAZIRISTAN, PAKISTAN

WANA, the capitol of South Waziristan, was a crossroads town forty kilometers from the Afghan border, surrounded by orchards and a vast Frontier Corps camp. Although the town was situated on a broad plain of the western flank of the Sulaiman mountains and more than four thousand five hundred feet above sea level, it was warm and stuffy inside the thick, ancient, mud brick walls of the madrassa. Even the high ceiling didn't dissipate the heat very well.

The people of South Waziristan were almost all orthodox Sunni Muslims, and a great majority of them were illiterate. To counter this, the religious leaders in Pakistan's tribal regions had opened dozens of *madrassas*, or Islamic schools, where young Mehsud and Wazir tribesmen were indoctrinated to participate in jihad. The madrassas were supported financially by the governments of Persian Gulf countries, especially Saudi Arabia. That meant that the students were constantly exposed to Wahhabism, a particularly austere and rigid form of Islam. Much less time was spent on the traditional madrassa curriculum such as the *Tafseer* (Interpretation of Holy Qur'an), *Hadith* (thousands of sayings of Prophet Muhammad), and *Fiqh* (Islamic Law), than on encouraging jihad. But the schools were especially popular among Pakistan's poorest families because they fed and housed their students.

Turan Salam's head was beginning to nod as Mullah Siddiqui droned on in Turan's native Pashto about *Shaitan* or *iJunoon*—the Great Satan. The lectures always descended into the same diatribe against the Jews and the West, especially the United States. Turan, age sixteen, had heard this speech so many times he could repeat it verbatim. But he knew he should pay attention because Mullah Siddiqui was an esteemed scholar of Islam. He also was a very powerful man, one of the top commanders in the Ahmedzai Taliban.

Just as sleep was about to overtake Turan, he felt a sharp pain on the top of his scalp, as the mullah bounced a small stone off his head. He jerked back in his hard wooden chair, eyes now wide open.

In a loud, angry voice Mullah Siddiqui said, "Is it your desire to remain an ignorant fool all your life, boy?"

"No, sir." Turan felt his face redden as the other students around him snickered.

"Then you had better pay attention. We are teaching you how to serve Allah, how to be a Holy Warrior, how to kill the enemies of the faith. There is no higher calling. Do you not want to slay the Jews, their despicable allies in the West, and the apostates and false-believers in our own faith?"

Turan bobbed his head vigorously. "Yes. Yes, of course." He wished he could melt into the chair and escape his embarrassment. But he didn't have to. Something else happened instead. With a deafening roar, the bare, dingy classroom exploded. Smoke and dust suddenly filled the space, choking the occupants. Chunks of brick and mortar shot through the room, killing some outright, wounding others—some mortally. A piece of brick struck Turan's head with a glancing blow and darkness rushed in.

Chapter 10
MACAO

THE KOREAN AIR 737 descended through the haze covering the Macau International Airport. It touched down just past the threshold of the sole runway. The strip had been built on reclaimed land in Zhujiang River Estuary, which opened into the South China Sea. At just under four hours, the flight from Incheon Airport near Seoul had been a short hop compared to the fourteen-hour flight from Toronto to Korea. And that didn't include the six-and-a-half-hour layover at Incheon. The huge man seated in the First-Class cabin was exhausted.

He deplaned and entered the terminal. It seemed smallish for a city of Macau's size and commerce. Having no luggage, he skirted the baggage claim area and headed for the sign that said "Ground Transportation" in Cantonese, Portuguese, and English. Near the door to the arrivals pick up area he saw a small Asian man holding a sign that read "Mr. Maxim." In his fatigued state, it irritated the new arrival. *Bastards not only are confusing my first name with my last, they can't even spell it correctly.* Then he remembered that in much of Asia the family name is always written first. But he'd never cared about local customs anywhere in the world.

He yanked the small sign from the man's hand, ripped it up, and said, "Let's go." He didn't wait to see whether the Asian man followed or not.

The limo was parked at the curb with the engine running. Two members of Macao's police force, or PSP, were dutifully guarding it. One of them hurried to open the door for Maksym, who could tell by the look on the cop's face that he was intimidated by the passenger's bulk and muscularity. Maksym was used to it. His appearance had been terrifying others since his early teens.

THE LIMO DRIVER cruised at a leisurely pace along Avenue Wai Long, around the Rotunda do Aeroporto, and past the enormity of the Venetian luxury resort and casino. It was the largest casino in the world, and the largest single structure hotel building in Asia, as well as the seventh-largest building in the world by floor area. Past the Venetian, the driver looped around the Rotunda do Itsmo onto Estrada da Baia de Nossa Senhora da Esperanca then turned left onto Avenida Marginal Flor de Lotus. Traffic was light. Maksym suspected the driver was purposely taking the long way, probably to show off his modern, growing city to this stranger in the backseat. But Maksym wasn't interested in Macao. He didn't plan to be there long. A meeting with his real employer and a good night's sleep, and he'd be on the next plane out.

He was aware that Macau had been a Portuguese territory from the mid-sixteenth century until it was returned to China in December 1999, two years after the handover of Hong Kong by the British. Today, like Hong Kong, it was a Special Administrative Region of the People's Republic of China.

Along the way from the airport, the road was lined intermittently with apartments and offices. Much of the remaining vacant land was under construction, and building cranes intruded on the developing skyline. It reminded Maksym of Dubai in its heyday. His lips peeled back from his teeth in a silent snarl. Not that long ago, the Russian buffoon Federov had been presented with an opportunity to kill Whelan and three of the other Dogs in Dubai; but he had failed. *Ultimately, Federov got off easy. He bled out quickly from a gunshot wound. I would have killed him slowly.*

Chapter 11
MACAO

As EXHAUSTED as Maksym was from the long, sleepless trip from New York to Macao, that wasn't what had been the most stressful event in the past two days. That event had occurred before the flight had even begun. It had started when Maksym gained a simple uninvited entry into a large three-story Federal-style home built in Georgetown in the eighteen hundreds. Technically, the act had constituted breaking and entering, even though the front door had been unlocked. The legal standard includes even the slightest amount of force, such as pushing open a door, if it's done without authorization. But Maksym's purpose in entering the home hadn't been burglary. His supposed employer, Harland Fairchilde, IV, chairman of the Alliance for Global Unity, or AGU, had sent him there to confirm a killing. The wet work was to be done by a rogue FBI agent on AGU's payroll. If the agent failed, Fairchilde had dispatched a second killer as backup, an ex-Spetsnaz operative named Federov. In an abundance of caution, Fairchilde also had sent Maksym to finish the job. The special attraction of the job was twofold. First, Maksym hated Federov and blamed the Russian for a botched assignment that had involved the two of them. Second, there had been a possibility that another man may have been at the home also. That man was Maksym's own brother, Brendan Whelan; the person he hated most of all in this world.

As things developed, another Bureau agent had killed the rogue agent. Federov had been outshot by his intended victim, Cliff Levell, a former Marine and CIA operative who headed an organization that was the mortal enemy of Fairchilde's group. On the bright side, Whelan indeed had been there. Unfortunately, one of his deadliest colleagues in the Sleeping Dogs unit, Marc Kirkland, had been there also. Kirkland's monk-like devotion to mastering all forms of martial arts combined with his genetic gifts made him one of the most dangerous men in the world. Before Maksym could kill Whelan and finish off Levell, he'd been surprised by Kirkland, who wounded him with a shuriken and a throwing knife. The shuriken had pierced the back of his right hand, causing him to drop the SIG he had been holding. The knife, a Smith & Wesson SWTK10CP, had been imbedded in his ridiculously muscled neck dangerously close to the carotid artery. As he yanked the knife free, blood began to flow freely from the wound. Kirkland, brandishing his fabled katana *doragon no chi,* or Dragon's Blood, had charged. Maksym had heard the rumors that Kirkland could halve a man from scalp to groin with a single blow of the weapon. Ordinarily Maksym feared no one, but under these circumstances, he chose discretion as the better part of valor. He dove through a window and sprinted through neighboring yards. Eventually he'd found a cab idling beneath a large shade tree while the driver ate his lunch. Maksym had quickly squeezed into the back seat and said, "I've had an accident. Get me to the hospital. Quick!"

The driver, with a half-eaten sandwich in front of his open mouth, stared at this huge, bleeding man for a couple of seconds. Then realizing how much of the cab's rear area the passenger filled, tossed the sandwich on the seat and stomped on the accelerator.

Several quick blocks down the street, Maksym said, "Pull over and park for a minute. I need to tell you what happened in case I'm unconscious when we get to the hospital."

The driver dutifully pulled to the curb and turned to look at his passenger.

"Put it in park," Maksym said. The driver, a recent immigrant from Somalia, complied.

As soon as the transmission was disengaged, Maksym clamped a huge, thick, bloody hand around the man's throat. He yanked him into the backseat before the driver could blow the horn, stomp the accelerator, or do anything else to call attention to his situation. Maksym snapped the man's neck with the ease of twisting a cap off a bottle of beer. He roughly sat the body up in a corner of the rear seat to make it appear the cab had a fare. He quickly emerged from the rear of the cab and climbed into the driver's seat. It was approximately four miles to Union Station. He covered it in about twenty minutes, and parked the cab a few blocks away, stashing the driver's body on the rear floor of the cab.

On the walk to the station he made a quick stop at a CVS and bought a small bottle of hydrogen peroxide, some bandages, and a triple extra-large tee shirt. It was the only shirt he could find that might fit him with reasonable comfort. It had the Washington Wizard's logo on it. He ducked into the men's room and cleaned up and dressed the wound as best he could. Next, he bought a ticket to Boston on the 4:00 p.m. Acela Express. Twenty minutes later the train pulled out of the station. When it reached Penn Station in New York City, he got off and contacted Fairchilde.

Two of Fairchilde's men, both large and well-dressed but clearly hired muscle, picked Maksym up in front of an Irish bar across from the railway station. They took him to a mid-range hotel a few blocks away. One of the men paid the desk clerk in cash for one night's lodging in a suite then the three of them went upstairs to the room. Maksym wasted no time getting into the shower. Thirty minutes later he was sitting in the suite's living area speaking with Fairchilde and wearing fresh clothes that had been delivered to the room while he was showering. The muscle was standing expressionlessly behind Fairchilde's sofa. The bulges in their jackets were unmistakable.

"Well, Maksym," Fairchilde said, "you came to us highly recommended, but I can't say I'm impressed by your recent performances. A year ago you participated in an attempt on the life of the president. It failed miserably. A few days ago, I gave you a simple assignment. In the event the first two people I sent to kill Clifford Levell failed, you were to complete the job. Earlier today all three of you failed. That boggles my mind. It's simply incomprehensible that all three of you could fail. And, for what we pay you, it's inexcusable."

Maksym smiled. It was thin and hard. "I have not failed. I merely didn't complete the assignment in your timeframe. But I will complete it in mine." He paused briefly and the smile vanished. "I didn't antici-pate the presence of the additional FBI agent or Marc Kirkland. That was my error. Next time I will be better prepared."

Fairchilde stared at Maksym for a long moment. Maksym was certain he could read the other man's thoughts. Fairchilde would be weighing the recent failures against Maksym's well-earned status as perhaps the deadliest hominin on the planet. On the one hand he would be considering Maksym to be a potential liability. On the other, there was a strong possibility that Maksym would kill all three men in the room with his bare hands, with Fairchilde saved for last.

When Fairchilde finally spoke he said, "I believe in second chances, Maksym. And I believe you do intend to kill Levell." He paused and made a circular motion with a hand, as if sorting out his thoughts. "I believe, however, that for the time being we need to get you out of the country. You need time to recover from your wounds..."

"They are nothing," Maksym interrupted. "I have had many worse than this."

"I'm sure you have," Fairchilde said with an empty smile. "But just the same, Levell and the others know of your attempt on his life. It's likely he'll have Whelan, Kirkland and the others hunting for you."

"Let them hunt." Maksym said it with a snarl. "It is my intention to kill them too."

"In good time, Maksym. In the meantime, the person who recom-mended you to us has requested some time with you."

"Zheng? The Chinese finance minister?"

Fairchilde nodded. "Yes. I'll arrange to have you flown by private jet to Toronto. From there you are to fly commercial to Macao for the meeting with Zheng. After your business with him is concluded, we'll revisit the Levell matter."

A trace of a smile flickered across Maksym's scarred face. *You have no idea it's Zheng who I really work for. Or that his plan is for me to kill you when he deems it appropriate.*

Chapter 12
WANA, SOUTH WAZIRISTAN, PAKISTAN

WHEN HE REGAINED CONSCIOUSNESS, Turan was lying on a filthy cot in Wana's cramped and dirty infirmary. He didn't know how badly he had been injured, but felt grateful to have a cot in the infirmary. The mullahs at the madrassa often had reminded the students how desperate things were in South Waziristan—one hospital bed for every twenty-two hundred people; one physician for every seventy-seven hundred people. These numbers were far worse than for Pakistan as a whole. He knew the FATA (the Federally Administered Tribal Areas, a semi-autonomous tribal region in the northwestern part of Pakistan) was the most impoverished part of the nation, with an annual per capita income well below one thousand dollars. Mullah Siddiqui had said repeatedly that the poverty was the fault of the Jews. Their goal was to kill all faithful Muslims by starvation and disease.

There was a bulky bandage around his aching head, and he was still wearing his now-bloody *kameez*, a long tunic-like shirt, and *shalwar*, the loose, baggy pajama-like trousers, wide at the top and narrow at the ankle worn by Pakistani men. He lay there, hovering along the edges of consciousness, trying to figure out what had happened. In his pain and confusion, he began to hallucinate that he had been flung back in time to the legendary Battle of Wana.

Turan Salam had been barely more than a toddler at the time, but he still had vivid memories of the intense fighting. Although Wana was the largest town of South Waziristan Agency and the summer head-quarters for the Agency's administration, it was still a small town of barely two thousand residents. But that didn't include a current head-count of the several hundred nonindigenous Islamist fighters. At times, that number swelled to a sum greater than the native population. The infamous weeklong battle hadn't changed the area's popularity as a staging ground for Taliban and al-Qaeda fighters.

The battle had started near the town of Wana following confirma-tion by Pakistan's ISI (Inter-Services Intelligence) Covert Action Divi-sion of the presence nearby of a High-Value Target (HVT). It was reported to be Ayman al-Zawahiri, al-Qaeda's second in command after Osama bin Laden. Fighting soon spread into the mountain fast-ness of the Sulaiman Range along the border with Afghanistan. There the jihadi warriors, under the leadership of the revered mujahideen Nek Muhammad, a member of the Ahmadzai Pashtun tribe, as was Turan, had fortified the caves and dug tunnels near the peaks. Some of the tunnels were believed to have been interconnected with the Black Caves (Tora Bora) region of Afghanistan. Turan had been told that there were at least five hundred Taliban and al-Qaeda fighters, maybe twice that many. By the end of the weeklong battle, they had been opposed by nearly seven thousand Pakistan Army regulars and elements of its special mountain troops. The soldiers had pushed into the mountains, encountering wave after wave of al-Qaeda counterat-tacks, as additional foreign jihadis continued to join the fight. After days of intense combat, the army had finally established control over the entire area, but sporadic fighting continued as the soldiers pursued the al-Qaeda fighters. The official word was that the army had suffered casualties of forty-nine soldiers dead, thirty-nine wounded, and eleven captured. The al-Qaeda forces lost fifty-five dead and one hundred forty-nine captured. Most of them were Uzbeks and Chechens. The government had never established whether there had been a HVT involved in the fighting. The Inter-Services Public Relations (ISPR), an administrative military media brand that broadcast and coordinated military news and information, claimed he had indeed been there, but had managed to escape into Afghanistan through the network of tunnels.

But, Turan knew from the stories told by the mullahs and others, the fighting had not ended with the conclusion of the Battle of Wana. It erupted again and again with hit-and-run raids on government troops. Fighting even broke out between the Pashtun tribal fighters led by Nek Muhammad and other Waziri Taliban leaders who declared jihad against foreign fighters from Uzbek, Chechnya, Tajikistan, Uyghur-dominated Xinjiang, and various Arab countries. Eventually, the government had been forced to strike a peace treaty with Nek Muhammad. It lasted barely a few weeks before fighting resumed. Two months later Nek Muhammad had been killed by an American missile while giving an interview by satellite phone to a foreign news organization. His legend, growing larger and more improbable by the day, had been a catalyst in drawing thousands of warriors from the Mehsud and Wazir tribes to South Waziristan to join the Taliban fighters who were already there.

To this day, the huts of villagers and farmers in the surrounding area bore the scars of the ceaseless fighting. In some areas along the road from Wana to Tank, the winter headquarters for the South Waziristan Agency, every one of the now-empty houses had been affected. Their twenty-feet-high sunbaked mud walls, studded with pebbles to withstand machinegun bursts, were perforated with perfect round shell-holes; mute testimony to the occasional presence of the army.

IN HIS SEMI-DELIRIOUS STATE, Turan sensed the presence of someone beside his cot. He forced his eyes open despite the searing pain in his head. It took a moment before he could make out the features of the man looking down at him. It was no one he recognized. Looking up from his cot close to the floor, the man looming over Turan seemed tall. Very tall. He wore Pashtun clothing with an ammo belt slung around his shoulders. There was an AK47 in his left hand. He looked young, only a few years older than Turan, but he had a world-weary aura of someone much older. The stranger wore a full beard, but Turan could distinguish scars that appeared fresh on his right cheek. He looked into the man's dark eyes and saw only ice. *Is he* Malak al-Maut (the Islamic Angel of Death, known in the West as the Grim Reaper) *come to collect my soul?* Turan shivered involuntarily and pressed back against the soiled cot.

The man stared at him in silence for a while, further unnerving Turan. Finally, he said, "What is your name?"

"Turan. Turan Salam." The boy stuttered as he said it. Even so, he was reassured by the fact that the man spoke in Turan's native Wazirwola Pashto dialect and not Urdu, the lingua franca of Pakistan.

The man smiled. "Turan is a good name. It means 'one who is brave'. Are you brave, Turan?"

The boy shrugged. "I don't know what happened. I don't know how I got here. I don't know if I did something brave."

Anger flashed in the man's cold eyes, further alarming Turan. *Did I do something wrong? Was I not brave? Is this man going to shoot me?*

"Because of the cowardly American infidels, you did not have a chance to be brave."

"What happened? I think I was in school listening to Mullah Siddiqui, then I don't remember what happened after that."

The man raised a fist in the air and shook it vigorously. "The American devils used a Hellfire missile from one of their accursed drones to kill Mullah Siddiqui. It also killed several of your classmates and, like you, wounded many others."

Turan was shocked. "But why would they kill Mullah Siddiqui? He was a man of God. A man of peace."

The man scoffed. "No, boy, he was much more than that. He was a true mujahideen who led many punishing raids against the Americans and their Western allies in Afghanistan." He stared down at Turan. "He was a true martyr."

Turan didn't know what to say, but he was afraid to say nothing. "Who are you?" he stammered.

"I am Bazir Haqqani."

"Bazir. That means 'keeper of eagles.'"

Bazir, with an icy sneer said, "Yes, and I have my eagles right here." He shook his AK47 for emphasis. "I send them to strike down infidels, apostates, sinners, and all those who refuse to accept the true words of the Prophet."

After several moments of silence, Turan said, "Why are you here? Do you seek something from me?"

Bazir nodded. "Yes. I want you to help me avenge the death of Mullah Siddiqui and all the other brave and noble martyrs who have sacrificed their lives in the name of Islam."

Now it was Turan who nodded his head, as vigorously as he could manage given the awful ache in his head. "I will do it. I want to do it. Just tell me what it is you want me to do."

"For now, you must recover from your wounds. Later I will return for you and others and take you to a camp. There you will be trained to become one of Allah's holy warriors. Depending on the level of skills you develop, you will be assigned a specific mission against the infidels.

"Our brother Pashtuns in Afghanistan have suffered invasions, first by the warmonger Soviets and then the detestable Americans and their allies. We must do all we can, make whatever sacrifice is necessary to help our brothers destroy these foreign infidels."

"I will be ready," Turan said. "I will serve the Taliban proudly."

Bazir smiled benignly and wagged his head slowly back and forth. "The Taliban are amateurs, as is al-Qaeda and its sycophants. I serve Mukhtar Rahim Khan. He has pledged his allegiance to the great Nadir Shah, founder of the Holy Army of the Caliphate."

Turan's eyes widen in surprise. "Mukhtar Rahim Khan! I have heard many great things about him. The Americans captured him on the battlefield in Afghanistan and held him prisoner for years in the place called Guantanamo."

"Mukhtar is recruiting warriors for the Holy Army of the Caliphate who are willing to give their lives for the caliphate. Willing to destroy all infidels including the Shia false-believers." He paused and stared hard at Turan for several moments, then said, "This is the only opportunity you will ever have to rise above the poverty into which you were born. And you can do it in the service of the true followers of Allah."

Chapter 13

ANTELOPE WELLS, NEW MEXICO

DAVID HIDALGO, eyes closed, sat very still in his desk chair, almost willing the struggling HVAC system to ratchet down the room temperature. The Border Patrol's Antelope Wells port of entry had been established by President Grant in 1872, but the current facility was new. The project included an 11,000-square-foot building where Hidalgo's office was located, and a 5,000-square-foot forward operating base (FOB) for agents and officers of the U.S. Customs and Border Protection agency (CBP). The $13 million in funds for the new structures were part of the multi-billion dollar American Recovery and Reinvestment Act of 2009 (ARRA); the infamous presidential stimulus package.

The border crossing was open every day from 8:00 AM to 4:00 PM solely for non-commercial traffic. On average, between four and a dozen vehicles crossed daily. Although New Mexico Highway 81 was a paved, two-lane road that ended at the crossing, its continuation on the Mexican side was a seven-mile stretch of dirt that connected with distant Route 2. The port was the only development for miles in either direction. In fact, the only permanent resident was a single CBP agent. The other agents made the more than two-hour commute from either Lordsburg or Deming.

Hidalgo glanced at his watch, confirming that it was only noon. He had four more hours of duty plus the long drive to his home in Lordsburg. This wasn't the glamorous career he'd envisioned when the CBP had recruited him following his discharge from the Army. His goal had been to become a part of the U.S. Border Patrol's Special Operations Group (SOG), headquartered in El Paso, Texas. He had been hooked by the agency's literature: "SOG's Mobile Response Unit (MRT) is a rapidly deployable asset capable of addressing problematic areas along the Nation's borders, providing an immediate-response capability to emergent and high-risk incidents requiring specialized skills and tactics." Its Selection and Training Course (BSTC) purposely was designed to mirror aspects of the U.S. Special Operations Forces' grueling selection courses. But, among other qualifications, there was a requirement that a candidate had to have a minimum of three years of continuous Border Patrol service in good standing. So, for the time being, he'd ended up here in the smallest and least-used border crossing of the forty-three ports of entry along the border with Mexico. *Hell,* he thought, *less than a dozen vehicles cross daily, on average, and that number is in a steady decline. The most excitement this port has ever had was the seizure of one hundred twenty-eight pounds of marijuana in 2013. Pretty damned puny when compared to the fifty-five thousand pounds seized in all of New Mexico that year, or the more than two million pounds for the entire southwestern border.* Still, he knew, there was no move afoot to close the Antelope Wells port of entry.

Outside it would have been at least 110° in the shade. If there'd been any shade. But the sun was directly overhead now, leaving the Border Patrol station incapable of generating a shadow. Not that he would have gone outside anyway. He'd grown up in Tucson where temperatures in the surrounding Sonoran Desert were even higher. Although its inland position provided a higher elevation for the Chihuahuan Desert beyond his office window, it was still hot as hell. He thought about his high school football practices in Arizona, the two-a-days that started in mid-August. He shook his head. *How the hell did I survive that? Maybe it was just the fact that I was a teenage kid and too naïve to think about how miserable it was.* He grinned. *Maybe it was the smoking-hot cheerleaders who were always hanging around the practice field.*

He opened his eyes and looked out the window at the shimmering heat broiling the desert landscape. He was convinced that his was the most boring job in CBP. He was a third generation Mexican-American, a graduate of Arizona State University, and a former member of the U.S. Army Military Police. When he'd joined the CBP he'd thought his life would be exciting; chasing down drug runners and illegals who weren't willing to take the legitimate path to citizenship like his grandparents had. At first, he'd been assigned to the port of entry in Nogales, Arizona, just an hour south of his hometown. But when his training period was up, he'd been reassigned to Antelope Wells. *What a joke! There aren't any antelope or wells anywhere near this shit-hole.*

Hidalgo stood and walked to the windows. His office was on the second floor in the southeastern corner of the port's new administration building. The windows provided views to the east and south across the border with Mexico. He swept his gaze slowly from left to right. He'd seen the same scenery countless times. From the razorback escarpment of U-Bar Ridge, south to the solitary mound of Sentinel Butte and beyond it the rugged terrain of Alamo Hueco and Pierce Peak. Further south were the dull grey hills of Eagle Mountain and Middle Mountain, almost straddling the border.

Even with the tinted windows, the sun's midday glare was fierce. Hidalgo blinked several times in reaction to the glare, then slipped his sunglasses on and swept the scene again. It was some of the ugliest territory he'd ever seen, and that included his tours of duty in Afghanistan and Iraq. When he was in middle school, his father had taken the family to see the Painted Desert in northeastern Arizona. It was interesting terrain. With a little creativity, it was possible to imagine that a divine artist had softened the harshness of the arid terrain with variegated pastels. But the colors of this, the Chihuahuan Desert, looked more like a drunk had smeared it with brown and gray vomit using a tar mop.

He found it ironic that Antelope Wells was located in Hidalgo County, and hoped it wasn't named after one of his ancestors. *If so, why couldn't it have been a county in Northern California, or South Florida, or better yet Hawaii? Not this godforsaken desert in south-western New Mexico, where most living things were designed to harm you—rattlesnakes, Gila monsters, scorpions, tarantulas, wolves, jaguars, and an infinite variety of cacti.*

He glanced to the south across the border with Mexico. The crossing checkpoint was just inside the American side. He could see the heads of the two agents inside the air-conditioned structure. Nothing moved around them. No vehicles had passed through the checkpoint in the past few hours. There were no dust clouds rising in the distance on the Mexican side to indicate any were approaching. *Another hellish day in the most boring shit-hole on the southern border. How'd I get so lucky?*

He caught motion out of the corner of his right eye and turned to see a white Jeep Grand Cherokee pull into a parking place below his office. The broad, diagonal green strip on the door identified it as a Border Patrol vehicle. Hidalgo watched the driver exit the truck and recognized him as Tom Donnelly, the FOB's Supervisory Border Patrol Agent and the man in charge of the Antelope Wells station. Hidalgo noted that Donnelly was wearing the CBP's rough duty (RD) uniform —a green, long-sleeve work shirt, green cargo pants, black work boots, and a green baseball cap with the CBP insignia above the bill. His spirits brightened. *Maybe something's going down for a change, besides the rare mind-numbingly boring search of vehicles crossing over from Mexico.*

Barely a minute later, the door opened and Donnelly walked in, nodding at Hidalgo. "Dave," he said. The walk from his truck to the entrance to the facility was only about fifty feet, but Donnelly's shirt was wet under the arms and beads of sweat dotted his forehead. He went straight to the small refrigerator and grabbed a cold bottle of water.

"You're not exactly dressed for a party, Boss. Something up tonight?"

Donnelly took a long pull on the water bottle, draining half its contents. He wiped his mouth with a shirtsleeve. "Yeah. We got word from one of our informants in the Federales," he said, using a slang term for the Mexican Federal Police or *Policía Federal*, an institution created to fight organized crime in the United Mexican States. "Says there's going to be a load of Mary Jane smuggled in tonight."

"I assume from your RD uniform it's gonna be somewhere around here."

Donnelly emptied the water bottle and tossed it in a wastebasket. "Yeah, about twelve klicks east of here."

"That should put it between Eagle and Middle Mountains."

"Yeah, there's an arroyo that splits the terrain between them. Starts right at the border and runs north for about four klicks, then a series of old ranch roads wind in a westerly direction to Highway 81, intersecting it maybe twelve klicks north of here. From there, it's smooth sailing to Lordsburg, Deming, and points beyond."

"So I take it I shouldn't plan on leaving at four," Hidalgo said with a grin.

Donnelly fished another water from the refrigerator. "No. Call the wife and tell her not to hold dinner. If the intel is right—for a change— I'm going to need you for a possible intercept tonight."

Hidalgo frowned. "It'll give her an evening alone with the kids. After being with them all day, I'm not sure she'll like that."

"You have two little girls, right?" Donnelly said.

"Yeah, ages two and four." Hidalgo smiled. "I never asked you, Boss; you got kids?"

Donnelly finished off the second bottle of water. "Yeah, a son and daughter, but they were already in college when their mother and I split up." He tossed the empty in the same wastebasket with the first one and said, "Better go put your RD on. And grab a helmet and vest too."

Hidalgo raised an eyebrow. "You expecting a firefight?"

"I don't know what to expect. It just pays to be cautious."

"Why? What did the Federale informant say?"

Donnelly shook his head. "It isn't what he said. I just don't trust any intel from south of the border. It's rarely accurate. Hell, half the time it's designed to throw us off what's really going down."

Hidalgo thought about the comment, then said, "What did the informant say was supposed to happen tonight?"

"The usual—a half dozen or so illegals doubling as mules to help pay the coyote's fees."

"Doesn't sound particularly dangerous. We bringing anyone else along?"

Donnelly nodded. "HQ seems to think there may be more to it than five or six peasants toting weed. They're sending a BORTAC (Border Patrol Tactical Unit) team by chopper. Should be here in about an hour."

"BORTAC? Shit, does HQ think the illegals are smuggling pot or WMDs?"

Donnelly's face screwed up in a pained expression. "I don't know what the fuck they think. I just know the last time I worked with BORTAC it turned into a colossal cluster fuck. They're as bad as the Bureau—got to be large and in charge. And they don't know shit about the terrain or the types of situations we locals deal with. They mostly just get in the way."

"I don't know, Boss; BORTAC doesn't usually get involved when it's just a handful of *peones* looking for a steady paycheck north of the border."

"Maybe, maybe not." He motioned to Hidalgo to follow him as he walked over to a large, high-resolution satellite photo tacked to an interior wall. "Here's us." He pointed to a yellow pin marking the location of the Antelope Wells FOB. Next, he pointed to a spot on the border about twenty miles west of Antelope Wells, and dragged his finger north another twenty miles. "Over here is the Animas Valley FOB, known as Camp Garza. Sittin' way the fuck up there, it's about as useful as tits on a boar when it comes to covering border traffic."

Donnelly repositioned his finger to a spot on the border about twenty-five miles west of Columbus, New Mexico. "This is the Camp Ramsey FOB. That's about sixty miles east of here." His finger circled a large area on both sides of the border surrounding New Mexico's southeastern Boot Heel. "That means we're responsible for about twenty-five hundred to three thousand square miles of some of the most desolate land in the Western Hemisphere."

He pointed to an area on the Mexican side of the border. "This is the village of San Luis in the northernmost reaches of the Sierra Madre Occidental mountains. It's maybe ten to twelve klicks over the border." He paused and stared at Hidalgo. "Guess what I just learned is very near the village."

Hidalgo shrugged. "I don't know."

"You're not supposed to know. I was just told by the CPA (Chief Patrol Agent) when I was in El Paso yesterday. I was ordered not to say anything to anyone else. But it may have something to do with tonight's operation, so I'm sharing it with you, but you need to keep this under your hat. That means don't share it with anyone else, not even the Mrs. Understood?"

Hidalgo nodded his head slowly. "Understood."

Donnelly turned back to the satellite photo and again put his finger on the spot that was labeled "San Luis." "Just west of this village and at a slightly higher elevation is a training and staging camp. As far as we know, it's been there for a year or more."

He turned and looked directly at Hidalgo. "It's operated by HAC, the Holy Army of the Caliphate."

Hidalgo clearly was stunned. "Holy shit! HAC is right here on our border?"

Donnelly nodded grimly. "And apparently it's not the only jihadi installation sitting a stone's throw away from the homeland."

"What the hell are they gonna do? Invade the U.S.?"

Donnelly scoffed. "I wish they were only that far along. The CPA told me several different jihadi groups have been slipping agents into the country for years; maybe since before 9/11. Most now have sworn allegiance to HAC. The CPA said DHS believes there are thousands of them scattered in cities and towns all across America—for the day the command comes down from their caliph to butcher us infidels."

"My God!" Hidalgo was staring at the satellite photo and shaking his head back and forth in disbelief. "That's the kind of thing that could bring the country to its knees. The shock, the confusion—we'd be sitting ducks for a well-organized force." He turned from the photo and looked at Donnelly. "If we've known about this for some time, why the hell haven't we done anything about it?" His words were laced with anger.

Now it was Donnelly's turn to shake his head. "You'll have to take that up with the geniuses inside the Beltway."

"So those bastards are playing politics with the lives of thousands —shit, maybe millions—of Americans, all so they can...can...what?" Hidalgo stared at the other man with a dazed look on his face.

Donnelly stared back for several moments, then said, "The CPA told me he'd heard a rumor that the current administration sees it as an opportunity to destroy the constitutional restraints on executive power and the congressional and judicial checks on that power."

"But how can that be?" Hidalgo said, raising his voice in outrage. "This is America! It's a democracy; the people run the country."

Donnelly shook his head, a sad look on his face. "That's what America was, Dave. It isn't what it's become. The lunatics really are running the asylum today."

Hidalgo slammed his fist against a desktop. "So you're telling me that we don't know what to expect tonight. We could intercept a handful of raggedy-assed Latinos each with a half-pound of pot shoved up his ass, or a couple of hundred black clad, sword waving towel-heads screaming 'Allahu Akbar?'"

Donnelly shrugged. "We've got ground sensors in the area."

"That's really helpful," Hidalgo said with sarcasm. "Arizona's got a system of towers topped with a package of sensors—radar as well as daytime and infrared cameras. If there's an alert, someone in the control room in Tucson can zoom in for a closer look. The damn cameras are high quality and have a range of eight to ten miles to show whether the bodies are carrying weapons. Plus they augment that with MVSS (mobile video surveillance systems) deployed on hilltops throughout the sector. But that's Arizona. Us, shit, we have no idea what we're walking into."

Donnelly made a calming motion with his hand. "It's not that bad. BORTAC's sending a drone with infrared sensors to scope the area."

"And can it detect the presence of weapons?"

"I don't know."

Hidalgo was quiet for a few moments then said, "I suppose BORTAC's gonna chopper in and let the illegals know they're coming when they're still miles away?"

"No, they're putting down on an old ranch road about four klicks north of the border. That's where we'll rendezvous with them. Then we'll all hike down the arroyo and interdict the illegals when they come across."

Chapter 14

MACAO

MAKSYM'S weary thoughts were interrupted as the limo turned into the entrance to the Banyan Tree Macau Hotel. It was a newly risen monument to *über* luxury on the Cotai Strip in Macau. The Strip itself was 5.2 square kilometers (2.0 square miles) of newly reclaimed land in Seac Pai Bay. The strip conjoined the Portuguese and Chinese named islands of Coloane and Taipa; hence its name. Cotai was a portmanteau of the islands. Its creation was mandated by a combination of the scarcity of land in Macau, the most densely populated region in the world with twenty-one thousand people per square kilometer (fifty-five thousand per square mile), and the burgeoning gaming industry in what had become the largest gambling center in the world. Despite the density, Macau was one of the world's richest cities and its GDP per capita by purchasing power parity was higher than that of any other country in the world. Oddly, despite its notoriously poor air quality, Macau's residents enjoyed the second highest life expectancy in the world.

The Cotai Strip was where the luxury resorts and casinos were being developed. It was so new that it had not yet been assigned to any of the freguesias, or civil parishes, in Macau.

Maksym was aware that where gaming was concerned, Zheng

fancied himself a player. His favorite casino was the Venetian on the Cotai Strip, but he preferred to stay at the ridiculously luxurious Banyan Tree. It was part of the holdings of the Galaxy Entertainment Group, a major hospitality developer, and only a third of a kilometer (339 yards) from the casino at the Venetian Macao. Zheng was a frequent guest at the Banyan Tree, and the management always put him up in the Sanctuary Pool Villa, a two-bedroom Eden surrounded by a private pool. It had floor to ceiling glass walls, a kitchen that would impress a Parisian chef, and a private spa treatment room with both in-and-outdoor jet pools.

When the exhausted Maksym checked in, he found that Zheng's minions had placed him in a much smaller suite on the opposite side of the hotel. Even so, it was luxurious beyond anything Maksym could recall seeing. He wasted no time in showering and collapsing naked on the appropriately king-sized bed.

THE RINGING of the room phone woke Maksym up three hours later. It was one of Zheng's aides advising him that the finance minister was ready to meet with him. At once. For the money they paid him, Maksym was accustomed to his employers ordering him around. But he never liked it. *One day*, he thought, *I'm going to kill them, each and every one.* He glanced at the elaborate entertainment device on the nightstand. Its clock said it was 8:00 p.m. local time. He stood up and put on the same clothes he'd worn since his meeting with Fairchilde in the New York hotel.

Ten minutes later he was in the Sanctuary Pool Villa, sitting on a clearly expensive, ultramodern, and damned uncomfortable, chair. He assumed it was supposed to be a work of art that could double as a chair. It was clear to him that the designer had never bothered to sit in it. Or perhaps the designer was a lithe, tiny Asian person who could contort comfortably into any position, not a six and a half foot, three hundred pound man with less than three percent body fat to cushion his ass.

After several minutes, Zheng entered the room. He was preceded by four large, expressionless Chinese men who took up positions around the room where they each could clearly watch Maksym. Each folded his meaty hands in front, where Maksym assumed they could quickly draw their weapons.

Zheng was short and slender with a round face and wire-rim glasses. His close-cropped hair was brown, not the ubiquitous midnight black of most Chinese. And there was something about his features that belied pure Chinese genetics. Among other things Maksym had noticed at their first meeting, the man's eyes were hazel with dark green around the edges and gold in the center. He suspected Zheng was Uyghur. That had raised Maksym's curiosity. He knew that most Uyghurs were Sunni Muslims. He wondered how much that influenced Zheng's political intentions.

"So, Mr. Kozak, I understand you have had a bad time of it lately?" Zheng said with the slightest trace of a sneer.

"Call me Maksym." It was said pleasantly.

"You are a servant. I will call you whatever I choose." There was a hard edge to Zheng's voice and the sneer was gone.

Maksym gave a barely perceptible shrug, as if conserving energy.

"I must tell you that I am shocked at the turn of events at Levell's home. Part of it I can understand. The FBI agent was a greedy dilettante; an ineffective fool who had been on AGU's payroll for some years. Federov, on the other hand was a natural killer, as are you. But he was handicapped by his enormous ego. It was only a matter of time before it got him killed."

Zheng paused briefly. His English was nearly flawless. Maksym wasn't surprised. He had googled Zheng's background. The man had earned his undergraduate degree at Princeton, and a master's and Ph.D. in finance from the Wharton School at the University of Pennsylvania.

Zheng continued. "Whereas I could foresee the possible failure of the first two would-be assassins, it's yours that truly surprises me, Mr. Kozak. Please explain."

Maksym stared impassively at the finance minister and said nothing. After several moments, Zheng's face began to color as his glance flitted between his four bodyguards.

Finally, when Maksym sensed Zheng was about to explode in anger, he appeared to stretch languidly then suddenly jumped to his feet and took a menacing step toward Zheng. Two of the bodyguards immediately rushed forward to restrain Maksym. In a move almost too fast for a human mind to comprehend, he grabbed their skulls and crushed them together with such force they split open and blood and brain matter burst out. Their corpses had just begun to fall as he yanked their weapons free. In a feat nearly impossible for a Norm, he simultaneously fired in opposite directions at the two remaining bodyguards, hitting each of them squarely in the middle of the chest. The slugs tore through their hearts, killing them instantly. He brought both weapons to bear on the stunned Zheng, who had leaped to his feet in shock.

"You see, you little fuck. Anytime I want you, you're mine. The whole fucking Red Army can't keep me from killing you."

Zheng's wobbling knees could barely support him. He reached down to brace himself with a hand on a coffee table. He just stared in speechless horror at the four spreading pools of blood. A wet stain widened rapidly across the front of his own trousers.

"Sit down, Zheng," Maksym said pleasantly. "This isn't about which one of us has the biggest cock. It's about business. Let's have a conversation."

He stuck the weapons in the waistband of his trousers then collected two more from the other bodyguards. Zheng sat quietly on a white leather loveseat that would never be quite the same again, as he finished wetting himself. Maksym poured four fingers of Johnny Walker Blue into a cut crystal tumbler. He handed it to Zheng then sat on the coffee table facing him.

"We'll chalk that fiasco at Levell's up to the old adage that too many cooks spoil the soup. I'm sure I can convince that arrogant asshole Fairchilde not to make that mistake again."

Zheng shuddered, as if imagining what Maksym might do to AGU's leader.

"What's important for your plans is that we stay a step or two ahead of AGU. You want them to do the heavy lifting; create global chaos. Then when all of the other world powers are on their knees, China ascends to the 'throne.' Right?"

The Johnny Walker had begun to calm Zheng. "Yes. It has always been China's destiny to rule the planet." He thought about that for a moment then said, "And beyond."

Maksym sneered and shook his head. "I don't give a fuck about China and its fantasies about world or interplanetary domination. Money speaks to me. Pay me what I want and I'll help you realize your daydreams."

Zheng nodded. Color was starting to return to his face.

"But it's not altruism on your part that causes you to want your beloved China to succeed under the governance of just anyone, is it, Minister Zheng?"

"No," Zheng said in a voice just above a whisper.

"You little pansy, you plan to take control of the People's government and run the whole show yourself, don't you?"

Still a bit shaken, Zheng nodded slowly.

"It's time you shared your plans with me. From now on, consider us partners."

Chapter 15
THE LODGE

FOLLOWING his earlier meeting with Levell at the Lodge, Mitch Christie spent the rest of the afternoon exploring the facility. He had been given a wristband to wear during the time he was on premises with instructions that it would be reclaimed when he left the following day. A tiny microchip in the band would allow him access to almost anywhere in the Lodge and adjacent facilities. Christie also knew the chip served a dual purpose. It allowed the security staff to track his every move. That didn't surprise him. In fact, he'd expected it.

The surveillance wasn't what bothered him. It was the overnight part of this visit. He had survived a very rough physical and emotional time in his life. His wife had left him and taken their two children. Failure on the job had resulted in demotion and reassignment to the boonies. And his digestive system had almost killed him. Now, however, his star was rising once again. Despite his attempt to kill Whelan, the Irishman had persuaded Levell to engineer Christie's path back into the Bureau's good graces. Once again, he was operating out of headquarters in Washington D.C. His stomach issues were history. And, best of all in his opinion, there was a special woman in his life.

That was the rub. He had been instructed to come to the Lodge alone. That meant having to leave Camila Ramirez behind. He realized it was only one night, but the two of them cherished every minute together. He'd tried to avoid spending the night, but Levell was intractable, insisting he attend a meeting that would probably last late into the evening. Camila had only recently switched jobs from the Bernalillo County Sheriff's Office in New Mexico to the U. S. Capitol Police, and moved into his apartment in Falls Church. As he looked around the grounds—the swimming pools, the tennis courts, the riding facilities—he realized how much she would have enjoyed being here. Even if he was in meetings most of the time, there was still the evening. Instead, he had come alone.

Thinking about Camila, he unconsciously pulled out his cell phone and started to speed dial her number. He stopped just in time when he realized the Lodge's security measures either would block the call or monitor it. He definitely didn't want to appear needy or clingy to Levell or Camila. He slid the phone back into a pocket and glanced at his watch. It was almost time for the meeting to start. He gave one last look around the sylvan setting, took a deep breath of fresh air—who knew when he'd get the next one—and headed back to the main building.

EVEN THOUGH THE buildings and other facilities that comprised the Lodge were virtually impervious to electronic eavesdropping, Levell was a stickler for taking every precaution to ensure confidentiality. The floor of the Lodge's library was made of six-inch thick, three-foot stone squares overlain with throw rugs that reflected Southwestern style and colors. The light switch on the wall beside the entrance to the library served a dual purpose. It did turn on the lights recessed in the lower part of the tray ceiling, providing accent for the fireplace and bookcases. But if flipped ten or more times in rapid succession, the switch activated an electrical motor. The motor caused one of the stone plates in the floor to recess and pull back under the adjoining flooring, revealing a set of steps leading down into a chamber beneath the library.

Bottles of fine wine were stacked and gathering dust in specially crafted shelving. The walls, floor, and ceiling of the chamber were lined with lead and other more sophisticated materials designed to reject any attempt to probe its activities. Although well-ventilated and climate-controlled, there was a faint mustiness appropriate to a wine cellar. The concealed room was furnished with a long, well-polished mahogany table and several comfortable chairs. Attendance at SAS meetings was always limited to only those members whose knowledge, position, or connections applied to a given meeting's business. It was on a strictly need-to-know basis, and Levell was the sole arbiter of who met that qualification. Tonight's meeting concerned an update on threats to the homeland. It also included the introduction of Mitch Christie and the role he would be expected to play in SAS operations.

Also attending the meeting were Gabriella Hamish, a senior fellow in a Washington, D.C., think tank that catered to a single client—the Department of Homeland Security. She sat in the middle of the table opposite Levell, who always chose a middle seat. In terms of group psychology, it was the weakest position, but so strong was the force of Levell's personality that he purposely chose it. Hamish was flanked by Chester Sturges, the Deputy Director of Operations for the CIA, and Harriman Floyd, head of the NSA's Associate Directorate for Security and Counterintelligence, also known as The Q Group. Navy Admiral Clayton Lawler, Vice Chair of the Joint Chiefs, sat at one end of the table in the chair that had been occupied in the recent past by Marine Corps Major General Roscoe "Buster" McCoy, Levell's closest friend and Lawler's former roommate at the Naval Academy. Levell, McCoy, and the Muellers had founded the SAS. A former Russian operative, Kirill Federov, had murdered McCoy a few months earlier. Federov also had been the assailant who had wounded Levell in a shootout at Levell's Georgetown home. But Levell had been the better shot, and mortally wounded Federov.

The table's other end seat always was occupied by one of the Mueller brothers. Tonight it was Tomas, the youngest at seventy-nine. The principal deputy director of National Intelligence, Damian Zarella, a Marine Corps four-star general, sat to Tomas's left. Levell was next to him. Mitch Christie occupied the seat on Levell's left.

Levell cleared his throat as a means of calling the meeting to order. It had no effect on the gravelly raspiness of his voice.

"Alright, lady," he nodded at Hamish, a stout woman with thick glasses and short, badly cut, salt and pepper hair, "and gentlemen. To plagiarize Robert Frost, we have 'miles to go before we sleep.' Let's get started."

Levell glanced at Christie. "First up, I want to introduce a new member of our organization, Special Agent Mitch Christie."

One by one, Christie made eye contact with everyone at the table.

"Which agency, FBI?" Zarella said.

Christie nodded.

"Special Agent? Hell, we have SAS people much higher up in the Bureau than that," Zarella said warily.

"True," Levell said, "but Mitch is the recently appointed deputy assistant director—the number two man—in the Counterterrorism Division. Prior to that he was the DAD in International Operations. He's an eighteen-year veteran of the Bureau, well-connected, and in a position to be a great asset for us."

Levell looked at everyone around the table, and pointedly at Zarella. "Let's move on." He paused briefly and leaned back in his wheelchair. "I've received an invitation from a most improbable source."

"What source?" Mueller said.

A cat-that-caught-the-mouse grin spread across Levell's craggy features. "Harland Fairchilde."

"Fairchilde?" Zarella spit the word out in surprise. "What does that sonofabitch want with you?"

Still grinning, Levell said, "Believe it or not, he wants to meet with me to discuss burying the hatchet."

"Where? In our skulls?" Sturges said.

"Why does he need to meet? He could simply call you," Floyd said.

The grin vanished from Levell's face. "I'm sure he doesn't want to use any form of communication that could be bugged or traced back to him." He turned toward Tomas Mueller. "He's asked that we meet on your ship, *The Captain Molly*. He knows it from the days when it was owned by Chaim Laski, and is aware of its impregnability from eavesdropping of any kind."

Mueller shrugged. "Of course, that shouldn't be a problem. Let me know when you'll be having your meeting and I'll make certain it's available to you."

"Tonight's meeting specifically concerns a critical domestic issue and is the reason for Ms. Hamish's presence. Because of its nature, I believe Agent Christie can be of great value."

"But didn't you say he just came over from the International Operations Division?" the CIA's Sturgis said.

"Yes, and that should be helpful, given that the Bureau and Agency don't share intel very well. Never hurts to have another source, does it, Chester?"

Sturgis looked around the table for support and got none.

"Alright, if we're finished with digressions, let's address the real issue. It concerns our all but wide open southern border."

"The war on drugs?" Lawler said.

"Drug smuggling is no longer the real issue, Admiral. It's much more complicated," Hamish said.

"Hard to fathom that," Lawler said. "We know from experience that drug usage weakens its users' will and perception of reality. It unmoors young adults from the traditional institutions of work, family, and civil society. They become distrustful of their fellow citizens. They become easy prey for the lies of a nation's enemies."

"I agree," Hamish said. "And the current administration's agenda appears to be aimed only at enacting laws decriminalizing drug possession and use. The real purpose, as you suggested, is to facilitate clouding the reason and weakening the political will of the users, principally the young. The bottom line is to control their voting behavior or lack of it. And we know whom that benefits."

The NSA's Harriman Floyd said, "Look, the drugs are bad enough, but the human smuggling is even more threatening to the safety and wellbeing of this country. And I'm not talking about illegals taking jobs from citizens, sending money out of the country, or using taxpayer provided services without paying any income taxes. Neither am I referring to the occasional killer, rapist, or other criminal who sneaks in, as a certain presidential candidate inarticulately pointed out."

Levell slapped the tabletop with his right hand, as if cutting off the comments. "I don't disagree with any of you, but drugs and illegal workers are among the least of our concerns. The border situation involves far worse than simply drugs and illegal workers. It's a principal reason why I asked Agent Christie to join us. But more on that later. First, I want you to hear what Gabby has to tell us." He looked across the table at Hamish and nodded.

All eyes turned toward the DHS consultant.

The small, dark eyes in her round face narrowed. "Some of you already know bits and pieces of what I'm going to tell you, but the full story is very disturbing."

She opened the iPad case in front of her, pressed the Home button, and slid an index finger across the bottom of the screen to activate the device. After using a thumbprint to unlock it, Hamish peered at the screen and selected an icon to access the notes she wanted.

Those at the table who knew Hamish had no doubts that the notes were merely a prop. They were well aware that she had an eidetic memory, and doubted she had ever forgotten a single image, sound, or object.

"Recently," she said, "CBP—the Customs and Border Patrol—made a number of disturbing findings in the deserts of Arizona and New Mexico. It happened on both sides of the border during a joint exercise involving the Mexican Army and U.S. law enforcement."

"I've been hearing rumors to that effect," Lawler said. "What exactly did they find?"

"Iranian Army uniforms, Islamic terrorist flags, prayer rugs, Qur'ans, and a book celebrating Islamic suicide bombings titled 'In Memory of Our Martyrs,' as well as other documents in Arabic and Urdu, the principal language of Pakistan."

There was silence at the table. After a while, Levell said, "Chester,

Harriman, did either of you know about this." The two men looked at each other.

The CIA's Sturgis said, "We've heard the rumors, of course; even asked DHS directly. Never got a straight answer."

"Same here," Harriman Floyd said. "Given what's at stake, there's no fucking excuse for that." He stared hard at Zarella, the Marine Corps general and principal deputy director of National Intelligence.

Levell turned to Zarella. "Damian, you're the PDD of National Intelligence, the president's top advisor on matters of national security. Your agency heads the seventeen separate entities that make up the country's intelligence community. Did you know about this?"

The general shook his head. "Like CIA and NSA, we heard stories, but couldn't get any hard intel from DHS. They gave the impression that they believed these were just unsubstantiated stories. Why in hell would they stonewall us?"

All heads turned toward Hamish.

Levell said, "Gabby, I doubt very seriously you knew anything about this before yesterday. What the hell is going on at DHS?" It was more of a demand than a question.

She smiled a hard little smile. "Politics."

"What the hell does that mean?" Lawler said.

"It means the secretary of DHS is a loyal and obedient servant of the Oval Office. We're all aware that our president and his handlers have their own agenda."

"And it's soft on jihadism and Marxism." Lawler said.

Hamish smiled again. It was an empty smile. "That's true, and it means that nothing is allowed to get out that might alarm the citizenry and result in calls for action. The secretary has been sitting on this under direct orders from the White House."

"How did you find out about it?" Tomas Mueller asked the question that was on everyone's mind.

"I have a close friend who's an EA in the office of the secretary of DHS. As you can imagine, she was stunned by this and passed it along to me at lunch yesterday." She paused briefly, then added, "But that's not the whole picture."

"What? There's more bad news?" Sturgis said.

Hamish nodded her head slowly up and down. "Indeed. Among other things of interest, detailed plans of Fort Bliss were recovered."

Lawler sat bolt upright, as if he'd been goosed. "Fort Bliss? Shit, that's the Army's second-largest installation and home to the First Armored Division. It covers some seventeen hundred square miles in Texas and New Mexico."

"And," Zarella said, "it's FORSCOM's (United States Army Forces Command) largest installation, too, as well as home to several other critical military units."

Levell said, "The headquarters for the El Paso Intelligence Center, a federal tactical operational intelligence center, also is hosted at Fort Bliss, as is the DoD (United States Department of Defense) counterpart, Joint Task Force North."

Mitch Christie, who had been quietly listening to the exchange, said, "If I'm hearing all this right, I think what Miss Hamish is saying is that the wide open southern border is a lot more problematic than drug smuggling and illegal workers sneaking into the country."

Several people around the table started to speak, but Levell silenced them with a hand motion. "It's all related," he said. "HAC, and before them other mujahideen organizations, have been working for years to infiltrate the U.S. They're aided by drug cartels, such as the Zetas, and criminal gangs like MS-13."

"Now we're getting into an area the Bureau tracks and I can offer some insight," Christie said. "We know that MS-13 has a presence in more than eleven hundred U.S. cities. The Zetas have a cooperative arrangement with MS-13 for smuggling jihadis into the U.S. To put some numbers on this, we know that al-Qaida, for example, would pay these gangs between thirty thousand and fifty thousand dollars for each sleeper agent smuggled across the border from Mexico. HAC is no different."

"Beats the hell out of the twenty-five hundred to four thousand bucks per illegal worker the patrones charge for a coyote's services," Floyd said.

Christie continued, "The sleepers are also provided with phony identification, most often bogus matricula consular ID cards."

"Bogus ma…what?" Lawler said.

"They're identification cards," Levell said, "issued by the Government of Mexico through its consulate offices to Mexican nationals residing outside of Mexico and essentially are indistinguishable from Mexico's official ID. They're commonly accepted in the U.S. to open bank accounts and obtain driver's licenses. But some of the Hezbollah and Iranian Revolutionary Guards also pick up fake passports in Venezuela."

"So the evidence is that there are what…maybe thousands of terrorists now living inside this country?" Mueller said.

"It gets worse," Christie said. "In addition to the HAC operatives, many of whom are former al-Quada and al-Shabbab followers, Iran's proxy terrorists have been operating out of Mexico for years too."

"Hezbollah?" Mueller said.

"Yes," Christie said.

"For those of you who may not be aware of this, Hezbollah is considered by many anti-terror experts to be the 'A' team of Muslim terrorist organizations," Levell said. "Some consider their operators to be the most skilled, the equals of the Russians, Chinese or Cubans because of their long-term strategic thinking. And they've been setting up shop in Mexico for the past fifteen to twenty years.

"We know, for example, that they're helping the drug cartels build smuggling tunnels under the US-Mexico border. According to satellite images, in some instances they're nearly identical to the maze of tunnels running under the Gaza-Egypt border. And, worse yet, Hezbollah is training the cartels' operatives to improve their bomb-making skills."

"So I'm getting that there are perhaps thousands of terrorist or mujahideen sleeper cells in cities, towns and villages all across America," Zarella said. "Presumably they're waiting for the signal to strike and amassing weapons and bombs, and identifying soft targets like schools, churches, malls, theaters, arenas, as well as police stations, military installations, and first responder facilities." He slumped in his chair. "A bloodbath. It'll be the beginning of the End of Times."

Levell's eyes were slitted and glittery, like those of a pissed-off snake. "Doesn't anyone want to ask the question?'

"What question?" Sturges said.

"The one the elephant in the middle of the room is sitting on. A bunch of mostly camel jockeys still stuck in the seventh century are pulling off this whole caliphate thing along with all these well-equipped, well-planned terrorist attacks around the world? All on their own?"

"Well," Lawler said slowly, as if afraid he might be giving the wrong answer. "They've got a lot of petrodollars behind them."

Tomas Mueller sighed and said, "And of course there are the machinations of AGU."

Levell smiled thinly, as if any more display than that would be painful. "Yes, Arab states from the Saudis to the Qataris and more are semi-secretly paying tribute to the HAC. And we all are well aware of AGU's relationship with Nadir Shah and his caliphate. But there's more. I see Chinese fingerprints all over this. They have the financial, military, and technological ability to provide the resources the Islamists don't have in-house." He paused for effect then said, "And, given their poorly disguised ambitions for world dominion, they stand to gain the most from the weakening of the West."

PART TWO—LONE WOLVES

It never troubles the wolf how many the sheep may be.

—Virgil

Chapter 16
PUEBLO, COLORADO

THE SIDEWALK CAFÉ was on a side street a half-block off the town's former main drag. The area had gone to seed, but was enjoying a nascent rebirth as a dining and artsy spot. The age and style of the buildings in the area were a dead giveaway that, in its younger days, this had been the town's central business district. The main street was lined with a mix of narrow, single-story shops and two-story buildings that had once provided live-above space for shopkeepers. Most of those upper floors were empty now, with stained blinds permanently affixed in the down position. The buildings were dated by their dull red brick façades, a building material commonly used in Colorado in the late nineteenth and early twentieth centuries. A few larger, tired-looking three-story structures occupied the corners. The ones still in operation had the look of former hotels turned flophouses.

It was past five in the afternoon and traffic was sparse, particularly on the side streets, where a mix of small retail shops and professional offices struggled to project the new "in-spot" atmosphere. On one of the side streets, a single story cafe with aging Art Deco embellishments looked out of place in the old western town. On the sidewalk in front of it, four young men sprawled in wrought iron chairs at a matching round table. The table top looked like the site of an empty beer bottle convention.

All of the men had long hair and carefully ungroomed whiskers. One wore a baggy, long-sleeved tee shirt that might once have been a shade of blue. The others wore collared shirts in faded shades that had been dull even when new. One wore sandals; two wore tattered running shoes. The fourth had on a scuffed and worn pair of desert boots. Each had a partially empty bottle of beer in his hand or on the table in front of him.

"Kev," the one in sandals said to the man in desert boots to his left, whose name was Kevin Johnson. "It's good to finally have you home." The speaker and the other two men raised their bottles in an informal salute, and all four took long pulls.

"So, dude," said the man in the tee shirt. "Guess you sure showed the fucking Army who's boss."

Johnson smiled. "Yep, Adam, I sure as hell did."

"Army? Shit, you showed this whole country of warmongering, capitalist pigs who's boss," said the fourth man, loudly. They'd each had several beers and the effects were becoming evident.

"Shit, Josh, somebody needed to do it. Why not me?" Johnson took another long pull on his beer.

.

THE SUN WAS FADING FAST behind the massive Rocky Mountains west of town. Three tables away a tall, husky man was sitting by himself. His medium brown hair was combed straight back forming a widow's peak. It made his aquiline features seem even sharper. He casually removed the sunglasses he'd been wearing. Anyone close enough to get a clear view of his eyes would have been startled by two things. They were a brilliant glacial blue. But even more arresting were the tiny dots of fiery red that glowed in the center of each eye. The man had a local newspaper spread on the table in front of him, but he wasn't reading it. A cup of long-cold coffee was nearby. He sat facing a direction where he could watch the four young men with his peripheral vision. He purposely never looked directly at them or showed any interest in their conversation, which was becoming louder with each beer. He'd been stalking the one named Kevin Johnson for the past three days.

"I GOTTA TELL YOU, Kev, when I seen that shit on TV 'bout you bein' a deserter, I figured they was gonna shoot your ass," Josh said. "I mean, you know, they was sayin' you left your post and joined up with them towelheads."

Johnson smiled and drained his bottle.

"Yeah, Kev," Zach said. "What exactly happened over there?"

Johnson shrugged and set the empty down in the midst of all the other dead soldiers. "Shit, dudes, the fuckin' Army was trying to get me killed. A fuckin' FOB—Forward Operating Base—in the middle of Taliban-land ain't a safe place to be."

The four men laughed.

"So, c'mon, tell us what really happened," Zach said again. "How'd you manage to scam the Army and end up safe and sound right here in little ol' Pueblo?"

"He's safe, but he ain't exactly 'sound'," Adam said, pointing to his own head. All the men laughed again.

"Well, it went somethin' like this," Johnson said, twisting in his chair and looking around for their waitress. "I figured it wasn't gonna be long before I got my ass shot off—hell, everybody else was getting' theirs shot off. Or worse. So I figured I'd make a deal with the Taliban —I'd tell 'em everything I know about the FOB, the personnel, the defense structure, strategy, everything—in turn, they'd get my ass safely to Canada and I'd live happily ever after."

"And the little fuckers didn't go for it, I guess," Josh said.

"Oh they went for it, just not the way I wanted. They beat the hell out of me."

"To get the information?" Adam said.

"Hell no. I would'a given that up without the beatings. They just

87

liked beatin' on me. Then the bastards kept me locked up and half-starved in a coupla' different shitholes for years. Canada was never on the table." There was a pout on Johnson's face that even the whiskers couldn't hide.

"Yeah, that part sucks," Zach said. "But it turned out okay; at least you got back home and the Army didn't shoot you. Now you're free as a bird."

"Sure as fuck took the Army a long time to get you back. I bet the bastards weren't trying real hard," Adam said.

"It wasn't the Army that got him sprung, doofus. It was the president. He traded a bunch of camel jockeys from Gitmo for him. Don't you remember the shitstorm that caused?"

Adam squinted his eyes as if trying to recall the event. "Yeah, I kinda do. But I don't remember you bein' locked up or nothin' when you first got back."

"I wasn't. I was assigned to a desk job sixty-five klicks up the road from here at Fort Carson. Took the Army damn near a year to get around to chargin' me with desertion and misbehavior before the enemy. There was an Article 32 hearing…"

"What the hell's that? Adam said.

"It's like them grand jury things in civilian court. Anyway, I was facin' life in the slammer at hard fuckin' labor. Woulda' been at Leavenworth, a very bad place to get sent to. But I got lucky and had some sharp lawyers."

"Lawyers ain't cheap. Where'n hell'd you get that kinda money?" Josh said.

Johnson smirked. "Didn't need no money. Turns out there's a lotta people who don't like this sorry-ass country and what it stands for. They think I'm a fuckin' hero because I stood up to The Man. Hell, I'm like that Edward Snowden guy in their eyes." Johnson leaned back in his chair with a smug expression. He saw the waitress looking his way and signaled for another round.

"And here you are drinking beer with us guys again, just like high school," Zach said. "How'd you get outta' that life sentence shit?"

"It was them hot shot lawyers. They plea-bargained. At first, the

Army wasn't having none of that shit. But my lawyers argued that I had suffered enough at the hands of the Taliban and that should count for time served. Then they got the Army to agree to let me plead to a lesser offense. Goin' AWOL. They convinced the dumbass Army lawyers that I got issues and would probably need mental healthcare the rest of my life." Johnson guffawed. "Like, did the government really wanna take mental health care away from a soldier who'd been held captive and tortured?"

"I read somethin' about all that, but I didn't really understand it; so, what did happen?" Adam said.

"I got busted down to E1, and shit, I had only just made E5—that's sergeant. And I got thrown out of the Army, but it was a general discharge for medical reasons, not a fuckin' dishonorable discharge."

"What the hell's the difference?" Josh said, shaking his head again.

"Dumbass," Johnson said. "It means I get healthcare the rest of my life and VA disability and other medical benefits. Thank you, taxpayers," he said with a sneer. "But I also got a form of probation. If I don't stay out of trouble for five years, I could still end up doin' hard time."

"Hangin' out with us ain't exactly a guarantee of stayin' out of trouble," Zach said. All four of the men laughed again.

"Life is good. I got a cush job as a runner for a law firm here in Pueblo. It gives me enough bread to rent a room and hang out drinkin' beer with my buds. What the fuck kind of trouble could I get into?"

"You ever worry that one of them super patriot type guys might want to hurt you, maybe even shoot you?" Josh said.

The four men were quiet for a while before Adam said, "You know, I never did understand why you joined the fucking Army anyway. Why would you want to defend this piece of shit country?"

"Yeah," Zach said. "If you ain't one of them rich-ass Wall Street people, you can't make enough money to make fuckin' ends meet."

"Like the man said, the rich get richer and the poor get poorer," Josh said.

"Is that the ninety-nine percent versus the one percent thing them Occupy Wall Street people was bitchin' about on TV?" Adam said.

"What this shitbag country needs is a good old-fashioned revolution," Johnson said. "Burn Wall Street to the ground and kill every sonofabitch making more than thirty K a year."

Josh and Zach shifted uncomfortably. "Well, ah, I'm makin' about thirty-five. But it sure as hell don't go very far," Zach said.

"Yeah," Josh said. "I'm pullin' down a little more than Zach, but it's a struggle by the time payday rolls around on Friday."

Adam didn't have a job. At twenty-seven he still lived at home on the largesse of his divorced mother.

"Well, what the fuck; then kill everybody making forty K a year," Johnson said.

AFTER THE WAITRESS brought another round of beers to the young men's table, she approached the man who had been watching them from three tables over. Years of training, followed by being on the run for many years, had given him an unusual sense of awareness of his surroundings at all times. He could recite, for instance, how many people in the past hour had walked past the café on either side of the street, their gender, appearance, clothing styles and colors, their gaits, and which direction they had taken after passing the café. He also had noted the make and model of every motor vehicle that passed by, its occupants, and whether it had parked or continued on out of sight. He was aware that the tables on the sidewalk were filling up with diners and he was a single occupying a four-top. As the waitress approached, he slipped his sunglasses back on, turned, and smiled at her.

Before she could speak, he said, "I'm ready to order dinner and some wine."

"Sure," she said with a tired smile, apparently pleased that this stranger wasn't going to tie up a full table during dinner hour and only nurse a cup of cold coffee. "Do you need a menu, or do you know what you want?"

"I'm good. Bring me a small green salad with lemon juice dressing, and the Colorado lamb chops medium."

"Something to drink? More coffee?"

"I saw Black Chicken Ranch Zin on the menu earlier."

"We only have it by the bottle, no glasses. Sorry."

"Bottle's fine."

As the waitress nodded and turned away to greet a party of four who were eyeballing the last empty table, the man slipped the sunglasses off again. *Don't know how much longer these four dim bulbs are going to guzzle beer. Hopefully, long enough for me to finish my meal. I don't like killing on an empty stomach.*

Chapter 17

NEAR SHAWAL, NORTH WAZIRISTAN, PAKISTAN

IT WAS EARLY SUMMER, but there already were snow flurries in the high altitude of the northern extension of Pakistan's Sulaiman Mountains. Turan Salam was used to cold temperatures in his native Wana, but this was different. The mountains here were higher and the air was bone-chillingly dry. The eastern slopes of the Sulaimans' rugged spine had drained almost all moisture from the humid winds blowing off the Indian Ocean. Turan shivered and tried to burrow deeper into the thin camo material of the baggy shalwar kameez he was wearing. It didn't work. The stiffness of the mottled green and brown uniform wouldn't cooperate. Only one more hour of sentry duty and he could retreat to the warmth of the cave he shared with the twenty or so other HAC recent recruits. A meal of cooked rice and maize bread awaited him. Although if their recruiter and trainer, Bazir Haqqani, was impressed with their training progress, they might be treated to pulao, a rice pilaf with roasted meat.

All of the recruits were young Pashtuns, and most were from the Waziri tribe. They had been together for almost three months. First, Bazir Haqqani had brought them to a staging area near Shawal in North Waziristan. It was only thirty-five kilometers, on a straight line from Turan's hometown of Wana. But a direct route through the mountains was impossible, so they had been driven more than one hundred kilometers in a caravan of battered Toyota Hilux pickup trucks. Bazir had told them that he'd seen a video on BBC television's Top Gear program testing the ruggedness of a Hilux that had over 300,000 kilometers on it. Among other tortures, it had been sunk in salt water, pounded with a wrecking ball, and set on fire. Afterwards, it had continued to perform despite heavy structural damage. It was the truck of choice for militants in the area.

Their stay near Shawal had been brief. A renewal of Operation Zarb-e-Azb by the Pakistani military, a comprehensive operation to flush militant groups from North Waziristan, had caused a change in plans. With air support and the Great Satan's drone attacks, the army had closed the noose around the areas south of Dattakhel towards the Afghan border and through the mountainous and forested Shawal Valley. The military had even enlisted help from Afghanistan to prevent militants from fleeing over the border. It marked a significant step forward in a thaw in relations that began when the new Afghan administration took office the previous year.

Many militants had been killed, including members of such groups as the Tehrik-i-Taliban Pakistan (TTP), Lashkar-i-Tayyiba, the Islamic Movement of Uzbekistan, the East Turkestan Islamic Movement, Lashkar-e-Jhangvi, and al-Qaeda. But Bazir Haqqani had led the small group away from the Shawal Valley, deeper into the lightly populated mountain fastness to the east, closer to Palgai. It was less than forty kilometers from Shawal, but the deeply forested ravines and barren, frozen peaks offered sanctuary from the final activities of Operation Zarb-e-Azb. Bazir had told them that the government's military campaign in North Waziristan had displaced more than one million local civilians from the region, yet the army still had not been able to decisively defeat the militants it was targeting. He'd said that the influx of Pashtun and Sindhi people into the city of Karachi, due to displacement caused by ongoing Pakistani military operations in the country's tribal areas, had swollen Karachi's population to twenty-five million people. The city had become the most populous metropolitan city in Pakistan, the largest city in the Muslim world, and the second-largest city in the world by population.

Bazir had belittled the other militant groups as weaklings and idiots. They were doomed to fail, he had said, because they were not as dedicated and well organized as the HAC. Still, Turan and some of the other recruits were uncomfortable with the knowledge that more than one hundred Islamic scholars had issued a joint fatwa in support of Operation Zarb-e-Azb, calling it a jihad against militants staining the peaceful nature of Islam. Bazir had cursed these men, calling them cowards and puppets of the Great Satan. He vowed that he would take great pleasure in personally beheading each of them when the opportunity presented itself.

The new campsite near Palgai was less hospitable than the Shawal area had been, but also far less perilous. It didn't appear to be included in the pincer movement of Pakistani military forces in the wrap-up of Operation Zarb-e-Azb. Better yet, no drone activity had been detected in the area. Even so, Turan and his fellow recruits lived in their camo shalwars and stayed in their caves when not going through training exercises. The drones reminded them of the folk tales of flying, fire-breathing dragons who dealt death from the skies. They vowed they would slay the dragons and their infidel masters.

Bazir told them they were being trained to serve in the Mujahideen Special Group. It was the HAC's version of special operations forces. Their various stages of instruction included weapons training; manufacturing explosives and ammunition, assembling and testing improvised explosive devices; assault drills; conducting assassinations using motorcycles; land navigation using global positioning systems; the use of social media for encrypting and encoding messages, as well as hacking signal communications; and first aid techniques. In addition, the recruits repeatedly were subjected to punishing physical training and navigating challenging obstacle courses. One part of the training puzzled the young recruits—evading drones and other technology said to be employed by the United States' Customs and Border Patrol.

Over the past three months, Turan had grown stronger and more muscular. He'd mastered the use of many different types of weapons and was becoming proficient in hand-to-hand combat techniques. What puzzled him most, however, were the courses in Spanish and English, as well as lessons on the customs of the crusaders. Why, he and his fellow recruits wondered, did they need to learn the corrupt languages and ways of the devils whom they were dedicated to killing?

Chapter 18
PUEBLO, COLORADO

Two young women were about to enter the café, when one of them, Taylor Mayol, gasped, and said, "Oh, my God, that's him. That's the guy."

Her friend, Madison Prosser, glanced around. "What guy? Where?"

"I told you about it. He tried to force me into his car last week. When I was leaving the club over on Union Street." There was a touch of a wail in her voice as she said, "What am I gonna do, Maddie?" She shrank back, trying to put her friend between the man and herself.

"Where is this guy?"

"Over there." She nodded toward the tables lining the sidewalk in front of the café. "He's with three other guys. They're drinking beer."

"I see them, but which one is him?"

"The one in the blue and yellow shirt. For God's sake don't stare. I don't want him to see me." Her voice was approaching a hysterical tone.

Madison turned to her frightened friend. "We're calling the cops. That bastard should be in jail. You were lucky you got away. The next girl might not be so lucky." She dug her cell phone out of her purse and tapped 911 on the keypad.

Taylor clutched Madison's arm as tightly as she could. "Please," she begged, "don't do this. I don't want any trouble. The cops never do anything. It's always the girl's fault. They turn the guy loose and he does something awful to her. It's always that way." The words came out in a rush. Tears began to slide down her soft, smooth twenty-two-year-old cheeks.

"Girl, you've been watching too many slasher movies." Madison turned back to the table where the four men were sitting and stared hard at Johnson. "Wait a minute, I think I know who that bastard is." She turned back to Taylor. "Yeah, his name is Kevin Johnson. I saw him on TV. He's that guy that deserted in Afghanistan. He was court-martialed and kicked out of the Army. What a low-life son of a bitch. He *should* be in jail."

A voice came on the other end of the phone connection. "Pueblo Police Department, this is Sergeant Casey. Who am I speaking with?"

Madison spoke with the sergeant for several moments. When she was finished, she turned to Taylor and said, "He said they're sending a unit over. We have to stay here and identify the guy. It won't be long."

"Noooo, Maddie," Taylor wailed. "Please, let's go. Please!"

"Dammit, Taylor Mayol, stop thinking only of yourself. This guy's a danger to all of us. Help the cops do their job."

Just then, Johnson stood up. He tossed a couple of twenties on the table and said to the other three men, "I gotta get goin'. Still got shit to do." He turned and began walking west along the side street that the café faced.

"Shit, he's leaving," Maddie said. She thought for a moment, then said, "I'll follow him. You stay here and wait for the cops. I'll stay in touch on my cell phone. We're going to get this bastard!"

A FEW TABLES AWAY, the waitress was just serving the man wearing sunglasses. He saw Johnson stand and toss the money on the table before heading down the street. In the process, he walked right past the seated man, who was partially blocked by the waitress. The man also saw the two girls standing by the entrance to the café. He knew that, on a few occasions in the past, Johnson had been accused of stalking women. The look of near-terror on one girl's face told him that she had experienced more than simply being stalked. A thin smile flashed across the man's face. Johnson was even more deserving of death than he'd originally thought. What bothered the man was the second girl. She had parted from her friend and clearly intended to follow Johnson. That was an unexpected complication. Sometimes collateral damage was unavoidable, but he preferred to kill only those who deserved it.

"Do you happen to have my bill handy?" the man said to the waitress who had started to move away.

She dug a small, faux leather folder from an apron pocket. "Aren't you going to eat your dinner?"

"I'm running a little late for a function and just want to avoid waiting for the bill later."

She offered him the folder.

"Just tell me what it comes to," he said.

"One-eighty. It's mostly the wine; I didn't charge you for the coffee," she added hastily.

He handed five fifties to her. "Keep the change," he said with a pleasant smile. The waitress returned the smile and moved off.

The man leisurely ate a few bites of a lamb chop, savoring its juicy perfection. He sipped about half of the Zin in his glass. He never looked directly at anyone, but he knew where everyone was. The other three young men remained at the table, one of them signaling for another round of beer. The girl with the frightened look cowered in the entranceway to the café staring after her friend. The other girl strolled down the side street in the same direction Johnson was moving, but half a block behind him.

The man in the sunglasses pulled a small plastic bag from a pants pocket. It contained a cloth that had been treated with a chemical solution. He used it surreptitiously to wipe off his knife and fork, the stem of the wine glass, and the handle of the coffee cup. He folded up his newspaper, tucked it under an arm, calmly rose to his feet, and began walking in the opposite direction that Johnson and the girl had taken.

He was dressed casually, like a sales clerk who might work in one of the area's small retail shops—probably a sporting goods store, judging from his muscularity. But no one paid any attention to him. When he reached the intersection with the old main street, he turned left. As soon as he was around the corner and out of sight of anyone at the café, he stuffed the newspaper into a trash receptacle and quickened his pace. To any observer, he appeared to be jogging. In reality, he was covering ground much more quickly than a jog would. He reached the intersection with the next side street and turned left again, moving parallel to the street the café was on. He picked up his pace and turned left again at the end of the second block, moving swiftly to the intersection with the café's street. He slowed to a walk and turned right. Ahead of him, he could see Johnson near the end of the next block. He had slowed down and the girl was much closer to him than before. She had one hand to the side of her head, speaking on her cell phone.

When Johnson reached the end of the block, he turned right and disappeared around the corner. The man knew what the girl was going to do, but he couldn't warn her. She quickened her pace out of fear of losing sight of Johnson. It was a bad decision. She reached the corner and turned right. The man with the strange eyes broke into a dead run. It was unnaturally fast, like a jaguar closing quickly on a peccary. He rounded the corner moments later and saw what he'd expected to find.

Johnson had the girl pinned against the wall of an old brick building, his forearm pressed against her throat and his lower body leaning into hers. He had ripped her blouse open and was groping at the hemline of her short skirt. Her breasts were heaving with the effort to breathe. She clawed at Johnson and he coldcocked her in the side of the head. Her knees buckled, the phone fell from her hand, and she sagged against the restraining forearm. Johnson snarled and reached back under her skirt.

He never got to his objective. The man in the sunglasses clamped his left hand onto the back of Johnson's neck and applied crushing force. Johnson straightened suddenly as if he'd been jolted with a heavy bolt of electricity. The girl slid down the wall and stared groggily at the two men.

The man dragged the temporarily paralyzed Johnson a short way down the block and into an alley. Johnson was six two and close to two hundred pounds, but the man flung him at a dumpster as if he were nothing more than a rag doll. Johnson caromed off the dumpster and caught a backhand from the man. It shattered his cheekbone, resulting in momentary unconsciousness. Johnson bounced off the wall on the opposite side of the alley and sprawled onto the filthy pavement in front of the dumpster.

As awareness returned, so did the pain. Johnson put a hand gingerly to the side of his broken face and looked up at the man. "What the fuck, man? I wasn't gonna hurt her." Speaking was so painful that he had to keep his jaws together, causing his words to slur. "Look, the little bitch was following me. I was just tryin' to find out why, that's all."

"This isn't about her. It's about you."

"Me? Who the fuck are you?" With his other hand, Johnson was fumbling in a pants pocket.

"You can think of me as the taxpayers' ombudsman," the man said as he removed the sunglasses and slipped them into a pants pocket.

"An om…what the fuck is that?"

"You owe this country a debt, a debt you should have been made to pay. But you skated, and I'm here to open a hole in the ice."

Johnson climbed shakily to his feet, still holding the side of his face. His other hand emerged from his pocket holding a switchblade knife. He pressed a button in the handle and a five-inch blade snapped out. He made an unsteady move toward the man and shoved the blade at him. That's when he noticed the man's eyes. They were a glacial shade of blue. With bright red centers that seemed to expand suddenly, as if a volcano had erupted.

The man moved with inhuman quickness, grabbing Johnson's knife hand in a grip that locked the knife in it. The edge of his left hand slammed into the crotch of Johnson's elbow, bending the forearm upward. The man swiftly guided the knife blade through the bottom of Johnson's chin all the way to its rudimentary hilt, and beyond. The speed and power of the blow drove the blade through muscle, sinew, and bone. It pierced Johnson's brain, but wasn't a kill shot. Still gripping Johnson's hand, the man pulled the blade free and, with speed too quick to fully perceive with the human eye, he repeatedly plunged it through Johnson's ribs and breastbone, perforating his heart like a sieve.

"Stop! Drop the weapon!" someone shouted from behind the killer, near the entranceway to the narrow alley.

The man gave Johnson's corpse a shove and it collapsed on the damp and bloody garbage that littered the floor of the alley. He turned and saw two uniformed members of the Pueblo Police Department aiming their service weapons at him. Off to one side, the girl who had been following Johnson was filming the scene with her cell phone.

Not exactly how I wanted to debut on YouTube, he thought. *Maybe Larsen's sarcasm was well-founded; no good deed goes unpunished.*

Chapter 19
NEAR SHAWAL, NORTH WAZIRISTAN, PAKISTAN

AT LAST TURAN'S frozen three-hour sentry shift was finished. He reeled down the steep mountain slope toward his cave. His feet were so numb that at first he couldn't feel the hard ground beneath them. The feeling was beginning to return as he entered the mouth of the cave. The first things he experienced were the warmth of the fires and the smells. Ten of the recruits and a supervisor shared the meager living quarters. The odors of weeks without bathing or washing their garments mingled with the damp smell of the cave, smoke from the fires, spent gunpowder, solvent and gun oil, and the aromas of meals past and present. He nodded at a couple of his cave mates as he drifted over to a fire pit. A big iron pot sat on some large, flat stones in the middle of the fire. From the odor emanating from the pot, Turan knew they were in luck. Meat! Tonight must be a celebration of some sort. They were having pulao.

He rested his AK-47 against the wall of the cave and sat down with his back against a large slab of rock that had been dislodged from the ceiling by some earthquake eons ago. Like him, the others had been recruited from among the lower classes and lower-middle classes of Pashtun tribes in the Afghan-Pakistan area. Because of the war in Afghanistan next door, a new kind of madrassa had emerged in the area. Bazir told them there now were one thousand or more madrassas in Karachi alone.

The students were peasant children who didn't have access to any kind of schooling other than what the madrassas offered. These madrassas weren't like the traditional ones. They were not concerned with scholarly pursuits. They were dedicated to training religious warriors. As such, they were a hotbed of recruiting for Taliban and other militant jihadi groups. The recruiters manipulated the youths through jihadist literature and lectures, leading them to believe they could go from a state of poverty and neglect to one of glory and lionization through jihad. Equally enticing for the young recruits was the promise of seventy-two houris each upon entering Paradise. Pointedly, the recruits were never made aware of the fact that the tale of the houris came not from the Qur'an, but from a hadith that was considered by many Islamic scholars to be apocryphal. What they and their families weren't told was that most of the graduates either were jobless or employed in jobs that paid less than one hundred dollars per month. In essence, the madrassas were creating a vast class of jobless young people. The hopelessness of their situations made them low-hanging fruit for hardline militants recruiting for jihad against the rest of the world.

Turan had become sufficiently warm and began to drift into sleep. He was awakened by an excited buzz from his cave mates that began to grow in intensity. Something big was happening. *Was it an attack by the Pakistani army or special operators for the hated crusaders? Perhaps drones had been spotted in the area.* He hurriedly sat straight up and grabbed the barrel of his AK-47.

Just then, Bazir Haqqani strode into the cave. Pashtuns were among the tallest tribesmen in South Asia, averaging about five feet nine inches in height. At six feet two, Haqqani towered over them. Behind him stood an older man who was inches taller than Bazir. He had a full, bushy gray beard, a thick torso, and wore faded but clean camos. A deep, ugly scar ran across the top of a pair of eyes that would be well suited for *Malak al-Maut,* the Islamic Angel of Death, known in the West as the Grim Reaper. To Turan and the others, the newcomer looked like a giant. They stared at him in fearful awe. A few uncon-sciously backed away from him.

Bazir held his AK-47 aloft and shook it. "We have a very special visitor. Tonight we will celebrate his presence!"

He turned and smiled at the giant, then looked around the cave at the recruits. "You are in the presence of a great man. I am honored to present Mukhtar Rahim Khan!"

There was a loud, collective gasp. All of the recruits had heard of the legendary exploits of one of Allah's finest warriors. Now in his 50s, he had been a Taliban commander who had been captured and detained in Guantanamo for several years. After his release, he had broken with the late Taliban emir Mullah Omar and sworn allegiance to the leader of HAC, Omar Kamel al-Bakr, who called himself Nadir Shah, caliph of a new and growing Islamic state. Shah was an appealing figure for young followers who had a jihadi mentality. His background as an Islamic scholar and former officer in Hosni Mubarak's Egyptian army made him one of the most admired men in the Middle East and Africa, and offered a strong role model for impres-sionable youth.

Shah's positioning of Mukhtar Rahim Khan in Pakistan, together with HAC's capture of vast amounts of territory stretching from Libya to Syria and Iraq, was a sign of the caliphate's global ambitions. Khan's experience was suitably martial. He had studied in Afghanistan, and starting in the late '70s fought against the country's occupation by the Soviet Union. He and the HAC were objects of awe to the battle weary militants in the Federally Administered Tribal Areas of North-western Pakistan. Their fantasies of global Islam and universal Sharia law seemed most achievable under a unified caliphate. It was multi-plying HAC's adherents in Pakistan and Afghanistan more dramati-cally than had efforts of the Taliban and al-Qaeda. The HAC brand offered jihadis access to richer sources of funding, recruiting cache, a distinction over rival groups, and a more realistic plan for success.

HAC's military successes had had a very seductive effect on Pakistani militants, not the least of them Bazir Haqqani. He moved a few steps back from Mukhtar Rahim Khan with a slight bow.

Khan took three slow, deliberate steps forward, paused and looked each of the recruits in the eye, holding his gaze for a few seconds with each one. He had a cruel face that made an impassive expression impossible.

"Know this, my would-be warriors. The supremacy of Islam is only possible through jihad, and the final crusade between Muslims and infidels is imminent. It is the sacred duty of every Muslim to follow the orders of the caliph and contribute in whatever capacity you can to assist the Holy Army of the Caliphate against *Taghoot* (the enemies).

"Some of you will serve in capacities such as recruiting." He held up a fistful of leaflets. "For instance, these are titled 'Fateh' (victory) and are printed in Pashto, Dari, and Farsi. HAC is distributing this recruiting collateral in big cities like Karachi, Islamabad, and Peshawar. It is an important service, one to be taken seriously."

He paused and laid the leaflets on a nearby rickety wood table, "For others of you, the fortunate few, you will be called upon to give your lives for the glory of Allah. As martyrs, you will be richly rewarded in Paradise."

That got everyone's attention. The recruits waited raptly for Khan to continue.

"The very best among you will be chosen to strike deep into the heart of the Great Satan. You will enter the crusaders' homeland and bring death to its infidel citizens. You will strike at their women and children. They are descended from pigs and monkeys. You will slaughter them by the thousands. You will render the infidels defenseless. You will drive indescribable fear into their evil hearts. The terror you create will destroy their will, their ability to fight. You will eliminate the Great Satan's presence forever. Islam will rule the world, as the Prophet intended!"

Chapter 20
THE LODGE

MANAGING the ever-expanding affairs of SAS had caused Cliff Levell to spend more and more time at the Lodge. It had become his primary residence. He had fashioned an office in one of the rooms that made up the administrative center for the Lodge. He was at his desk, studying SIGINT and HUMINT from a number of SAS sources within various government agencies at home and abroad, when his phone rang.

"Levell," he said, impatience making his raspy voice even gruffer. *Fucking interruptions are the scourge of modern life.*

It was Kayla, a member of the Lodge's office staff. "I'm sorry to disturb you, Mr. Levell. There's a man asking for you on line seven; a Mr. Nishioki. He says you worked together on a special project twenty years ago."

"It's alright, Kayla, but I need a favor. Please call him back on a secure line and patch it through to me."

A few moments later Levell's phone rang again. "Bill?"

The voice on the other end sounded warm and pleasant, but older than Levell remembered. "Cliff, I hope I'm not interrupting your efforts to save the world."

Levell chuckled. "Too late for that. But no, I always have time for an old friend." Levell paused and his voice softened. "I know it's been a few years, Bill, but I'm so sorry about Isamu. It must have been a terrible loss for you."

There was a pause at Nishioki's end of the line. When he spoke, Levell thought he detected a catch in his friend's voice. "She was the personification of her name—vigorous, robust, energetic. And then she was gone. At least it was mercifully short; she didn't suffer long."

"I don't know what to say, Bill. I wish I did. And I wish I could have been able to attend the ceremony."

"It's just a part of life, Cliff. I do appreciate the flowers and note you sent. It meant a great deal to me and my family."

Levell glanced at his watch and shifted conversational gears. "What's the occasion for a call from the leading geneticist of his era? After all these years, I doubt you're just calling on a whim." He tried to make his tone sound lighthearted.

"I ran across something that I thought might be of interest to you."

"Something to do with the last project you and I worked on?"

"Yes. The Dogs."

"I'm all ears."

"Over the past year or so, I've had a couple of conversations with an FBI agent."

"Mitchell Christie?"

"Yes. I see you are still on top of *everything*. You never cease to amaze me."

Levell brushed off the compliment. "What's the old saw—'It's a dirty job, but someone has to do it?'"

"Cliff, I do sleep better at night knowing you're still fighting the good fight."

"It's not a one-man show by any means. There are a lot of good people taking enormous personal risks to try and save the people of this country from their own foolishness and greed."

"And, based on what I've learned from Agent Christie, the Sleeping Dogs are among those people."

"Well, I wish I could say unequivocally yes; but unfortunately the situation with those genetic freaks is in a state of flux. You know how hardheaded those bastards can be."

"Quintessential individualists."

"You're being polite. So, what is it you have to tell me that you think may concern the Dogs?"

"As I'm sure you know, I may be retired but I like to stay current in my field. I've recently returned from a conference on genetics. While there, I had dinner one evening with an old friend and former colleague who now lives in Australia. He was aware of the work Jake Horowitz and I did, and our theory of quantum leap genetic mutation."

"I thought your fellow geneticists considered your theory to be something akin to voodoo."

"That was true twenty years ago, but in light of recent research and findings, its image has softened a bit. My colleague shared something with me that's intriguing. He was doing similar research, and one of his graduate students told him about a unique individual. From the description, he sounded very much like one of our Dogs."

"I don't think that surprises me. We always knew the rare genetic mutation that produced Whelan and the others wasn't limited geographically to the U.S."

"Indeed not. Jake and I traced it to people descended from early inhabitants of Western Europe. Their descendants colonized Australia as well as the U.S., Canada, and other countries."

"Tell me about this 'unique individual,' this Aussie."

"Unfortunately, there's a certain aura surrounding him that smacks of mythology. It's hard to tell where reality leaves off and the apocryphal begins."

"Not surprising. We know how that works from the experiences of our own Sleeping Dogs. When you're that physically superior to us mere Norms, people tend to regard you as almost godlike, a member of Aesir or some similar pantheon."

"Yes, but if you'll recall, that physical and intellectual superiority comes with a heavy price. You don't fit in—you can't, because Norms can't understand these gifts. They're either frightened by them or try to manipulate your skills for their own benefit. These gifted ones become reclusive at an early age. The Dogs, to a man, were loners by choice, finding a spirit of comradeship only with their own kind."

"That's true. Every college football coach in the country was salivating over those guys. Larsen and Thomas signed with Miami—the U —simply because Whelan did. They didn't want to play against each other."

"Exactly. And remember how easy it was to recruit them for our program."

"Basically, we just offered them the opportunity to use their abilities to the fullest and not be subjected to public scrutiny."

"Indeed," Nishioki said.

Levell paused momentarily in thought, then said, "So, I assume our Australian demigod is something of a recluse, hard to find. That means somewhere in the Outback, well away from society."

"That's true. My colleague said the grad student told him the man worked on a cattle station in the Northern Territory. A long way from anywhere."

"Did your former colleague share anything more specific regarding this person's genetics?"

"As a matter of fact, he did. It seems that his own research led him to identify a certain genetic marker. It's the same one Jake and I identified more than twenty years ago, but never publicized."

"Because the Agency paid you quite handsomely not to."

"Yes, but here's the crucial point. My Australian colleague, through his graduate assistant who knows the man, was able to obtain a DNA sample…from a cigar butt, I think."

"Let me guess. He found the marker in the DNA."

"Correct."

"What's the name of this Aussie version of our Sleeping Dogs?"

"Liam Stone."

"Find out which station he works on, and get back to me."

Chapter 22
ABOARD THE CAPTAIN MOLLY,
BALTIMORE HARBOR

THE CAPTAIN MOLLY, formerly known as *The Feral*, was one of the most luxurious yachts in the world. The billionaire arbitrager Chaim Laski had owned it until Whelan and the Dogs had killed him. Ironically, Tomas Mueller, one of the three multibillionaire Mueller brothers who underwrote much of SAS's operations, had purchased it from Laski's estate. He had renamed it *The Captain Molly*. Many people assumed it was named in honor of his wife or mother, a daughter, or perhaps a paramour. In fact, he had named it after a largely unsung heroine of the American Revolution. Margaret Cochran 'Captain Molly' Corbin had led the defenders of Fort Washington in 1776. When British and Hessian troops attacked the fort, her husband John took over as gunner until he was killed. Captain Molly had no time to mourn. She manned the cannon and continued firing until she was severely wounded.

The ship was three hundred and sixty feet in length, with an aluminum superstructure atop a steel hull. Her twin MTU 20V 1163TB engines were capable of generating almost nine thousand horsepower. Originally, it had been custom made by one of the top shipyards in Germany for a billionaire Russian oligarch. The Russian had sold it to

Laski for a reputed price of two hundred million dollars. Thomas Mueller had paid a fraction of that at the estate sale.

Certain specifications had been inherited from the Russian oligarch. They included bombproof windows and armor plating. In addition, there were two helipads. The most important feature, however, lay behind the walls of the boardroom. Richly paneled in Honduran mahogany, the walls —like those at the Lodge—were lined with materials designed to prevent penetration by infrared, ultrasound, and other surveillance methods. The same materials underlay the deck beneath the cabin. Even its tray ceiling was lined. It was an ideal place to conduct sensitive discussions.

A stocky, well-dressed man in his mid-thirties pushed an older man with close-cropped, iron gray hair in a wheelchair. They passed two large, heavily armed sentries and went up a boarding ramp onto the main deck of the ship. Unseen were three additional guards on nearby rooftops and elsewhere. The older man may have been confined to a wheelchair, but his ramrod posture, square jawline, and bright gray eyes attested to his vigor. From the top of the ramp, the younger man rolled the wheelchair along the deck to the entryway to the main salon.

Once inside, the man in the wheelchair turned his head and said, "This is fine right here, Nando. You know what to do, right?"

"Yes, Mr. Levell. There will be no interruptions or disturbances. I'll see to that." He spoke with a slight Latino accent. Nando took up a position in the middle of the salon. From there, he could scan the surrounding area through the ubiquitous panoramic windows made of bombproof glass.

Levell propelled the wheelchair down a passageway to an elevator, which he took to an upper deck. He rolled down another passageway and entered the seagoing boardroom. There was one other occupant in the room.

Levell nodded at the other man and, with obvious distaste, said, "It's been a while, Harland. How are you?"

"It does no good to complain, Clifford. No one ever listens," Harland Fairchilde said with an attempt at a smile.

Levell grunted. It was accompanied by a hostile look on his

leathery face. "What would you have to complain about anyway? You're filthy rich, born with a diamond encrusted, platinum spoon shoved all the way up your dilettante ass. You're the head of the wealthiest bunch of thieving bastards on the planet, all dedicated to destroying the concept of nation-states and replacing it with a one-world environment in which you and your pals control all the wealth. You're a lawless, greedy prick."

"Tell me, Clifford, how do you really feel?" This time the smile was almost genuine.

"Don't waste my time with small talk, Fairchilde," Levell said with a growl. "You asked for this meeting. Say your piece and then drag your ass back under a rock."

"Always the ex-Marine, aren't we? Very well, Clifford, I'm sure you must know the purpose of my visit." He shifted gears and said, "By the way, I've already made a major concession by agreeing to meet you on this boat."

"Ship! Anything over fifty feet is a ship, not a boat. I would have thought a blue-blood like you would know that."

"My point is, I agreed to meet you on your turf, so to speak."

"So what? That's no concession. This meeting was never going to take place anywhere that's comfortable for you."

"I'm not uncomfortable here. I was on this boat…ship…on several occasions when Chaim owned it. I'm aware of its virtual impregnability, particularly where electronic eavesdropping is concerned."

"Good for you. Get on with it."

Fairchilde smiled the fake smile and crossed his legs. The bright sunlight flooding through the large picture windows bounced brightly off his immaculately polished shoes. He folded his hands and rested them in his lap atop the trousers of his fifteen-thousand-dollar bespoke suit. "Very well, Clifford, I wanted to meet with you to offer a proposition."

"Not interested," Levell said snappishly. "Save your breath for when this fool's errand of yours backfires and the Islamists, or Chinese, or whomever, come after your miserable ass."

"You and I have been adversaries for a long time, Clifford. We know each other well; so well, in fact, that it should be possible that we could reach some sort of amicable arrangement. Instead of devoting so much energy and resources in this constant struggle of point-counterpoint, we could work together to achieve an end result that accommodates each of our goals."

"You need to stop sniffing the glue on envelopes when you seal them, Harland. You're beginning to hallucinate."

"I assure you, I don't seal my own envelopes; I never have. I employ staff and domestics for those menial tasks." Fairchilde sounded somewhat miffed by Levell's comment. "But to stay on topic, here's my assessment of our situation. You are right. My colleagues in the financial markets and I do intend to totally transform all of the planet's societies into something much more cohesive and efficient. With the end of nation-states, as you noted, there will no longer be any basis for wars and disputes. There will be no large standing armies, no power-mad individuals attacking their neighbors and commercial rivals, no wasting of precious assets or blood, no competing economies. There will be a single global government and a single economy that treats all of the world's citizens equally."

Levell made a face, like he had just bitten into something rotten. "Please, you sanctimonious sonofabitch, spare me the bullshit. This is all about you getting your claws on all of the world's wealth, as if you didn't already have enough. This inane crap about a world at peace, about playing with unicorns, holding hands across the globe and singing Kumbaya, is just another iteration of Marxist lunacy.

"You are as mindful as I am that, in all of history, hell, all of nature, there has never been any such thing as peace. Humans aren't some sort of exalted creatures. We're just a more accomplished, more emotional species of animal. While all other animals on this planet only fight or kill out of a sense of survival, we humans are given to fighting to take what we want—food, territory, power, wealth, mates. Everything. You can impose governmental dictates by force, but you can't purge humans of their instinct to resort to violence out of a sense of greed. The best you can do is identify those most prone to commit acts of violence and lock them up or kill them."

Fairchilde laughed. It was a hollow sound. "Same old hawk, Clifford. In a way, it's refreshing to know that some things don't change. Nevertheless, I believe there is a way by which we can bury the hatchet, so to speak.

"A one-world economy, governed by a single, global entity is inevitable. It's not 'if', but 'when', and the sooner it happens the more lives will be spared. However, I don't disagree with your assessment of human nature. That will continue to be an issue even for a singular, global society. It's in that context that I believe we can find common ground."

"You're talking through your ass, Fairchilde. We have nothing in common other than a desire to rid this planet of each other."

"There does seem to be that, of course. But bear with me for a moment." Fairchilde paused and glanced down at his still-folded, impeccably manicured hands, as if in thought. When he looked back at Levell, he said, "Clifford, you and certain members of your organization, with its far-flung network of military and intelligence operatives, would be the ideal mechanism to identify and eliminate troublemakers, real and potential, who threaten a global peace during and following the transformation."

"No doubt we'd take our marching orders directly from you."

Fairchilde shook his head. "No, actually, you'd operate under the direction of the democratically elected world governing body."

Levell scoffed. "Democratically elected, my ass. Just like this country's current administration and congress were democratically elected? Like you and your minions didn't manipulate the media, the vote counts in crucial districts, and anything else that could be bought or intimidated into achieving the election results that benefitted your agenda?"

"My, Clifford, you have such a negative view of things," Fairchilde said chidingly. "Look, I didn't expect you to accept my proposal immediately. Actually, I anticipated its rejection, but I do expect you will spend at least some time reconsidering it. Talk it over with your most trusted colleagues. Offer a modified counterproposal, if you deem fit.

This truly can be a means for each of our organizations to achieve its respective goals."

Levell pointedly looked at his watch.

Fairchild rose to his feet. "Thank you for your time, Clifford. I shall look forward to furthering this discussion when you're ready. In the meantime, I know the way; I can show myself out."

"I'll be sure to get back to you, Fairchilde," Levell said with a large measure of sarcasm, as he watched the other man's retreating back.

Chapter 21
CLEVELAND, TENNESSEE

TULLY'S TAVERN was an ersatz Irish bar on the western end of a financially failing shopping plaza. It was about a quarter of a mile east of Interstate 75 on Twenty-Fifth Avenue Northwest. An old, grungy service station partially hid it from view, making it mostly a locals' hangout. You either had to know it was there or have a drunk's inexplicable intuition for finding watering holes. The two men, hunched over their drinks at the far end of the bar, fell into the latter category. They had come in before noon about twenty minutes apart. Except for the bartender and a few fellow sots, the place was empty. The two men had struck up a conversation with each other and traded off buying rounds. Now it was approaching midafternoon and both men had run out of money.

"Shit, Bill, I'm tapped," said the shorter of the two men, who was rummaging through his pockets hoping to find some loose change. His gray hair was long and unkempt, and looked like it hadn't been washed in a while. He was about six feet tall and thickly built, but a paunch rested on the scuffed leather belt that held his dirty jeans up. His face looked old; older than it should have, like something in addition to his lifestyle was aging him more rapidly than would be expected. There was a hangdog aura about him, and a haunted look in his eyes—startlingly glacial blue eyes.

The other man was about the same age, but two inches taller and much leaner. His dark hair was rapidly receding from his forehead, and a bald patch was spreading outward from the crown of his head. He was wearing loafers, khaki pants, and a short sleeve, light blue plaid shirt worn untucked. He shrugged and said, "No sweat, Rafe. Maybe I got a few more bucks somewhere. He searched through his pants and shirt pockets, but came up with nothing.

After a few minutes of the fruitless searching, Rafe shrugged and said, "Fuck it, maybe it was time to stop drinkin' anyway." He sighed in frustration.

"Maybe not. I got an idea. You got a car?"

Rafe nodded. "Yeah, it's a piece of shit, but it runs. Why, you know someplace we can drink for free?"

Bill flashed an unctuous grin. "Better yet. I got some money in the bank. You drive me to it and I'll cash a check."

"Yeah? Where's the bank?"

"Any fucking bank will do."

Rafe crinkled his nose in confusion. "Don't you have to cash a check at the bank that has your money?"

"Not this time, dude. It's a cashier's check, good at any bank."

Rafe slid off his bar stool. "C'mon. What are we waiting for? There's booze to be drunk and pussy to chase."

THEY WERE IN LUCK. The nearest bank was the Ocoee Valley Community Bank. It was on Twenty-Fifth Avenue Northwest, just across from the bar. There was a circular drive in front of the bank with a poorly landscaped island in the middle. A slightly tilting flagpole was centered in the island.

Rafe drove around the island and dropped his new BFF at the front door.

Bill got out, then leaned back through the open window of the rusted, decade-old jalopy. "I wouldn't park this thing here."

"Why not? This ain't gonna take long, is it?"

"It's not that; I just don't want to catch grief from the banker because he or she thinks you're blocking traffic." He turned and strode into the bank like he owned it.

Rafe pulled around the island where the road widened and paused, facing down the driveway toward Twenty-Fifth Avenue. The rear of the car, with the license plate, faced the bank.

A few minutes later Bill burst through the front entrance to the bank with a bag in his hand and sprinted out to the car. He ripped open the passenger side door and jumped in. "Go, motherfucker, go!" he said.

Rafe slipped the transmission into drive and began to pull away from the curb. "What the hell's the big hurry? The bar's just across the street."

"Fuck the bar. We'll find a new one down the road. Just get the hell out of here!"

Rafe hit the accelerator and the old car begrudgingly began to gather speed. He turned right at the end of the driveway and headed west on Twenty-Fifth Avenue, passing under the I-75 overpass. "What the fuck did you do? Rob the bank?" He chuckled at his own joke.

Bill grinned and pulled open the sack he was carrying. The sack had the bank's name and logo on it. "What do you think?"

Rafe glanced into the sack. It was filled with currency. And a 9 mm Glock 17. He guessed Bill must have had it hidden under his shirt in the bar. His eyes snapped up to the rearview mirror. "You asshole. What the fuck have you gotten me into?"

"Shit, you'll be thanking me soon enough. This little stash will tide us over for a while." Bill's grin quickly faded. "But we got to change venues."

"Yeah? Where we headed now?"

"Keep going straight ahead. There's a little mom-and-pop motel about a quarter mile out. I been staying there for the last coupla' days while I was figuring out where I was going to get my next payday.

Thanks to you and this piece of shit car, that problem's been solved for a while."

When they reached the small, rundown motel, Rafe pulled into the empty parking lot and eased to a stop in front of Bill's unit. They went inside and Bill walked into the cramped bathroom with the money and the gun, and locked the door. He took a quick shower and emerged a few minutes later wearing fresh clothes. His thinning hair was still wet.

"Man, I'm powerful hungry. Whatsay we head down the Interstate to Chattanooga and find a first class restaurant. And bar." He didn't wait for an answer. He grabbed a small suitcase and walked out the door, climbing into Rafe's car on the passenger side. He casually tossed the sack containing the money onto the back seat where some of the cash spilled out. He placed the Glock in his lap.

Rafe followed him to the car. He drove out of the motel parking lot and turned east, back toward the town of Cleveland to intercept the freeway to Chattanooga. He didn't notice the sheriff's cruiser that settled into a position one or two cars behind him. He also failed to notice that there no longer was any traffic coming from the opposite direction.

Just before the on-ramp to the interstate, the four-lane divided highway they were on was blocked by an assortment of police and fire department vehicles. All had their lights flashing.

"Shit! This doesn't look good," Rafe said. He craned his neck to the left and right, looking for an alternative path. There was none.

He heard the siren go off behind him and looked in the rearview mirror. The trailing sheriff's cruiser had blocked his car's retreat. The driver and passenger scrambled out of the cruiser and pointed their service revolvers at Rafe and the other man. Up ahead, a dozen sheriff's deputies and city police officers were aiming an assortment of assault rifles and shotguns at the two men. One cop, wearing a vest that had "SWAT" on it in large, yellow block letters had a rifle with a sniper scope pointed in their direction.

Another cop using a battery-powered bullhorn said, "Exit the vehicle slowly. Now. Keep your hands in the air where we can see them."

Rafe turned to Bill. "See what you got us into, you asshole. We're fucked. I didn't know you were gonna rob the fucking bank. Now I'm gonna do time because of you. I oughta' kick your sorry ass right here and now."

Bill's hand closed around the butt of the Glock. He grinned. "How do you think that'll turn out for you?"

"So what're you gonna do? Shoot me then shoot it out with the cops?"

"Hell no. I'm a robber, not a killer. And I don't have a death wish. Besides, I always liked jail. Three squares a day and television." He paused momentarily. "What about you? Ever been in jail?"

Rafe shook his head. "Not really. I went through some training a long time ago where we had to go through simulated imprisonment and torture. Still it ain't a place I ever wanted to go."

"Well, if you're the badass you claim you are, you'll be just fine. If not, you'll be some motherfucker's girlfriend by the end of your first day."

"Thanks for the pep talk, asshole." Rafe slowly opened the driver's side door and eased out of the car with his hands over his head. He knelt in the roadway and waited while one of the deputies came up from behind, pulled his arms back, and, one at a time, cuffed them behind him.

On the other side, Bill did the same, wisely leaving the Glock on the front seat.

Chapter 23
CHICAGO

THE MAN OPENED the door to McGillicuddy's Pub, a neighborhood corner bar on West Irving Park Road. The cool air inside rushed out to battle the steaming humidity of a late spring afternoon in Chicago's North Center community. On one side of the long, narrow room was an ancient, dark wood bar lined with stools that were upholstered in dark green imitation leather. Most of them were empty at this hour of the day. Later in the evening the place would fill up with a mix of ages, mostly from the neighborhood.

Gaggles of beer taps were clustered at two stations along the bar, offering a brew for every taste from light beers to double IPAs. A long mirror in an ornate frame was anchored behind the bar. Wood booths with padded seats ran the length of the other side of the room near mullioned windows overlooking the side street. There was a lot of highly polished brass mixed with Irish paraphernalia and scattered about with an affected casualness. Faux antique metal tiles lined the high ceiling. The wood floor was partially covered with a big green carpet that looked like it had been designed for an indoor putting green. In the rear, near the doors to the restrooms, was a small stage that was used a couple of nights a week by whichever local band was available cheap. A jukebox sat next to the stage. A well-used air hockey table occupied a corner near the entrance. Strings of festive, multicolored bulbs crisscrossed the ceiling and ran above the seating area along the bar.

The newcomer's skin was a deep, rich umber color. He stood a couple of inches over six feet in height. The lightweight fabric of his modestly priced gray suit didn't disguise his muscularity. He had on a white long-sleeved shirt and a dark blue tie. His left hand clutched the handle of a well-worn cordovan-colored leather briefcase. A couple of patrons looked up when he entered. One of them recognized him and raised his mug in greeting. The man in the gray suit nodded in return and strolled to the rear of the bar, settling onto the last stool. He dropped the briefcase beside the stool and rested his elbows on the bar.

A heavily tattooed and pierced young woman with bright purple hair was working the midafternoon shift behind the bar. She had been talking with an older man who was nursing a beer at mid-bar. She looked up, saw the man in the suit and walked over to him. "Quentin, you're right on time. I like punctuality." Her face lit up in a genuine smile.

He returned the smile. "Thanks, Tasha. If a man's going to have vices, he might as well be disciplined about it."

"The usual?"

"Yeah, for starters."

Tasha moved down the bar and poured a shot of Jack Daniels, then drew a mug of Budweiser. She walked back and placed them in front of Quentin, who picked up the shot glass with a hand that shook slightly, took a sniff, and tossed back the shot in a single gulp. He pushed the glass toward her, indicating a refill.

While she was pouring it, he swallowed half the beer. "Better get me another of these, too, Tasha."

"Tough day?" she asked as she set the new drinks in front of him.

"They're all tough anymore."

"You're a teacher, right?"

"Yeah," he said as he finished off the first beer.

"What do you teach?"

"Comparative religion. Pretty funny for a Catholic school, huh?"

"St. Dom's?"

"Yeah."

"That's what, two blocks away?"

"Yeah, about that."

"So we're probably the closest bar to the school."

"Lucky for me. I'm not sure I could make it much farther." He grinned.

"Yeah? Where do you live?"

He took a long pull from the second beer. "I have a small apartment over on North Claremont, about four blocks from here."

"That's a nice street," she said. "Big canopy of mature elms, lotsa shade."

"Yeah, it'll do for the time being. But the street's double loaded with parking. Turns it into a narrow, one-lane chute."

She glanced down at the bar for a moment, then looked into his eyes. They were an unusual color for anyone, especially an African-American—a glacial blue. "So, Quentin, it sounds like you're not that much into teaching. Did you ever do something else?"

He knocked back the second shot and pushed the empty toward her again. His face became expressionless and he squinted his eyes, as if peering into the past. "A long time ago I was a soldier of sorts."

"What exactly is a 'soldier of sorts?' I thought people either were soldiers or they weren't."

"It's complicated. We were a special purpose unit. The missions were, and remain, highly classified." He looked down at the beer mug and his voice dropped to a hoarse whisper. "The things I've done. The things I've seen." He shook his head as if trying to shake free of certain memories.

Tasha smiled beguilingly and said, "What kind of things? I won't tell anybody, I promise."

He shook his head and changed the subject. "My favorite job was teaching in college."

"College? Wow, you must be really smart. Where was that?"

"Vanderbilt University. It's in Nashville."

"What did you teach? Comparative religions?"

He shrugged slightly. "Similar. It was Eastern philosophies."

"You're pretty cool," she said as she put the new shot in front of him. "You've been coming in here just about every day after school and on the weekends, and I didn't know any of this about you."

"What can I say? I'm an international man of mystery."

"Should I call you 'Austin Powers?'" she said with a mischievous smile.

"Call me anything you want, just keep the drinks coming."

"I only know you as Quentin. What's your last name?"

"Thomas," he said.

She poured a third draft and slid it in front of him. "That college gig sounds pretty good. What happened? A good-looking hunk like you probably drove those little college girls crazy. Did one of them get you fired?" she said, teasingly.

Quentin blanched visibly. He turned his head and stared out the bar's front door toward West Irving Park Road where going-home traffic was beginning to build. Soon the place would begin slowly filling up.

"Did I say something I shouldn't have? I'm sorry. Sometimes I can be a little too nosy." Tasha sounded genuinely penitent.

He turned back around but didn't look at her. His eyes were focused on the empty shot glass in his hand. "It wasn't anything like that. I didn't get fired. I quit." He held up the shot glass and pointed to it.

She took the hint and refilled it. As she walked back to him, she said, "Like I said, I don't mean to pry, but that gig at Vanderbilt had to be a lot better than the one at St. Dom's. You mind me asking why you quit?"

"It's a long story. Someone blew up my classroom."

"Oh my God! Was it one of your students?"

He grinned and said, "I wasn't that bad a teacher." Wagging his head slowly back and forth, he said, "No. Someone wanted me dead and thought it was best accomplished by blowing up a class full of students."

Confusion was clearly written on her face. "But...but you're not dead."

"No, I had taken the day off to attend to some personal business. I had a TA running the class that day. She was killed along with the students. Thirty bright, innocent, young souls...gone." He tossed back the last shot.

Tasha was silent for several moments. "Is that why you drink? To erase the memory?"

He smiled wanly. "Yeah, I guess I am beginning to feel like a character in a background scene from Hogarth's *A Rake's Progress*." He twirled the empty shot glass in his hand for a few moments.

Tasha went to the other end of the bar to draw a beer for another patron. When she returned, she said, "You ready for another one?"

"I think I'll wait a while and nurse this beer. I'm starting to feel the buzz." He took a small sip and said, "I had the perfect job, a really great girlfriend, and the life I'd always dreamed of. Then it was gone, all of it. I haven't been able to deal with it very well, I'm afraid. I don't even work out anymore. I'm going to seed."

She reached across the bar and gently put her hand on his arm. She could feel the solid, grapefruit-sized bicep. "Maybe you've got that PTSD thing. You said you were a soldier...of some kind. Maybe you can get some counseling through the VA."

He looked up at her. "We were never officially a part of the military. There are no benefits." He shook his head. "The irony is that many African Americans and Native Americans have a genetic disposition—it's called alcohol dehydrogenase allele ADH1 B asterisk 3—that causes a more rapid metabolism of alcohol." He shrugged. "Wouldn't you know, I don't have it. I get just as drunk, just as fast as any Caucasian. And I'm just as susceptible to alcoholism."

Chapter 24
ANTELOPE WELLS, N.M.

Bᴏᴜɴᴄɪɴɢ along the deeply rutted ranch road behind the wheel of a modern paddy wagon, Border Patrol Agent David Hidalgo was both disappointed and relieved at the same time. The disappointment stemmed from the fact that the raid the previous evening had only netted a low level coyote and the twenty-odd AMMs (Adult Mexican Males) he'd been trying to smuggle across the border. The relief derived from the same event—it was only AAMs, not the OTMs (Other Than Mexicans) they feared might be encountered. In this case, the intel from a contact within the Mexican Federal Police had warned that the OTMs possibly were Islamic terrorists.

Once in a while, a coyote or one of the AMMs would spark a fire-fight with the Border Patrol, particularly if drugs and gangs were involved. But those situations usually were manageable. The Agents were trained and equipped for it. The Islamists were a different story. They were very well trained, often by Hezbollah, the Iranian-backed terrorist group whose members were on a par with Quds forces as fighters. Even though Hidalgo and his fellow agents had been supported by a BORTAC (Border Patrol Tactical Unit) team, it would have been an unusually hazardous situation.

It had been a long night for Hidalgo and the other agents, but they weren't through yet. The prisoners had to be interrogated and processed. With any luck, they all would qualify for and elect to go through the Administrative Return process. This meant they wouldn't face any charges for illegal entry, and would be eligible for administrative deportation—no judicial proceeding and no jail time. Under this proceeding, the AMMs would be transported back into Mexico within hours. Hidalgo had no doubts that the individual AMMs would attempt to sneak back into the States within days, maybe even hours. He knew that the border situation had gotten much worse just during his two years as a Border Patrol agent. ISBN (people smuggling) largely had been merged with drug trafficking by the Mexican drug cartels. More and more often, the illegal immigrants were being forced to act as mules. It was becoming part of the price of passage over the border. It had begun in the late 1990s when the cartels started charging the coyotes for crossing their lands on the way to the border. For reasons that escaped Hidalgo, little had changed policy-wise. The Border Patrol's efforts continued to focus on apprehending and deporting individual illegals, instead of combating the large and powerful organizations that ran the smuggling operations.

Compounding the problem was the growing relationship between the Mexican drug cartels and radical Islamists. Much of the heroin being smuggled across the unguarded nineteen hundred or so miles of America's southern border originated in jihadist-controlled areas of Pakistan and Afghanistan. The chain of control of these drugs resided with the radical Islamists and ultimately the Mexican drug cartels. Hidalgo was well aware of the fears that jihadist operatives were smuggling everything from deadly diseases to nuclear weapons into America.

The truck finally reached the intersection with New Mexico Highway 81 and Hidalgo turned left toward the Antelope Wells Port of Entry. The truck was one of the better ones in the Border Patrol's fleet. Its rear cargo area was paneled in stainless steel. There were bench seats on both sides with seat belts to secure the passengers. The space was fully air conditioned in the summer and heated in the winter. *We wouldn't want these desert rats to suffer*, he thought sarcastically.

Hidalgo was grateful for the double HEPA air filtration system that cleansed the air the driver breathed. It wasn't unheard of for an illegal to be suffering from a highly communicable disease, including smallpox.

Hidalgo's portable prison was transporting ten illegals in the back. Each had been handcuffed with plastic cuffs and their shoes had been removed. For the purpose of marching them from the point of capture to the truck, they'd been cuffed together in one long line. One prisoner's right hand had been cuffed to another one's right hand. He in turn had been cuffed left hand to left hand with the third prisoner and so on. This had every other man facing in the opposite direction. Effectively, that made running all but impossible.

Hidalgo pulled to a stop in the parking lot of the new facilities at the Antelope Wells FOB. Another prison truck and three Suburbans pulled in behind him and agents began herding the prisoners into a holding tank. They were uncuffed from each other and placed two or three to a cell. Their shoes were returned sans laces, but their hands remained cuffed behind them, making it difficult at best to slip them back on.

Another agent assisted Hidalgo in hauling the coyote to an interrogation room. The man said his name was El Chichón. It was the name of an active volcano in Chiapas, the southernmost state in Mexico, just above the Guatemalan border. The coyote was big and ugly with a perpetual sneer on his badly scared face. According to the Border Patrol's computer banks, El Chichón had a long history as a coyote. He had a reputation for violence, which had resulted in the nickname. He had been arrested many times and knew the drill. Hidalgo wasted little time with the interrogation.

After returning El Chichón to his cell, Hidalgo pulled one of the prisoners who had tried to sneak across the border. The man seemed to be terrified, as if this was his first attempt to enter illegally and wasn't sure what was going to happen to him.

Hidalgo decided to play the good cop role. After uncuffing the man's hands and getting him seated in the interrogation room, Hidalgo offered him water and a trail bar. The prisoner seemed shy and hesitant at first, but it had been too long since his last meal. He devoured the bar in two bites, then looked around. *He's probably never been in a building so modern and clean,* the agent thought.

Speaking in Spanish, Hidalgo said, "What's your name, amigo?"

"Sixto." His terror caused him to stammer.

"Last name?"

"Alvarez."

The man turned out to be from Santa Cruz Xoxocotlán, a town a few kilometers from Oaxaca. His story was typical of the millions of Mexicans and others from Latin America who tried to enter the United States—he had a family and wanted to create a better life for them. Hidalgo asked him to detail his journey from Oaxaca State to the border. It sounded like standard fare with one exception. It was the staging area just before the final run to the border. Whatever Sixto Alvarez had seen there clearly had frightened him.

"Tell me about this place, Sixto. What did you see there?"

Alvarez was a small, thin man who looked like he hadn't slept in a week. Or bathed either. He was leaning forward on the edge of his chair, his body tense, fidgety. He kept wringing his hands and his eyes darted around the room as if seeking some means to avoid the question. After several moments, he said, "It was in a small village that looked like an old, mostly abandoned mining town. I think it was called San Luis."

Hidalgo perked up. His boss, Tom Donnelly, had shared some confidential information with him just yesterday. There was strong and credible evidence that the Holy Army of the Caliphate had established a training camp and staging area just west of San Luis in the mountains above the town.

"What did you see in this village, Sixto?"

Alvarez began to rock back and forth, staring at his knees. "There were people there…men…who didn't belong."

"I don't understand, Sixto. Why didn't they belong?"

"They were not Mexicans."

"What were they? Europeans? Asians?"

"No, they didn't look like they were from Europe. They weren't white people, but they definitely weren't Asian."

"African?"

"No. They were dark, but not that dark. And they had long hair and much whiskers on their faces."

Hidalgo paused and Googled something on his computer. "Here, look at this, Sixto. Did they look like these men?" He spun the monitor so Alvarez could see it.

The Mexican's face paled visibly. "Yes! That is what they looked like. That was how they were dressed!" He was staring at a recent photo of HAC soldiers in their black battle dress uniforms.

"How many of these men do you think were there, Sixto?"

Alvarez shook his head rapidly back and forth. "I don't know. We weren't there long; less than a day. But there were many of these men, dozens, maybe more."

"Did you notice if any of them were armed?"

This time Alvarez nodded his head vigorously. "Yes, yes; all of them it seems. They were carrying weapons like the men on your television." He pointed at the computer screen. The men in the photograph on it were brandishing AK-47s.

It was a few hours later and Hidalgo was sitting in Tom Donnelly's office. They each were nursing a tall Scotch and water. None of the illegals they had apprehended earlier were known to have attempted previous entries. As a result, all had opted for administrative voluntary departure, also known as "voluntary return," a summary deportation procedure by which a non-citizen agrees to removal from the United States without a formal removal order. The Mexicans had been loaded aboard a Border Patrol prisoner bus and hauled under armed guard the one hundred and seventy-five miles to the Border Patrol station in El Paso, Texas. There they would be turned over to the Mexican authorities at the border.

The two men had been discussing Sixto Alvarez's revelations.

Hidalgo rested the hand that held his glass on a knee and said, "That about sums it up, Tom. Alvarez swears he saw a large number of 'strange' people. He identified them as Middle Easterners."

Donnelly gazed pensively at the ceiling for a couple of moments while absentmindedly gnawing on a pencil eraser. "And you showed him photos of HAC people?"

Hidalgo nodded.

"You think maybe he was mistaken? Like, maybe they were Mexican gangbangers? Those fuckers usually pack some pretty heavy-duty firepower. And they'd be likely to hang out near the border because of the drug trade."

"Hell, Tom, Alvarez *is* Mexican. He would know if those guys were Mexicans, too."

Donnelly started chewing on the eraser again.

Hidalgo wondered how the taste of the rubber mixed with the smoky bite of the Scotch. He took a long sip of his own drink, then said, "Shit, that little village, San Luis, is only maybe thirty klicks from here as the crow flies. And, what, maybe ten klicks or so below the border?"

"Yeah, about that."

"It doesn't take a rocket scientist to figure out what's going on. Those fucking ragheads are staging just over our border for only one purpose—an incursion. Hell, Tom, they're going to attack us, kill our people right here in the homeland. What should we be doing about it?"

Donnelly took a swig of his drink and said, "The only thing we can do is report it up the chain. The situation is way above our pay grades."

The other man shook his head vigorously. "That'll drag on forever and those candy-ass politicians won't take any action. The fucking administration seems content to sit on its ass and let bad things happen to America."

Donnelly shrugged noncommittally. "Ours not to reason why. We're just the hired help."

"Yeah, and when those sonsofbitches do make their move and attack us, what do we do then? Run up a white flag? Put out a picnic spread for them?"

"We do whatever we're instructed to do. It's that simple."

"And if one night we assume we're rounding up Mexican illegals and it turns out to be these Islamists, what do we do then? We get our asses shot off, that's what."

"I know you're frustrated and angry, David, but it is what it is. Look, our intel for last night's intercept said it might involve some dangerous types. So HQ sent BORTAC along. Those guys are like special ops. They're trained for this kind of stuff. Given the situation now, I'm sure we'll be seeing more of them on our operations."

Hidalgo drained his glass and stood up. "Don't count on it. Last night was a wild goose chase for them, a false alarm. I don't expect we'll see them again for a long time."

Donnelly shrugged. "Then we'll just have to deal with it ourselves."

Chapter 25
CHICAGO

THE FRONT DOOR to McGillicuddy's Pub was flung open and a half-dozen young men swaggered into the bar. They all looked pretty much the same, with lean builds, completely shaved heads, and bleach-splattered jeans rolled high to show off their tall Dr. Martens boots. Some wore white tee shirts; others wore skimpier white tank top undershirts. A few were wearing denim jackets, also splattered with bleach—urban camo. Stenciled across the back of each were the words 'Aryan Lords.' They all were sporting white power symbols, including the Confederate flag and the former flags of apartheid South Africa and Rhodesia. The wide, deep red suspenders they wore denoted their affiliation within the white supremacist structure. One had on a black Trilby hat with a red band that matched the suspenders. Another wore a dark gray wool cap with the edge folded back about halfway up his head. Several of them had lengths of chain strung around belt loops in their jeans. On all of them, the areas of exposed skin, including their scalps, were covered with tattoos. The designs were racist, from swastikas to explicit statements to combinations of numbers or letters such as "18" in which 1 stood for A, the first letter of the alphabet, and 8 stood for H, as in "Adolf Hitler." Some had "33/5" tattooed on them, where the 33 represented the eleventh letter of the alphabet, K, tripled, as in

KKK. The 5 stood for the fifth era of the Klan, which was its current iteration.

Their leader was a big man whose sleeveless tank top had been cropped at the waist to display his impressive abs. He stood with his companions just inside the doorway and looked around. His gaze came to rest on Quentin at the far end of the bar. A look of rage came over his face and he stared long and hard at him for about twenty seconds, taking slow, deep breaths. Finally, he shifted his gaze to Tasha, who was talking to Quentin, and said in a loud voice, "What the hell's a man got to do to get a fuckin' drink around here? This *is* a bar, ain't it?"

There were choruses of shouts from the other skinheads. One of them said, "Yeah, if you can drag your ass away from that darky long enough."

The other customers in the bar stirred uneasily. A couple of them looked like they wanted to get up and leave, but the skinheads were clustered around the door.

Quentin looked at Tasha and said, "Looks like things might get a little tense around here. Maybe if I leave, it'll settle down."

Tasha shook her head. "No, you're a regular. I've never seen these guys in here before." She moved back up the bar and said to the group's leader, "Look, this is a friendly neighborhood bar. Everybody's welcome, but if you're looking for trouble, go someplace else. Understand?"

The leader grinned, and it was clear that he was missing a couple of teeth, like they'd been knocked out in fights. He held his arms out in a "who, me?" expression. "Shit, We ain't looking for trouble; we're just looking to do some serious drinking." He paused and looked around the bar. "In fact, we're gonna buy everyone in here a fuckin' drink."

One of his companions said, "That ain't exactly right, Deke. We ain't buyin' no drink for the fuckin' nigger."

"That does it!" Tasha pointed toward the door behind the group. "Get out. Now!"

"Shit," Deke said, "Bo here didn't mean to say that." He turned and looked at the other man. "Did you, Bo?"

Bo was slow to respond. His expression turned pouty and he said, "Yeah, it just kind of slipped out. I didn't mean nothin' by it."

"See?" Deke said. "We'll even buy the brother a drink, too, to show there ain't no hard feelings."

Tasha turned and looked at Quentin, as if seeking guidance in the situation.

He shrugged. "I've been called worse than that. And a free drink salves a lot of wounds."

The collective sigh of relief from the other patrons was almost audible

Deke threw a hundred-dollar bill on the bar and said to Tasha, "Take the round out of that, then keep pouring for me and my men. When it gets low, let me know and I'll throw another hundred down."

When Tasha had poured a round for everyone in the bar, she started to pick up a shot and a beer and take it down the bar to Quentin. Deke grabbed the mug and shot glass from her and said. "This for him?" He nodded in Quentin's direction.

"Yeah. I'll serve it to him. That's my job."

"Nah, you got enough to do. I bought it for him, I'll give it to him."

He walked down to where Quentin was sitting and put the two drinks on the bar in front of him. "There you go, brother." He stood there grinning a missing-tooth grin and staring at Quentin.

Quentin saw something in Deke's brown eyes, something dark and malevolent; more than just a bully's arrogance. *Where the hell is this going to go?* he wondered. *I've already had too much to drink if things get twitchy.* He picked up the mug and raised it in Deke's direction. "Thanks."

Deke continued to stare at him. "You're dressed mighty fine. What kinda work you do?"

"I teach school."

"No shit? Well, you must be one of them *ed-yoo-cated* black folks." He said the word almost derisively.

"Something like that."

Deke's fellow skinheads had gathered around him.

"I guess getting' an *ed-yoo-cation* is no big deal for black folks."

"Yeah? Why's that?" Almost instantly, Quentin regretted saying it. It was like opening the door for something he really didn't care to hear.

"Shit, in this fuckin' country everything's easy as hell for the blacks. I mean, that Affirmative Action shit. It takes jobs and money and schoolin' away from us white people and fuckin' hands it to you blacks. Ain't that right?" That brought snickers from his entourage.

"For what it's worth, I don't support Affirmative Action. It's an insult to my race."

Deke looked surprised. "Insult? How do you figure that?"

"It was set up by elite whites on the premise that blacks aren't as smart or capable as whites, and we need to have 'special status' in order to compete."

"Well, I'll be goddamned. Maybe you ain't as dumb as you look."

Tasha walked up behind the bar. "Any problems here?"

Deke looked at her then at Quentin. "She sure seems interested in you. You fuckin' this skank, boy?"

"You asshole, get out of here. All of you," Tasha said.

Deke grinned again. "Or what?"

"Or I'll call the cops and have them drag you out." Her left hand was resting on the bar as she pointed toward the door with her right.

Deke's left hand swept out and grabbed Tasha's left wrist. He was a big man, and powerful. He yanked her up onto the bar and grabbed her throat with his right hand, knocking over the shot glass and beer mug in front of Quentin. His companions looked around the bar at the other patrons. One of the customers had pulled out a cell phone. A skinhead grabbed the chain looped around his belt and shook it in the man's direction. The cell phone disappeared back into the patron's pocket.

"Bitch, I am sick and fuckin' tired of your attitude," Deke said with a snarl. "Bo, get behind the bar and start servin' 'til I say stop. Crazy Bob, you drag this fuckin' skank over to the corner and make sure she don't say or do another fuckin' thing. If she does, beat the shit out of her." He reached his right hand into his jeans pocket.

Quentin rose to his feet a bit unsteadily. *Damn, I'm feeling those drinks. Not a good situation.* "Leave her alone, Deke, and get out."

"What the fuck's this? An uppity nigger? Me and my posse don't like no uppity niggers." His hand came out of the pocket clutching brass knuckles, and he swung at Quentin.

Deke was quick, but ordinarily a Norm's quickness would seem more like slow motion to Quentin Thomas. At the moment, though, Thomas's own reaction time was distorted by the alcohol in his system. He tried to move to his right but the bar blocked his motion. He partially blocked the blow with his left arm, but it landed hard enough to numb the arm, then glanced off it and grazed the side of his head. He momentarily saw stars and his knees felt wobbly. He had enough presence of mind to grab the beer mug.

Deke grabbed Thomas's tie and the front of his shirt with his left hand and attempted to throw another punch with his right. Thomas shook his head to clear it and slammed the mug into Deke's face. It took out a couple more of the skinhead's dwindling number of teeth. He staggered back into the arms of one of his gang members.

Another member came at Thomas from the left, swinging a length of chain. Thomas grabbed it, but his timing was off and he grabbed it too close to the assailant's hand. The free end of the chain continued in its quick arc and sliced the skin under Thomas's left eye to the bone. Thomas yanked the chain from the man's hand and snap kicked him in the groin. The skinhead gasped loudly, his eyes squinted shut in pain, and he fell to his knees, then toppled over and lay curled in a fetal position holding his injured privates with both hands.

Deke snarled and came at Thomas again with another big right hand punch, blood flowing freely from his mouth. At the same time, Bo came at him on the left with a bar stool raised high above his head. Thomas snapped his right arm around in a short arc, upper arm parallel to the ground, forearm perpendicular. It brought his forearm into contact with Deke's punch while shifting Thomas's position out of the path of the intended blow. Thomas had aimed for Deke's elbow joint in order to dislocate it. He missed the joint, but struck the man's lower arm with such force that it snapped both the radius and the ulna. He continued the technique with a back-fist strike by the same hand that caught Deke flush on the nose and flattened it, snapping his head back and rendering him unconsciousness. The skinhead leader's body flew backwards and landed in a gory heap.

With his left hand, Thomas grabbed the stool he'd been sitting on and threw it with force at Bo. It slammed into the skinhead and knocked him to the floor, where he lay still. Preparing for the remaining three, Thomas was relieved to see them sprinting for the door in unison. Despite the burning pain beneath his left eye and the throbbing in his head, he had an epiphany. *This felt really good. This is what's been missing. It's time I stopped running from the truth and accepted it. This is the way my life is supposed to be lived. And I like it.*

There was a moment of complete silence, then the other patrons burst into applause and cheered loudly. Thomas suddenly realized how tired he was. He sagged against the bar, then noticed the blood dripping from his cheek and puddling on the top of the bar.

Tasha came around the bar with a towel packed with ice and held it gently against the wound. "Quentin," she said, "the police are on their way. You better get out of here. You know what the Chicago cops will do to a black man who just beat the hell out of three white boys…even if they were trash."

He nodded slowly and took the ice pack from her.

"Use the back door. It'll lock automatically when it closes behind you."

IT HAD BEEN RAINING all day. The winds whipping across Lake Michigan picked up a steady diet of moisture and dumped it on the Windy City. Now, it was evening, a little after eight, and the stocky, well-dressed man under the black umbrella stood on the wet sidewalk in front of the parish hall. There was a butterfly bandage under his left eye. The eye itself was swollen almost shut. He'd been there for several minutes, debating whether to join the meeting in progress inside. Finally, he took a deep breath and exhaled gradually. He slowly plodded up the three steps to the front entrance and went in. He passed through an antechamber and paused at the doorway to the large gathering space beyond it. There were more than a dozen people sitting on folding chairs in a circle. He recognized a few of them. That startled him. He had expected total anonymity, not familiar faces. He started to back away when a burly man in a plaid flannel shirt looked up and saw him.

The man, who had a face full of salt and pepper whiskers, said in a deep, booming voice, "Welcome, stranger!" He made a vigorous beckoning motion with his hand. "Come in, come in; we always have room." He pointed to a few empty seats.

The newcomer reluctantly walked across the room and took a seat. His cheeks were burning. He definitely felt all eyes staring at him. *I asked for this by coming here. Might as well carry through with it.*

The burly man said, "Everyone here has already introduced themselves. Tell us who you are."

The newcomer shuffled his feet uneasily. "My name is Quentin."

The group chorused, "Welcome, Quentin."

"And I'm an alcoholic," he said.

Chapter 26
WASHINGTON, D.C.

CAMILA RAMIREZ ARRIVED at the restaurant a few minutes before her dinner companion. It was early enough in the day that a few booths still were available. She and Mitch Christie preferred the intimacy of a booth, so she decided to let the hostess seat her, confident that Mitch was only a few minutes behind her. From her long, well-shaped legs to her thick, lustrous mane of dark hair, she was a striking looking woman and used to men staring at her. Tonight was no exception. Heads turned as she followed the hostess past several tables where members of the business and political classes were seated. The high heels and short white silk sheath she'd changed into after work accented her legs, olive skin, and dark hair.

Camila slid gracefully into the booth's smooth, soft, leather covered bench seat and placed her purse on the seat beside her. She knew better than to glance around the dark, clubby, richly appointed steakhouse. That would send the wrong message to the room full of alpha males and wannabe alpha males trying to cut deals over expense account dinners. Already fueled by considerable alcohol, any number of them would be trying to buy her a drink and strike up a conversation that was intended to lead directly to the bedroom. She'd played that game in earlier years, and it usually had been fun. Then. Now, at thirty-five and divorced, she was in a different place. Camila had entered into a relationship with a man she really loved; someone who appreciated her and made her feel special. The relationship was serious enough that she'd left her job with the Bernalillo County Sheriff's Department in Albuquerque and moved to Washington. She now worked for the U.S. Capitol Police and had moved in with her lover, an FBI agent.

A server passed by carrying a tray of steaks, still sizzling loudly from the heat of the grill. A waiter appeared at her side and said that a couple of gentlemen wanted to buy her a drink. He nodded in their direction. Camila knew better than to look or smile, even if waving off the offer.

"No, my fiancé and I will buy our own drinks," she said to the waiter. The pervasive smell of cooked meat teased her appetite. It definitely put her in a red meat mood this evening. After all, it was a steakhouse. "I'd like a glass of red wine, a Cab."

"There are several on the menu, miss. Would you like any one in particular?"

"Surprise me."

Only seconds after the waiter left, Mitch Christie arrived. He kissed her long and passionately full on the lips, aware that, as usual, most of the men in the restaurant were watching enviously. He stood back and slowly looked her up and down. Camila blushed prettily.

"Wow, sweetheart!" he said softly, leaning over so that only she could hear. "I don't know if I can make it all the way through dinner without leaping over the table and taking you right here in this booth."

Her blush deepened. "Promises, promises."

Christie slid onto the seat opposite her. A moment later, the hostess reappeared. She removed the white napkin from in front of him and replaced it with a black one that wouldn't leave white lint on his dark suit. Moments later the waiter arrived with Camila's drink.

"Welcome, sir. Will you be ordering a bottle of wine this evening?"

Christie shook his head, never taking his eyes off his companion. "Just bring me a glass of whatever she's having."

"It's a Honig Cabernet Sauvignon. It has delightful notes of ripe berries and plums with a rich mid-palate and a long, smooth tannic finish."

"Yeah. Great. That's fine." Christie subconsciously made a small dismissive gesture with his right hand, as if wishing the waiter away.

"Very good, sir," the waiter said and glided away to get the wine.

Camila tossed her hair provocatively, the ambient light catching the highlights and sparkling. She leaned into the table. "Mitch," she said with a beguiling smile, "you're staring at me. Everyone is noticing it."

"Let 'em."

"It's starting to embarrass me." She said with a giggle.

"When I get you home, believe me, I'm going to do more than stare at you."

Her giggle morphed into a girlish laugh and she sat back in her seat. "You're such a bad boy. What am I going to do with you?"

Christie smiled slyly. "Do you really want me to tell you here, in front of all these people?"

"No, I think I have a pretty good idea. Maybe it's best if we change the subject…until we get home."

"Coward," he said teasingly.

"Why don't you tell me how your day went, Mr. Federal Bureau of Investigation?"

"Meh," he said and shrugged. "A lot of my focus has been shifted from the usual Middle East hotspots to the domestic scene; namely the southern border."

"You've said before that much of what you do is confidential and you can't talk about it with me or anyone else who's not a Bureau employee. Is that also true with this new focus?"

"Pretty much, but some of it is so well known that it's almost a part of the public domain. I don't have a problem discussing things that any citizen can find just by googling."

"Then tell me about that part. I like to know what the man in my life does with his days."

He made a face. "A lot of what I do is boring as hell, staring at a computer screen, shuffling paperwork."

"Can you talk about your work involving the border? My Mexican blood is curious."

"Yeah, you told me, your grandparents—both sets—immigrated to the States from Mexico."

Camila smiled prettily. "Yes, and I'll remind you, Mr. FBI man, my parents as well as my siblings and I were all born on *this* side of the Rio Grande."

"Shoot, there goes my chance to arrest you and hold you in special detention."

"Like your apartment?"

"Absolutely."

"Not to worry; you've already done that with my heart, *mi amor*." Her dark eyes flashed with an unspoken promise of things to come later in the evening.

The waiter returned with Christie's wine and took their dinner orders. When he'd left, Christie said, "What's making my job so challenging is the wide open nature of the border with Mexico. Just about anyone can come across, and that's a frightening scenario."

Camila shook her head. "I don't see it that way, Mitch. There are jobs here that need to be filled. How can you blame someone for wanting to improve their life and the lives of their loved ones?"

"Relax, Camila. That's not something we disagree on. The American economy works better when jobs are filled. To the extent that natives don't or won't do them, there should be an effective policy that accommodates foreign workers. Documented foreign workers." He leaned in toward her side of the table. "Look, we need to know who's here and where they are. The current immigration policies are an outdated disaster. Even if they were being enforced, and they're not."

"So, what would you do with this twelve million or so undocumented workers who are already here?"

Christie opened his hands palms up and shrugged. "Honestly, I don't know. That's way above my pay grade. But what I do know is that maybe fifty percent of the people who have slipped across the border in recent years are here seeking work. The other half is a different story."

Camila nodded her head slowly. "Tell me about it. Remember, I was with the Bernalillo County SO for almost ten years. We worked with ICE and DHS, among others. I'm familiar with the stories about non-Mexicans—OTMs—crossing the border. Is that what you're working on?"

"Yeah, given that we now know many of the OTMs are coming from my former area of concentration, the Middle East, we merged some personnel and efforts."

With a serious look on her face and concern in her eyes, Camila said, "Are we in trouble…America? Are we in real danger?"

"I can't share those details with you because of the confidential nature of the work we're doing. But I can tell you that we in America are in deep shit. The bad guys, the Islamists, are here. A lot of them. And more are arriving literally every day."

"How bad do you think it will get?" There was fear in her eyes now.

Christie took in a deep breath and let it out slowly, like a deep sigh. "We don't know for sure, but something big is brewing. If we can't stop it, it's going to make 9/11 look insignificant in comparison."

Chapter 27
HONG KONG

THE PEOPLE'S REPUBLIC of China took control of the former British crown colony on July 1, 1997, establishing it as China's first Special Administrative Region or SAR. As a function of the turnover, the Brits and the Chinese entered into the Sino-British Joint Declaration. Its purpose was to recognize the principle of "one country, two systems." The document stipulates that the SAR is to maintain an economic system based on capitalism for at least 50 years following the transfer of ownership. In an effort to insure the maintenance of a "high degree of autonomy as a special administrative region in all areas except defense and foreign affairs," the Declaration also established the Executive Council, the Civil Service, the Legislative Council, and the Judiciary as the primary pillars of the new government.

But in its inherent paranoia, the new owner also set up three governmental agencies to administer the SAR—and protect China against the heretical capitalism of this tiny outpost. The three agencies were the Central Government Liaison Office, the Office of the Commissioner of the Ministry of Foreign Affairs, and the Hong Kong Garrison of the Chinese People's Liberation Army. Of these, the Liaison Office was the most active and influential. Ostensibly, the principal responsibilities of the Liaison Office were to act as intermediary with the other two agencies in Hong Kong. It also was responsible, among other things, for facilitating economic, cultural, educational, technology and sport exchanges and co-operation between Hong Kong and Mainland China. But the real function of the Liaison Office was to remind the people of the SAR who it is that held ultimate control over the territory—Beijing. It was no coincidence that the Liaison Office also was the headquarters of the People's Republic of China's United Front in Hong Kong, and therefore the origin of all propaganda efforts carried out in the territory to "win the minds and the hearts" of Hong Kong's citizens.

It was the Liaison Office's facilitation of economic cooperation that, on the surface, was the reason for Finance Minister Zheng Bao Xun's visit to Hong Kong. But he had a more pressing reason—a meeting with Maksym Kozak. The memory of his last meeting with Maksym, in Macao a few weeks earlier, was etched indelibly into his primordial fears. Maksym had killed all four of Zheng's bodyguards in an instant and seemingly without effort. Then the hulking genetic freak had told him that he and Zheng were now "partners." Today's meeting would be different. Although Maksym terrified Zheng, the brute was all but indispensable for the finance minister's plans. After all, it was the sheer ruthless and relentless killer in Maksym that had encouraged Zheng to hire him in the first place. His actions in Macao had served to reaffirm his confidence in the man's special talents. Maksym indeed was the right person to send to Fairchilde and to keep an eye on the affairs of AGU. And when the time was right, Maksym would be the right man in the right place to eliminate Fairchilde and AGU's other top people, further clearing Zheng's path to assuming leadership of a devastated world that would be under the control of the People's Liberation Army.

The key to today's meeting was to regain the upper hand, to remind Maksym that it was he, Zheng, who called the shots. While there might be a substantial reward for Maksym's usefulness, there would be no partnership. With the memory of the sudden slaughter in Macao fresh in his mind, Zheng had placed twenty of the PLA's top special operations troops throughout strategic positions in the Liaison Office's building on Connaught Road West. An additional thirty of them would be with him in the office he had commandeered for the meeting from the director of the Liaison Office. The soldiers all were members of the elite Arrow Unit, formerly known as Divine Sword. He was well aware of Maksym's extraordinary skill set, but confident that this small army was more than sufficient to insure the man's demise if Zheng desired it.

The finance minister glanced at his watch. It was exactly 3:00 p.m. Hong Kong Time. As if on cue, the double doors to the luxurious office suite swung open. The hulking mass of Maksym seemed to fill most of the doorway. Zheng shot a quick glance at the PLA captain in charge of the fifty-man detail. The officer's face was satisfactorily inscrutable. If he found Maksym's physicality to be intimidating, he hid it well. The captain and the thirty other soldiers were armed with the latest models of the QBZ assault rifle chambering 5.8 x 42 mm rounds in thirty round magazines.

Zheng was seated at a large, teakwood desk. He looked at Maksym and motioned to a chair in front of it. As the huge man strode toward it, the captain spoke quietly into the mic nestled against his cheek at the end of a tiny boom extending from the headset he was wearing. After a moment, he spoke into it again. A few seconds later he glanced up at Zheng and spoke again, this time pressing a finger against the bud in his right ear. The previously implacable expression morphed into one of puzzlement. The captain turned to one of his subordinates and said something, motioning with his right hand for the man to leave the room. Then he turned and stared at Maksym, tightening the grip on his weapon.

Maksym returned the soldier's stare briefly, then smiled and sat facing Zheng. He said nothing.

"As usual, you are looking well, Maksym," Zheng said.

The big man gave a barely perceptible nod in response. "Your time is valuable, as is mine, Zheng. Skip the social bullshit and get to the point."

Zheng's dark-complected face colored even deeper. He smiled a thin, disingenuous smile and said, "As you wish. We are indeed busy men. I have my nation's global financial affairs to manage, and you have people to kill." His disdain was unmistakable. He glanced at the PLA captain's stony expression, and wrestled with the decision whether to order Maksym's death on the spot. On the other hand, he was not oblivious to the usefulness of Maksym's skills. Ultimately, he decided to continue the conversation. He could have Maksym killed at any time, should he choose to do so.

"At our recent meeting in Macao, we discussed expanding your activities to a more encompassing level, my friend."

Maksym's smile was slight, but decidedly mocking. He nodded for Zheng to continue.

"Your current role is very important to the success of my country's future plans. AGU's activities are progressing toward creating complete chaos in other parts of the world. Anarchy is its natural offspring. You and I understand that when that stage is reached, you will kill Fairchilde and anyone else of consequence in AGU."

"And China will then use its military power to restore order and, in the process, impose its might in recreating a stable global society. Ruled by China," Maksym said calmly.

Zheng's disingenuous smile softened around the corners of his mouth. He nodded his head twice. "Yes, that is how it should be. It has always been China's destiny to rule the world."

"I suspect your Russian neighbors have a different opinion."

Zheng spread his hands. "Ah, yes, our good friends the Russians. You need not worry about those ignorant peasants. We have plans for them."

"Plans?"

"Yes. Currently, we are disarming their egocentric idiot of a president with charm and the appearance of cooperation."

"Looks to me like you're soft-pedalling your own military capabilities to them while carefully appraising theirs."

Zheng laughed. "Your perceptiveness never ceases to amaze me.

On the surface you appear to be a thug, a killer. Behind that façade, there is genuine prescience."

"You better hope you're as clever as you think you are, Zheng. Your president has become a little Mao, grabbing more power that any Chinese president in decades. To realize your ambitions to run the whole show, you'll have to displace him."

Zheng's face showed just a hint of a smile, Mona Lisa-like. "That... ah, shall we say transfer, is already under way. As Finance Minister, I have taken steps to manipulate our stock market and other important financial institutions to create an extremely adverse effect on China's economy. The resulting turmoil already is roiling markets globally. Eventually, it will bring him down. Afterwards, I will present the plan for restoring order in the financial markets. In so doing, the presidency will be mine."

"That's fine for you, Zheng, but what's in this for me?"

The finance minister sat back in his chair and crossed his left knee over his right. It appeared effeminate to Maksym. He also noticed the Chinese man's feet were extraordinarily small. His highly polished wingtips appeared to be no more than a size six.

"You are a talented and valuable man, Maksym. Consequently, I am prepared to offer you the position of Governor of the Western territories."

"Western territories?"

"Yes, that is what we shall call Europe and the Americas after the Peoples Republic of China has established our dominion there."

"What would my role be as 'Governor?'"

"You will report directly to me, and be responsible for maintaining our rule in these territories. By whatever means are necessary."

Maksym was silent for several moments. Finally, he shook his large head and said, "No. Not good enough. I want the highest rank a general officer can hold *and* I want to be in charge of all elite Chinese forces."

Zheng stared at Maksym, the color once again darkening his cheeks. When he was able to speak, he leaned forward, and in a loud voice, said, "You ungrateful bastard! I..., we, don't owe you anything. My offer was almost ludicrous in its generosity." He paused as he struggled to regain control of his anger. "Look around you. I have more men here than you can deal with. I can have them shoot you down as you sit there in the chair."

The PLA captain cleared his throat and Zheng glanced at him. He was shaking his head back and forth. The soldier he had sent from the room had returned and stood next to him.

"What?" Zheng demanded in Mandarin.

"A word with you, Mr. Minister," the officer said.

"Speak up."

"Privately, sir."

Zheng, glaring at Maksym, rose from his chair and stormed over to the captain and the other soldier. "If you value your commission, Captain, this had better be good."

The officer swallowed hard and nodded at the other soldier. "When I could not raise the other men on the radio, I sent Sergeant Chou to investigate."

The anger fled from Zheng's face, replaced by confusion and a trace of fear. He looked at Chou. "What is it?"

The man seemed reluctant to speak. He shot a quick, fearful glance at Maksym.

"Speak!" Zheng demanded.

For a moment, the man's mouth moved, but no words came out. Then he said, "They are dead."

"Dead?" Zheng spoke the words as if in a trance.

"Yes sir, all of them. Twenty men."

"How is that possible?"

Chou said, "Their throats had been slashed. All of them."

The captain and Chou glanced back toward the chair Maksym had been sitting in. It was empty. Then their eyes opened wide as they stared at a spot immediately behind Zheng.

The finance minister saw it and whispered, "He's here, isn't he?"

Both soldiers nodded.

"Do something!" The words came out of Zheng's mouth like a hissing sound. Then he felt the muzzle of Maksym's weapon against the back of his head. As had been the case in Macao, he lost sphincter control.

"Unless you're intent on dying here and now, Zheng, you might want to rescind that order."

Zheng's knees were shaking so badly that he began to collapse. The captain and Chou grabbed him and held him up. "Yes, yes," Zheng said. "Don't shoot him. Don't do anything." It sounded like he was near tears.

Maksym held up a small device that looked like a cell phone. A thin wire ran from it to a bud in his left ear. "This uses an app that picks up speech in any major language and translates it into English." He prodded the back of Zheng's head with the muzzle of his Beretta 92FS. "So you speak to your men in Mandarin or Cantonese and I'll be following everything you say. If you disobey me, or use any language or dialect that the app can't translate, I will blow your little round head off its pencil neck. Understand?"

Zheng nodded his head gingerly. The muzzle was cutting into his scalp.

"Tell the men—all of them—to activate the safeties on all of their weapons, and then throw them into the center of the room. After that, they are to leave by the main entrance and keep going until they're back at their base." Maksym paused for effect. "Otherwise I start killing, and guess who the first victim will be."

Zheng gave the instructions and the soldiers followed them.

After they had left, Zheng said, "You are a clever man, finding that translation app for your cell phone."

Maksym spun the finance minister around to face him. "I don't know if there is any such app. I had no idea what you were saying. I just watched the men. If any of them had twitched the wrong muscle, I would have started killing them. But you first."

Zheng's eyes opened wide. "You...you didn't know what I was saying?" He seemed to gain some confidence. "I will not fall for that ruse again, but you may need it to get out of this place."

"As my Irish luck would have it, on my way in here, I ran into the late occupant of this office, the agency's director. His parting gift was to tell me about a private elevator in rear of the building. We'll be leaving that way."

Zheng was starting to shake again. "What...do you...plan to do to me?"

"I'm hungry. Let's go to dinner and celebrate our *new* understanding."

Chapter 28
DINGLE, IRELAND

THE MAN WAS ALMOST the size of Maksym. His massive body was a few inches shorter but no less muscular. He stepped casually off the train in Tralee, the seat, or county town, of County Kerry. There was a large duffle bag in his right hand. It sagged noticeably at both ends, indicating its substantial weight. It looked like something a normal man would struggle with both hands to pick up. Or maybe need a fork-lift. But the thickly built stranger carried it easily in one hand, like a kindergartener might carry an empty lunch pail.

A light drizzle was falling as he walked down the covered station platform toward the depot. His pace was measured; not too fast, not too slow. People looked at him out of the corners of their eyes. His intimidating aura made a direct look unthinkable. Only the little children, with the innocence of the very young, stared at him. As he neared the building, he saw a couple of cars parked to one side. They each had a green and blue "TAXI" sticker on the front doors. The word *TACSAÍ* was painted beneath it. He assumed it was the Gaelic form of the word "taxi".

The driver of the first car in line was leaning against the left front fender reading a newspaper. He approached the driver and said, "Is this cab available?" The driver, a middle-aged man with fine features and short salt-and-pepper hair, laid the paper aside and said, "It is. Where are you going?" He looked up at the stranger and was stunned by his sheer muscularity—and his eyes. They were the color of glacial ice, and just as frigid.

"Dingle."

"The town or somewhere else on the peninsula?"

"The town."

The driver reached for the man's duffle to put it in the vehicle's trunk. But the man said, "Better let me do that. You just pop the lid."

When he set the bag in the trunk, the driver noticed that the rear of the car sank an inch or two. "What have you got in there?" he said, pointing at the bag. "A Russian tank?" The big man smiled. His teeth were white and perfectly even. An orthodontist had enjoyed a big payday sometime in the past. "Just some clothes and workout gear."

"Yes, you do look like a weightlifter, a very serious one."

The stranger turned and looked at the cabbie, fixing him with those icy blue eyes. "I don't lift weights. Never have."

The cabbie shook his head. "Well, whatever you've been doing, it seems to have agreed with you."

THE CAB WAS A RELATIVELY new Mercedes A 160 CID. The rear compartment was a tight fit for the fare. It looked as if he filled most of its space. If he was uncomfortable, it didn't show. He sat in the middle of the back seat and watched the driver's eyes in the rear view mirror.

The town of Dingle was approximately halfway down the southerly side of the peninsula of the same name. The road out of Tralee was the N86, a National Secondary Road. It was two lanes, but well graded and paved. As they left the town behind, the driver began a fact and myth filled monologue about the Dingle Peninsula. He glanced frequently in the mirror at the passenger. The man seemed disinterested in the surrounding countryside. He kept his eyes unwaveringly on the driver. It began to unnerve the cabbie.

"So what is the purpose for your visit to Dingle, if you don't mind me asking?"

"The Customs people already asked me that at the airport."

"Oh. Well, it wasn't my intention to pry."

The big man sighed softly. "It's not a big deal. I'm here to meet an acquaintance, that's all. Now, why don't you tell me more about this place."

Just past the outpost of Derrymore, the road began to follow the inner curve of a bay. About half way around it, the road forked. N86 went left while another, narrower road continued along the edge of the bay.

"You taking a shortcut?" The big man said.

"In a manner of speaking. This is the R560, a Regional Road. It's a bit more scenic than the N86."

"And longer?"

"It is that, by about five or six kilometers, but I won't charge you for the extra distance." He glanced back at the passenger again. "I like to show folks the heart of Ireland, and this is it—green and glorious."

As they continued on, the cabbie gave a running narrative of the natural and historic phenomena they passed.

"Did you know that it was the Irish monks on the Dingle Peninsula that preserved civilization, as we know it, during the Dark Ages? They were peace loving and scholarly, and came here to the fringe of the known world to escape the butchery occurring on the continent. Without their effort, God knows where we'd be today."

The big man grunted.

The driver was mystified as to its meaning, so he continued. "The monks lived in small, round, low buildings. They look for all the world like beehives. You see them scattered all over the peninsula."

They drove on for a few more kilometers. The big man occasionally looked out the windows. While it was clear that the driver wanted him to focus on the lush green landscape, the passenger also noticed that parts of the peninsula were bleak and desolate. He spotted a series of high, vertical ridges as the car climbed a steep series of switchbacks. "What are those?" he said.

"Potato beds were planted there, but they've not been touched since 1845."

"Why not? Too hard to tend?"

"No. That was the year of the Great Potato Famine. It was devastating. Because of it, either through starvation or emigration, Ireland lost one-quarter of its population."

The passenger's comment was another indecipherable grunt.

A few minutes later the road, now twisty and one-laned, crested the Brandon Mountains at Conor Pass, the highest mountain pass in Ireland at 456 meters (1,496 feet).

"This view here is reason enough to take this route. Don't you agree?" the driver said as he pointed out the windscreen.

The rugged mountainside was stark and boulder-strewn, with sheer drop-offs in some places. The valley below was green and dotted with loughs—Irish lakes. They shimmered when the sun managed to break through the thick patches of moisture-laden clouds. In the distance, lay the town of Dingle with the dark waters of the North Atlantic just beyond it.

The cab dropped down the flank of the mountains into rich farmland. Houses became more frequent. At the outskirts of town, they passed a sign that said *An Daingean*.

"What does that mean?" the passenger said.

"This is Gaeltacht country, meaning that the Irish language, Gaelic, is the primary language. An Daingean is the Irish name for Dingle."

Chapter 29
LONG ISLAND

Harland Fairchilde IV had worn the mantle of leadership of the Alliance for Global Unity for many years, having been handpicked by his predecessor. Fairchilde took more than pride in the progress AGU had achieved on his watch. On the surface it was a think tank and advisor to various governments on the subject of international integration of political, economic, and social activities. Many of AGU's rank and file members believed that its purpose was to eliminate the bases for the animosities that led to wars and the destruction and hardships they caused.

The organization's ruling elite of international financiers and national and central bankers knew better. The real purpose was to fan the flames of discord and hatred into global chaos. It would be followed by a brief state of anarchy worldwide. That would provide the AGU hierarchy with the opportunity to create a one-world government, one in which they would control all things financial. There would never again be any catalyst, such as a recession or depression, which could affect their wealth. The über rich would become even richer. All of the billions of other people, those who survived the global holocaust, would be all but nameless souls with no individual rights or freedoms, subject to the all-pervasive dictates of the global state. That entity would be run by AGU's elite, principally Harland Fairchilde IV.

The biggest obstacle over the years had been the strength and size of the middle class, particularly in America. It had taken almost a century of two-steps-forward-one-step-back, but now the endgame was close. Over the years, AGU had co-opted academia, the labor unions, the entertainment industry, the news media, and, most important, one of the two principal political parties in America. Through its manipulation of the political system, AGU had been able to adversely affect the nation's economic system. Capitalism and the entrepreneurial class that created jobs in the private sector had been demonized and badly crippled. The effect of dwindling job creation impacted the middle class profoundly. It also killed off America's fabled economic and social mobility. Now there was only one direction for most Americans —downward.

Fairchilde had led the AGU to the brink of achieving its goal. The United States was the last obstacle. But not for long. Its economy was headed irrevocably toward a final collapse. In addition, AGU had made well-orchestrated moves internationally that assured the inevitable global conflagration. One was the ever-expanding crisis in the Middle East. Another was the infiltration into the United States of thousands of Islamic extremists across the porous southern border, all awaiting the command to destroy soft targets and inflict terror on the nation. There was China's aggression in Asia, as well as the megalomaniacal ambitions of the Russian president. And there were all the myriad of other hotspots around the globe. America had held the Free World together with its economic and military strength. But those days were past thanks to AGU's efforts. There really was only one annoying impediment—the Society of Adam Smith and its leader—that damned Clifford Levell.

Fairchilde also was becoming irritated with certain members of the governing board of AGU. He wasn't used to having his decision-making questioned by anyone. Ever. What had Fairchilde so irritated was the context of a discussion he'd had earlier that morning with a few influential fellow members of the AGU board. The topic had been

Levell and the SAS. He had shared with them his plan to solve the SAS problem by co-opting the SAS. That meant either appealing to Levell's sense of greed, if the fool had one; or his awareness of the certainty that his cause was lost. In retrospect, it had been a mistake to share those thoughts. The other board members had pressed him to admit that he hadn't heard a word from Levell since making the offer to him aboard the *Captain Molly* in Baltimore Harbor.

One of the board members had suggested that Fairchilde should communicate with Levell again and demand a response. But the other two had nixed the idea. They insisted that Fairchilde had wasted enough time and a more direct and permanent action was called for. Without Levell's leadership, SAS would flounder. While outraged that his leadership and actions would be questioned, Fairchilde knew what he had to do. That was the reason that he had contacted Andrei Ulyanin.

The renegade Russian SVR soldier and former Middle East mercenary was working out well as Fairchilde's replacement for the late Kirill Federov. He was punctual, respectful, and followed orders precisely. Best of all, he seemed to have no moral standards whatsoever. That was a most valuable trait for the kinds of tasks Fairchilde needed to have performed on behalf of AGU. But then, he also had Maksym in reserve for the heavy lifting.

Ulyanin arrived a few minutes early for the meeting at Fairchilde's Brookville estate. A domestic showed him to the den where Fairchilde was waiting.

"Good afternoon, Andrei." Fairchilde waved him to a chair in front of his mammoth teakwood desk.

Ulyanin nodded in return.

Fairchilde had come to believe that the Russians were a cold, emotionless race. Ulyanin had done nothing to dissuade him. He was grateful that the man at least didn't project Federov's annoying arrogance.

"You're looking well, Andrei. There's barely a trace of limp. I trust the wound is almost healed."

Again, Ulyanin merely nodded.

"My, aren't we the talkative one?" Fairchilde said with evident sarcasm. "Well, no matter. I have an assignment for you; an opportunity for you to earn a substantial bonus in addition to your very substantial salary."

Ulyanin crossed his right leg over the left and cocked his head slightly to one side. "Good, I was getting bored."

That brought a smile to Fairchilde's thin, patrician features. "Your services are important to our organization's current operations. We can't let your skill sets erode, now can we?"

Ulyanin just stared expressionlessly at the other man.

"I have decided to send a message to someone who's been a bit slow to respond to an offer."

"And you want me to kill this 'someone'."

"Not yet, although that may become necessary at some point. For this assignment, I want you to kill a person close to him; someone he relies upon for his own personal protection." Fairchilde paused and smiled a thin smile, almost a sneer. "That should draw a response, don't you think?"

"We will see."

"There is one thing, however. I don't want you to do the actual … ah, job. I wouldn't want anything to be traceable back to me. Understand? Engage the services of someone suitable, but they are not to know of my role."

"I am thinking of someone now. Two people, actually."

"They are trustworthy and competent, yes?"

Ulyanin nodded.

"And you know them how?"

"They are Russian illegals, childhood acquaintances from my old neighborhood of Perovo. It's one of Moscow's worst slums, a real shithole. People like us were called *gopniki*. Children of slums. Like me, they grew up in violence, filth, and misery. I managed to improve my lot through the military; for them, not so much. They literally would kill someone for as little as a hundred dollars, maybe less."

"I think we can be a bit more generous than that. How soon can you arrange for them to do the job?"

With his unblinking gaze still on Fairchilde, the Russian said, "As soon as you wish."

Fairchilde's features registered an element of satisfaction. "That's excellent because tomorrow is one of the best opportunities they will have."

Ulyanin shrugged. "Tell me who it is you want them to kill and where they can find him, and it will be done."

"His name is Luiz Fernando Correia, or simply Nando. He's the bodyguard, valet, driver, and personal assistant for the person to whom I am sending this 'message'."

"Bodyguard? Is he good?"

"Not so good that bullets wouldn't have the same effect on him that they do on anyone else. However, he is reputedly a very skilled martial artist. I would caution against getting too close or trying to subdue him manually."

"Good to know," Ulyanin said. "Where can they find this Nando person?"

The man he works for, Clifford Levell, has a home in the Georgetown section of Washington. It's where your late colleague, Colonel Federov, was dispatched. By Levell himself. Since then, however, he rarely stays there, although it's been heavily fortified with electronic and surveillance devices, as well as additional security personnel."

Ulyanin shook his head and smiled. "Security personnel are not a problem."

"Don't be so smug, Andrei. These are the best of the best, retired special operations personnel—SEALs, Green Berets, Deltas, Recon Marines, Rangers. Like so many other members of the American military, they grew disgusted with the way the current administration has gutted the services. Those actions, I'm pleased to say, are the result of AGU's influence. Now, these people use their skills in the private sector for a much greater return; much like you are doing."

Ulyanin just continued to stare at Fairchilde, but said nothing.

"At any rate, Levell is rarely at his home these days. He spends most of his time at a location in Northern Virginia known as the Lodge. Unfortunately, the place is absolutely impenetrable."

"So how are my men supposed to kill this Nando person?"

"Ah, on that front the news is much better. There is a capoeira school in Fredericksburg that he visits on Mondays, his day off. It's perhaps a fifteen- or twenty-mile drive from the Lodge depending on which route he takes; there are several. Because the location of the school is unambiguous, I would suggest that it is the place to engage Senhor Correia, however briefly."

Ulyanin studied Fairchilde for a few moments then said, "Tomorrow is Monday. I'll make the arrangements today. Be assured, your message will be sent."

Chapter 30
DOHA, QATAR

THE LARGE DHOW cruised slowly under power into the harbor at Doha, Qatar. Its size and structure classified it as a *boum*, a double-masted boat with quadrilateral sails that looked triangular when rigged. It had a raised hull and a sharp pointed bow like most dhows, but its stern also tapered, giving it a more symmetrical, double-ended shape. That dated the ship. Most modern boums had adopted a square stern, basically a product of European influence beginning in the sixteenth century with the arrival of the Portuguese and other Europeans in the Persian Gulf.

This dhow was thirty meters in length—about one hundred feet. It had a beam of eight meters—twenty-six feet. Its weather-beaten hull and decks were made of Ekki, also known as red ironwood, a wood found in the forests of Africa. The masts were made of teak. Boums had been important in maritime commerce for centuries. This particular ship hauled goods of all kinds, as well as the occasional passenger, between the Arab states in the Persian Gulf region.

As it slowly approached the crowded docks of Doha's Dhow Harbour, a lone passenger seemed to struggle to get to his feet. He had boarded the ship at Muscat, Oman, and traveled about seven hundred miles—more than eleven hundred kilometers, with stops at Dubai and

Abu Dhabi. By his appearance, he was an elderly man. His posture was stooped by age, his beard long and gray. He wore sunglasses and used a wooden staff, about seventy-two inches long, to assist him in walking. Anyone watching him would immediately assume from the sunglasses, the way he used the staff, and his movements that the old man was blind. He wore the traditional summer dress for men in that part of the Arab world, an old and worn white cotton *thobe*. It was loose, long-sleeved, and ankle length. There was a white knitted skull-cap, called a *taqiyah*, covering his head.

A crewman helped the old man disembark from the ship. Other than the staff and the clothes he was wearing, he had only one possession: a case such as a musician might carry for an instrument. It was about thirty-six inches long. Eyes shielded behind the almost opaque sunglasses and tapping his path with the staff, the old man trudged slowly up the docks toward Al Corniche Street. Along the way his senses were assaulted by the clamor of people hollering from boat to boat, kids yelling, dogs barking, and the myriad of closely moored ships gently creaking as the tide rocked them together in a rhythmical dance. And there were the smells: food cooking on the decks of the live-aboard boats, long dead sea life, and other pungent odors of the Persian Gulf. He didn't need his eyes to know that the men he passed would be garbed in a variety of clothing styles; some Western, some more traditionally Middle Eastern. The women would uniformly be dressed in the *abaya*, the large, traditionally black square of fabric draped from the shoulders or head that covered the whole body except the face, feet, and hands. Many of the women also would be wearing the *niqāb*, a face veil that covered all but their eyes.

The old man knew he had reached the foot of the docks and Al Corniche Street when he heard the sound of waterfalls, the clicking of cameras, and the oohs and aahs of tourists. The Pearl Monument was a tribute to the old pearling business that had sustained the Qatari for generations before fossil fuels blessed the small nation with the highest GDP per capita in the world. He was aware that some fourteen percent of Qatari households were millionaires in dollar terms. He also knew that in the nation's population of almost two million, little more than an eighth were native Qataris. The huge majority of the populace was made up of non-Arab expatriates, and over half a million of them were Indians.

The Pearl Monument was a giant oyster with a huge pearl inside. The old man turned left at its base and walked along Al Corniche. He appeared to be counting his steps until he reached bus stop number 76. He wanted the bus that would take him north along Al Corniche to the Katara Cultural Village. The drivers of the first two buses to arrive advised him that they were on different routes. The third bus was the charm. He climbed slowly aboard, dug a Karwa Smartcard from a pocket in his worn thobe, and handed it to the driver. When the driver returned it, the old man asked him to let him know when the bus had reached the Katara Cultural Village.

The Doha bus fleet was modern and air-conditioned. The old man welcomed the cool air after enduring the 110° temperature of Doha in late May. Inside, the areas at the front of the bus were reserved for women and children. He moved slowly to the rear of the bus and sat down.

Some ten kilometers later he disembarked at the Katara Cultural Village, the largest and most multidimensional cultural project in Qatar. With its magnificent concert halls, theaters, museums, and exhibition galleries, it intentionally was designed to be a place where people could come together to experience the cultures of the world. It seemed an odd way for the Al Thani family, rulers of Qatar since the mid-1800s, to spend a portion of its billions of petrol dollars. Encouraging an appreciation of world cultures seemed to the old man to be at odds with the jihadist bent of the Salafi version of Sunni Islam that a majority of Qataris followed. He was aware that the Al Jazeera Media Network was owned by the Qatari government and based in Doha. He knew of the government's reputation as having mainly Islamist perspectives, such as promoting the Muslim Brotherhood and other Islamist organizations.

After exiting the bus, he walked slowly through the superheated air along the westerly perimeter of the Village. When he came abreast of the Katara Mosque, he sat for a while in the thick grass, seemingly resting. He listened to the sounds all around him—the heavy traffic on Al Moasses Street, excited tourists chirping in a wild mixture of languages, tired, hot babies screaming and their tired, hot parents irritably screaming back at them. Eventually, he rose and began trudging in a northwesterly direction toward Shakespeare Street. His route took him past the Opera House and down a narrow alleyway that ran behind a series of high luxury retail shops. A group of rough-looking young men blocked the alley about halfway down.

Chapter 31
DINGLE, IRELAND

As the cab entered the small coastal village, the R559 picked up a new name. The signposts read *An Meal*. The cabbie said it was Gaelic for The Mall. The road entered an area where the buildings were much more densely spaced. The mostly two- and three-story buildings were painted in a riot of colors, as if someone on a psychedelic high had selected the palette. Most of them appeared to house pubs and B&Bs. Many of them sported Gaelic names with no corresponding English version. They passed a sprawling whitewashed structure with a sign that identified it as The Captain's House. It was mostly screened from the road by thick, almost jungled landscaping. The cab's passenger studied it, as if contemplating staying there. As the cab approached an intersection with the bay visible beyond it, the buildings lining the street appeared more staid. They had the appearance of private residences. The cab entered the intersection and curved along a roundabout past the Garda station. The big man in the back seat appraised it quickly. *Two-story pile of pinkish stucco and brick. Two cop cars parked in front.*

As they rolled through the roundabout, the man took a long, hard look to his left, up N86. At the top of the rise, a little over two hundred meters away, was the object of his attention, a two-story bed and breakfast. It was named the Fianna House. The cab exited the round-about still on R559 and continued about two hundred fifty meters to an intersection with Strand Street, passing a large grocery store and small buildings that housed gift shops on one side, with the bay and commercial fishing enterprises on the other. The cab made a left at the intersection and rolled to a stop at the curb two doors past it.

Dingle Bay Hotel was an aging structure of two and three stories and looked as if two separate buildings had been combined sometime in the past. The building had been painted a bright, fire engine red. The window casings, sashes, and sills were a sharply contrasting white. The double doors in front were wide-open and painted a garish yellow.

The stranger paid the cabbie in Euros before exiting the cab. The driver started to get out, but the big man said, "Just pop the trunk. I'll get the bag."

For all his muscular bulk, the passenger moved swiftly and smoothly. He seemed to flow from the cab, picked up his heavy duffle with no apparent strain, and stepped quickly through the double doors into the small hotel's dark interior. It looked like management had tried to renovate the place in the recent past, but it still had an old, tired aura about it. There was a musty smell in the small lobby. It mingled with the odor of stale alcoholic beverages and bar food emanating from the adjacent pub that was accessible directly from the lobby through a doorless entryway. The place suited the man perfectly.

The desk clerk, a young, thin, dark-haired girl, looked up and smiled. When her gaze reached the man's eyes, her smile froze and she stiffened noticeably, as if the countertop suddenly didn't seem nearly wide enough.

"I seem to have that effect on a lot of people," the stranger said with a smile of his own, but it was hard and devoid of warmth. "I have a reservation. Smith. John." He slid a fistful of Euro bills on the counter, pulled the registry to him, and signed in.

He held his hand out. "Key."

The young woman recovered enough to stammer, "Do you have some identification? The hotel likes to know that the reserved room went to the person who reserved it. It's the hotel's policy, not mine."

She said the words all in a rush, hoping they didn't anger the massive man.

He flipped open a passport and held it in front of her.

She glanced at it quickly and handed him a key, nearly dropping it in her haste to get the new guest on his way. "It's on the second floor, third room on your right."

The man nodded and walked quickly over to the well-worn staircase and disappeared up it.

Chapter 32
LONG ISLAND

It was Monday evening and Harland Fairchilde, IV, was relaxing in his elegant den. He'd had the room remodeled recently at a cost in excess of two hundred thousand dollars. He was enjoying the solitude of the huge manor house while his wife was in Europe vacationing with some of her lady friends. At the moment, he was sipping his second glass of 1963 Taylor Scion Very Old Port. He had paid almost four thousand dollars a bottle for it. He believed that a man of his means, who could afford anything he wanted, should have it. He took another sip and let it float on his tongue as he savored the flavors of coffee, chocolate, dried yellow raisins, orange citrus, and overtones of nuts and spices. *How ironic*, he thought, *that I'm enjoying this magnificent fortified wine from Portugal in celebration of the demise of Nando Correia, himself a Brazilian descendent of Portuguese émigrés.*

His thoughts were interrupted by the approach of his butler.

"I'm sorry to disturb you, Mr. Fairchilde, but there are some police here asking to speak with you."

Fairchilde flinched at the announcement, spilling a few drops of the precious port on the shawl collar of his silk smoking jacket. He brushed nervously at it and said, "Did they say what they want with me?"

"No sir. I did not inquire. They are waiting in the library. Shall I tell them you'll be there directly?"

Fairchilde's head bobbed nervously. "Yes, yes. Let me change out of this damn jacket and I'll be there shortly." The port's delicious finish had suddenly soured in his mouth.

When he arrived in the library, the two cops rose to meet him. One said, "I'm Detective Haddon and this is Detective Lewinski." He nodded at the other officer and handed Fairchilde his card.

"Is there something wrong? How may I assist you, gentlemen?" Fairchilde struggled to appear relaxed and casual. *Something must have gone amiss with the Nando thing. That damn Ulyanin.*

"We received an anonymous phone call about thirty minutes ago. The caller said there was a car parked in front of this residence on Cedar Swamp Road. And that there were two dead men in it."

Fairchilde didn't have to feign shock. "My God! Do you ..., I mean, was the caller correct?'

"Yeah. The car's there and so are the corpses."

"Late model Buick Enclave," Lewinski said. "That sound familiar to you?"

Fairchilde shook his head vigorously. "No. I mean, I certainly don't own such a vehicle. Never have."

"Do you have any idea why the car with the bodies would be parked in front of your home, Mr. Fairchilde?" Haddon said.

Fairchilde continued to shake his head. "No, I certainly do not." He paused momentarily then said, "These dead people, who are, ah...were they?"

Haddon shrugged. "We haven't ID'ed 'em yet. Forensics is dusting for prints and taking DNA samples. We should know something pretty soon."

"I'm willing to bet those guys are in a database somewhere," Lewinski said. "They're rough looking customers. Not exactly the choirboy type."

Haddon eyed Fairchilde for a few moments. "They were killed execution style—a single gunshot wound to the back of the head at close range."

"Why that's terrible," Fairchilde said. "What would people like that be doing in this neighborhood?"

"Judging from the small amount of blood in the car, it appears they were shot somewhere else and bled out there. Later the car, with them in it, was brought here and parked in front of your place," Haddon said.

"Let me ask you something, Mr. Fairchilde," Lewinski said. "You got any enemies that would want to send you a message like that?"

Chapter 33
DOHA, QATAR

THE GROUP of six surly-looking young men had been idling in the shade of the alleyway. The youths, ranging in age between eighteen and twenty-one, were not members of the fortunate Qatari households worth millions of dollars. They weren't even Qataris, but they had grown up in the tiny Arab nation and spoke decent Arabic. Their parents were Tamils who had fled the long, bloody civil war in Sri Lanka. The availability of jobs and a growing group of Tamil émigrés had drawn them to Qatar. But these boys, though poorly educated and unskilled, believed the work that was available was beneath them.

They spent much of their time, day and night, looking for ways to scrounge up money. The easiest way was simply to take it, by whatever means necessary, from others who had earned it. But they had to be careful—each of them had managed to develop lengthy records with the Police Force of the State of Qatar. Some had done jail time, and the Qatari prisons were brutal, crowded, and filthy.

One of the boys, Mukut, started to walk back down the alley. "I'm hungry. There's a street vendor at the end of the alley. I'm going to get some *pakki*," he said, referring to a type of biryani in which cooked meat and rice were layered.

Takshak, their leader and the tallest member of the group, watched him go and said, "If you don't want your ass kicked, you better bring me some, too." Takshak's name in Tamil meant cobra. It suited the boy's nature.

The other boys laughed obsequiously. They'd all experienced Takshak's bullying personally.

One of the other boys, Chodhi, glanced back up the alley in the other direction. "Hey, look," he said, pointing.

They all turned to see an elderly man shuffling slowly toward them. He appeared to be blind, with sunglasses and a long staff that he used to slowly sweep across the area in front of him. He was carrying a battered case of some kind in his other hand.

"Maybe he's got something of value that we can take," Chodhi said.

"Are you crazy? He looks like a fucking beggar. Look at his clothes, his appearance," Takshak said.

"Well, maybe there's something in that case," Chodhi said sulkily. "Maybe he's been begging all morning and keeps the money in it."

Takshak said, "Let's find out." He strode briskly up the alley toward the old man. The other boys followed eagerly. They encircled the prospective victim, laughing at how easy this would be. None of them were particularly religious, although their families were Muslim. But if there was a God, he had just blessed them with a gift. Even if the old man had no money, there must be something in the battered case that they could sell.

Takshak stood in front of the elderly man and said with a snarl, "Who are you, old man?"

"As-salaam 'alaykum (Peace be upon you)," the man said.

"Yeah, yeah, Wa-Alaikum-Salaam (upon you be peace), and all that," Takshak said impatiently. "What is your name?"

"Akhund Farid Ahmadzai."

Takshak wrinkled is nose. "What kind of name is that?"

The old man smiled easily. "Pashto. I am from Pakistan."

"That explains your stupid accented Arabic." Takshak grinned and looked around at his companions. They all returned his grin.

"What is the meaning of your name, old man?"

"Akhund is a title. It means I serve Allah, like an imam. Farid means 'unique'. Ahmadzai is my tribal name."

"Unique, huh? You are old, poor, dirty, and blind. I'd say that is pretty unique." Takshak's followers all snickered.

"Appearances can be deceiving. I am the most blessed of men. I get to serve Allah each and every day."

The grin faded from Takshak's face. "What are you doing here, old man?"

The smile never left the man's face. "Here? Just passing through."

"No, you fool! What are you doing *here*? In Qatar? You are Pakistani."

"As I said, I am in the service of Allah, the Merciful One. He has arranged for me to be invited to sing and teach holy songs at the Katara Mosque during Ramadan."

"What a waste of everyone's time," Takshak said. "What is in that case you're carrying?"

"It is my oud, a stringed instrument I play when I sing."

"Is it worth anything?"

"Alas, it is old, very used, and barely capable of rendering acceptable sounds."

Takshak stared at the battered case for a few moments. "I'll be the judge of its value. Open it up." He leaned down to snatch it from the old man's hand.

Like a mythical djinni, the man no longer appeared to be so old. He wasn't stooped and bent. He dropped the case and instantly straightened his posture. His chest, shoulders, arms, and legs appeared to be thick with muscle. The six-foot walking stick in his right hand became a bō staff. Moving with mesmerizing speed, it crashed into the side of Takshak's head, dropping him as if he'd taken a hollow-point slug from a high-powered rifle. Before the other four youths could react, the man had struck, swept, thrust, and finished them. His footwork was a blur. His movements displayed perfect balance and control. The magnitude of his strength and speed was terrifying.

The action took slightly less than five seconds. The five would-be attackers were motionless on the ground. Two were dead; the other three critically injured. Despite the frenzied activity and the oppressive heat, the man hadn't broken a sweat. He quickly glanced around then bent down and grabbed the handle of the case. Folding into a stooped posture, he began trudging slowly down the alley toward the open area of the Cultural Village.

Chapter 34

DINGLE, IRELAND

PADRAIG MURPHY, the Sergeant in Charge of the Garda station in Dingle had just finished his lunch at Darragh's Pub. It was about a two hundred fifty-meter stroll back to the station. He stepped out onto the street, stretched, and looked around. Something caught his eye. Two doors down the street—barely fifty meters away—he saw an extraordinarily powerful-looking man moving quickly from a cab through the entryway to the Dingle Bay Hotel. It was only a quick glance, but something about the man struck a familiar chord. He waved the cabbie down just as he was pulling away from the curb.

"The man you just dropped off, who was he?"

"Don't know. Didn't say much of anything, just listened mostly."

"He say where he was from?"

"No, but I think he's a Yank."

"Why?"

The cabbie shrugged. "He had that flat kind of accent Yanks have. Different from Canadians, you know?"

"Where did you pick him up?"

"At the train station in Tralee."

"Did he say why he was coming to Dingle?"

"He seemed a bit touchy about that, but did say he was here to meet an acquaintance."

"That's it? Did he say anything else?"

"Not really. He was a quiet sort of a fella, but not unpleasant."

Murphy handed the cabbie one of his Garda cards. "If something else comes to mind, call me."

"Why? Do you know that bloke?" the cabbie said, but the cop already had walked away.

Murphy entered the hotel and went directly to the registration desk. The clerk, still shaken from her experience with the huge guest who had just disappeared up the stairs toward his room, seemed visibly relieved to see the officer.

"A large man just came in here," Murphy said.

The clerk's head bobbed up and down in agreement. "Yes, very large." She nodded toward the stairs.

Murphy pulled the registry over and spun it around. "This him? John Smith?"

"Yes. Is there a problem?" Her eyes nervously searched the cop's face.

"I don't know yet. I think I may have seen him before." He pushed the registry book back to the clerk. "Where's he from?"

"He had a Canadian passport." She said it almost questioningly, as if she hoped it was an answer that pleased the cop.

"Where did he go?"

She repeated the same instructions she'd given the big man for reaching his room.

Murphy looked at the staircase thoughtfully for several moments, then turned back to the clerk, a local resident. He'd known her family for many years. "Maire, it may be the gent's here for a reasonable purpose. We'll give him the benefit of the doubt for now. But if you see or hear something that doesn't seem right, or if there are any problems where he's concerned, call me at once."

Maire's head bobbed up and down vigorously. "I will, I will."

THE MIDDAY TEMPERATURE was a comfortable 17° Celsius—mid-sixties Fahrenheit. The damp breeze blowing in from the southwest was redolent with the smell of the sea and the commercial fishing operations in the harbor. Padraig Murphy strode briskly along the quay and part way through the roundabout. On his left was the Garda station, where his office as sergeant in charge was in a corner of the second floor. He turned up Mail Road. Two hundred meters later he was knocking on the front door of a bed and breakfast. The sign near the entranceway identified it as the Fianna House.

A striking-looking woman with thick, black hair, peaches and cream skin, and bright emerald green eyes opened the door. "Paddy!" she said with delight and gave her brother a big hug. She said teasingly, "Is this a social visit or did you come to arrest my handsome husband?"

Paddy Murphy's smile was brief. "Actually, Cait, I came to talk to Brendan about something. Is he here?"

Caitlin gazed at her brother through narrowed eyes. "Now don't you be dragging Bren into town to help you keep the peace. He may be the toughest man anywhere, but he's not paid to be a police officer."

"I just want a moment of his time."

Caitlin brightened and took her brother's arm, pulling him into the house. "And you'll be staying for a cup of tea, too."

She led him into the kitchen and pointed to a chair at the kitchen table. "Have a seat. I'll get your tea and then go find Brendan. She dropped a K-cup of Earl Grey tea into a shiny Keurig machine sitting on a counter, slid a cup beneath the spout, and hit the brew button. "It's not the same as fresh brewed from a tea bag, but it's quite handy." She left the room.

A couple of minutes later, Caitlin returned. Brendan Whelan was right behind her. He shook Paddy's hand and said, "Cait told me you have something you want to discuss with me."

"I do," Paddy said and motioned for Whelan to take the chair opposite his own. "About a year ago, several of your colleagues from America stayed with you for a while."

Whelan watched Paddy's eyes, but said nothing.

"They were a most unusual bunch of fellas. Like you, really. Fearsomely stronger and quicker than any human clearly should be. Local folks were saying that maybe you were Fionn mac Cumhaill back from the dead, and those men were his legendary Fianna warriors. Frankly, it scared the bejesus out of a lot of folks. After all, the legend has it that Fionn and his band would return only when the world was on the eve of destruction."

A faint smile played across Whelan's lips. "What are you getting at, Paddy?"

"I saw a man today. He seems to be staying at the Dingle Bay." He paused while Caitlin slid a cup of tea in front of him.

"What about him?" Whelan said.

The cop shifted uncomfortably in his seat. "Bren, I think he might have been one of those fellas that was here last year."

"From my old unit, the Sleeping Dogs?"

Paddy nodded slightly as he sipped the hot tea.

Whelan said, "Which one?"

Paddy set the cup down and looked straight at his brother-in-law. "The big, scary looking one."

The faint smile flickered across Whelan's features again. "Hell, Paddy, we're all big and scary." The image of Rafe Almeida flashed through his mind. "Mostly."

"The *big* one. Shaved head. Never smiles. Looks like he could pick up a fully loaded freight car and toss it over a building. That fella."

Whelan leaned back in his chair and said, "Sounds like Sven Larsen."

"Yeah, that would be the one. Larsen." Paddy took another sip of tea.

Whelan said nothing, but his eyes narrowed as if thoughts were spinning through his head at warp speed.

"Did you know he was coming?" Caitlin said.

Whelan shook his head. "He dropped out of sight months ago along with everyone else except Marc Kirkland. Said they didn't want to be involved in the unit anymore. Wanted to find normal lives. Except for

Sven. He was obsessed with finding the man responsible for the killing of his wife and sons."

"And that man would be Maksym," Caitlin said with a shiver.

"You have any idea why this Larsen fella would suddenly show up here and not let you know he was coming?" Paddy said.

Whelan shook his head again, slowly. "Not really."

Paddy cleared his throat and pushed the empty teacup toward the center of the table.

"Would you like another cup, Paddy?" Caitlin said.

"No thank you, Cait, but I would like to ask a favor of Brendan."

"Sure," Whelan said with a shrug.

Paddy leaned forward with both elbows on the tabletop. "It's one thing for someone of your kind to settle down here, raise a family, run a business, become one of us. But when another one just drops in suddenly with no particular reason to be here, it causes a bit of concern."

"And you'd like me to go have a talk with him, find out why he's here."

Paddy glanced at his sister apologetically, then looked at Whelan. "Would you mind?"

Caitlin set her teacup down gently and turned to her brother. "And why would that be Bren's task? You're the policeman in Dingle." Her disapproval was clear.

Whelan reached for her hand under the table. "It's alright, Cait. I'd like to know why he's here, too."

Chapter 35
LONG ISLAND

TUESDAY HAD BEEN a rough day for Fairchilde. He'd had his personal assistant cancel his various scheduled meetings in the city while he stayed home in Brookville, trying to raise Ulyanin. Finally, about four in the afternoon, the Russian showed up at his estate. A domestic showed Ulyanin to Fairchilde's den.

Once the servant had closed the door and departed, Fairchilde said, "Dammit Andrei, what the hell happened?"

Ulyanin stretched languidly and said, "You have apparently underestimated your friend Levell."

Fairchilde was instantly livid. "I do not underestimate anything! Your incompetent thugs fucked this up royally. For God's sake, the police were here. In my house. Asking me questions as if I knew something about those men or what had happened to them."

Ulyanin stared at Fairchilde with cold, hard eyes, his face expressionless. "You give the police too much credit. They have no reason to suspect that you are implicated in any way. There is nothing to lead them to you."

"Except for the goddamned car in front of my house with two dead bodies in it!"

"Again," Ulyanin said patiently, "there is no connection between those men and you. You are wasting time and energy on nothing. If I were you, my efforts would be better spent trying to figure out how this Levell person, or his bodyguard, made this happen. The two men I hired, Yuri and Grigori, were not easy men to kill."

Before Fairchilde could respond, the phone on his desk buzzed. He picked it up, "Yes, what is it? I'm very busy at the moment."

It was one of servants advising that Detective Haddon was on the line asking to speak to him.

Even more livid than before, Fairchild glared at Ulyanin and mouthed the words, "It's the damn police."

Ulyanin gave a casual shrug and said, "So what? They know nothing."

Fairchilde punched a blinking button on his phone and said, "Yes, this is Mr. Fairchilde."

The voice on the other end said, "This is Haddon, with Second Precinct. We spoke last evening."

"Yes, I remember speaking with you Detective Haddon, and Detective Lewinski as well. Have you made progress in the case?"

"That's the purpose for my call." There was a brief pause then Haddon said, "The victims were Russian illegals…"

"Undocumented," Fairchilde interrupted, unable to restrain his progressivism.

"Whatever. They were in this country illegally. Thanks to INTERPOL's database we've been able to ID them. Just thought you'd want to know."

"That's very good work, Detective, and expeditious. Do you have any theories that might suggest why they were killed and left in front of my house, of all places?"

"That's still under investigation, but I can tell you that we've ID'ed the perp."

Fairchilde's face paled and he shot a glance at Ulyanin. *If they've implicated Andrei, he will probably sell me out to cover his own ass*, he thought, as panic swiftly rose. Just as swiftly, he had a calming thought. *Andrei wouldn't have killed his own men. It had to be Nando, of course. This may work out almost as well as if the two thugs* had *been able to kill him. Nando in jail was almost as good as Nando dead.*

"Based on hair fibers on the upholstery and a thumbprint on the steering wheel," Haddon said, "we've identified the shooter as a renegade former Russian diplomat and ex-Spetsnaz Colonel by the name of Kirill Federov."

Chapter 36
DOHA, QATAR

STREET VENDORS WERE OFFICIALLY BANNED from Doha's roadways; at least those streets likely to be trafficked by tourists and the city's more well-to-do-citizenry. This included the Katara Cultural Village. But a living had to be made, and oftentimes that involved risk. The thing about risk was its reciprocal: the higher the risk, the greater the reward. So street vendors sneaked into the Village and lurked just off the streets at the head of alleys and narrow passageways. They moved their wheeled carts frequently, but relied on the aroma of their wares to do the necessary marketing.

While Mukut was waiting for the street vendor to dish up his biryani, he glanced across the street and up the alley opposite where he was standing. He saw his five colleagues surrounding an old man, and smiled. When Takshak and the others were through with him, he would be lucky to have anything left, including his clothes and his teeth. He looked away as the vendor handed him a steaming plate of highly seasoned biryani.

After paying the man, Mukut started back across the street to rejoin his friends in the alley. He looked up, expecting to see the old man on the ground and the other boys dividing the meager spoils. What he saw stopped him in his tracks. The old man was shuffling out of the alley, turning left on the wide street and heading toward the roundabout at the intersection of Shakespeare Street and the Lusail Expressway. Mukut turned and looked up the alley. His five companions lay motionless on the ground.

Mukut was stunned. He almost dropped his plate of biryani. What had this old man done? There had been no gunshots, at least no audible ones. What could have happened? What kind of an old man could do such a thing? He was torn. He felt the urge to go to his friends and try to help them, but they weren't really friends, especially the bully, Takshak. Yet he also felt the urge to follow the mysterious old man, to see what he was up to. Perhaps he was a master mugger, one who disguised himself as an old man to disarm his victims, then preyed on their naiveté. The other five boys were of no use to him now. Perhaps he could learn some valuable skills from observing the old man, or whatever he was. He decided to follow him, but at a discreet distance for his own safety.

To Mukut's amazement, the elderly man was able somehow to cross the congested intersection with Lusail Expressway in spite of his apparent visual infirmities. He continued his slow shuffle westward along the northerly side of West Bay Lagoon Street, seemingly oblivious to the traffic streaming past him only a few feet away. He passed several side streets leading into the luxurious West Bay Lagoon development, a new area of massive villas and towering high rises. Finally, he began to move away from the road and toward the perimeter of the development. Because of the affluence of the development's residents, Mukut knew the community was gated and its private security staff was good. He slipped his cellphone from a back pocket of his jeans and quickly snapped a photo of his quarry. He thought it might prove useful somehow.

Mukut, who had been following some distance behind and on the opposite side of the road, stopped and looked around. He didn't see any sign of the Police Force of the State of Qatar or the private security force engaged by the homeowners' association. He waited for a break in traffic, then moved swiftly across the road and toward the first ring of landscaping that surrounded the development. West Bay Lagoon, like much of the newer parts of Doha, was a lush, tropical paradise in the midst of an otherwise barren desert. Following the old man's lead, Mukut slipped into the thickly landscaped area. He was glad to have the cover. It would shield him from the view of traffic on the busy road, and in particular the police, but it also caused him to temporarily lose sight of the old man. He quickened his pace. Shortly, he came to Al Buhaira Street, a four-lane divided road that ran parallel with West Bay Lagoon Street and formed a perimeter road around the ritzy development. Looking to the west, he saw that the old man had crossed Al Buhaira and was disappearing into the even lusher landscaping that encircled West Bay Lagoon. Mukut dashed across Al Buhaira and into the thick shrubbery and trees.

Chapter 37

DINGLE, IRELAND

AFTER DINNER with Caitlin and their two sons, Sean and Declan, Whelan strolled down the hill to the Dingle Bay Hotel. There had been a break in the drizzle, but the air was still sodden, and descending into a nighttime chill. He entered the pub that adjoined the hotel and looked around. It was still early evening and a number of families with kids in tow were enjoying their meals. There was a jovial crowd at the bar. Whelan knew all of them. The bartender, a bewhiskered, middle-aged man named Éamon, recognized him immediately and waved Whelan over. As he reached the bar, Éamon slid a pint of Guinness in front of him.

"Evenin' Brendan. Cait and the lads not with you tonight?"

"No, I'm looking for someone. He's staying at the hotel. An old acquaintance."

Éamon, who was wiping the bar with a white cloth, looked up. "Might he be one of your kind?" It wasn't said out of disrespect. In fact, it was the opposite. Most of the residents of Dingle were aware of Whelan's unusual gifts of strength, speed, and cunning. If anything, they appreciated how he had used it over the years to assist towns- people and to help Paddy and the Garda keep the peace. "He's big like you are, even bigger, and looks every bit as capable."

Whelan took a sip of his beer and nodded. "Might be."

"I expect you'll find him over there." Éamon motioned with his head.

Whelan saw a larger-than-life man in a dark corner, nursing a pint. Sven Larsen. He walked toward Larsen through the growing crowd of patrons, acknowledging friends and neighbors as he did, but not pausing to talk. Out of respect for his size, strength, and reputation, the crowd parted before him like the Red Sea deferring to Moses and the Israelites. As he would have expected, Larsen was aware of his approach. Whelan doubted that anything had slipped past the other man's notice the entire time he had been in the bar. Hyperawareness was one of the traits of their genetic construct.

At one point, Larsen and Whelan had been the closest of friends, almost like brothers. Whelan was best man when Larsen and his late wife had eloped during their freshman year at Miami, the U. Larsen had been the first of the Dogs to follow Whelan in joining the unit that Levell and other unconventional warfare experts had put together. They had saved each other's lives on countless occasions. Despite that history together, Larsen showed no sign of friendliness as Whelan approached. His face was almost expressionless, showing just a trace of a scowl.

Whelan pulled a chair out and sat in it, leaning over closer to Larsen to ensure their conversation would be private. He nodded at the glass Larsen was holding. "Beer? The Sven Larsen I knew rarely drank alcohol."

Larsen took a small sip of his beer, but never took his eyes off Whelan. He set the glass on the table. "Maybe that Sven Larsen no longer exists." He paused, then said, "And I didn't invite you to sit down."

"You want to take that boulder-sized chip on your shoulder out to the street and watch me whittle it down?"

Larsen made a snorting noise. It sounded like something that might have come out of a large, angry bison. "That's not possible."

"Sure it is. You just get up and walk out the front door. It's easy."

"That's not what I meant!" This time it was a deep growl.

"I know what you meant, Sven. We've always wondered which of us would win if we ever really got into it. I'm offering you a chance to find out."

Larsen just stared at him. He had two smiles. One was merely sinister. That was his good smile. This smile was his bad one; the one that had been known to cause complete sphincter failure in the baddest of badasses. Finally, he said, "Are you that eager to widow that beautiful wife of yours?"

Whelan's eyes narrowed. "That's really the issue, isn't it Sven? My wife and sons are alive and yours aren't." He leaned back in his chair and shook his head as they continued to stare at each other. "You might want to remember that when you lost your family, I was here killing the men Maksym had sent to murder my family and me."

"Yeah, but your family is alive and mine isn't."

"That's because I was home when the bastards came. In your case, you had been called into work. Maksym's goons couldn't have anticipated that. If you'd been there, I have no doubt that you'd have killed the whole fucking lot of them. Sharon and the boys would be alive today, and you and I would be laughing and telling war stories."

Larsen broke off the stare-down and looked down at his beer. He raised it to his lips with a hand that was surprisingly smallish for all his bulk. The way he held it was oddly delicate, as if he feared his very grip would shatter it. He took another small sip, set it down, and said, "Where are the other guys?"

With a slight shrug of his shoulders, Whelan said, "Marc was through here a couple of days ago. Said he was going to the Middle East. Stensen, Thomas, Almeida…I have no idea."

"You think maybe Levell knows where they are?"

"Cliff knows everything. Always has."

"Think he knows I'm here?"

"You could ask him."

"Always a wiseass," Larsen said sullenly. "Speaking of being here, do you think you could have found a more out-in-the-middle-of-nowhere place in all of Ireland?"

"You might have a point. The next parish over is a place called Boston."

Larsen smiled his good smile. It was the one that merely caused women and children to faint.

"But," Whelan said, "you *are* here. I'd like to know why."

Larsen shrugged his massive shoulders. "You're at the top of Maksym's list. Sooner or later he's going to come for you. When he does, I'll kill him. Slowly, over a period of days, maybe weeks. Not suddenly like he did to Sharon, Rolf and Erik."

Whelan wagged his head slowly back and forth. "Not a good idea, Sven. Cait and I have friends, neighbors, and relatives all armed to the teeth and watching our place around the clock. You might get in the way, be more of a problem than a helper. Besides, when and if Maksym comes, he's mine."

"Yeah? What makes you think that your right to kill him trumps mine?"

"For one thing, he's my brother."

Chapter 38
DOHA, QATAR

AS THE AGED cleric slipped into the dense vegetation, his appearance underwent a transformation. His body appeared to be strong and straight and much younger. He effortlessly leaped over a six-foot high wall that enclosed the exclusive community and crept to within a few feet of a point where the landscaping ended at the outer edge of a broad, green yard that surrounded a massive, two-story, arabesque villa. He estimated that it must have contained more than four hundred square meters—forty-five hundred square feet—under air. There was an ornate fountain in the middle of the yard, surrounded by a large area of reddish colored pavers. He squatted and studied the exterior of the building for several minutes. This side of the dwelling was mostly glass on the first floor, overhung with covered balconies with wrought iron railings and fancy fenestrations. Through wide glass sliders, he could see a well-equipped gym in the left corner of the villa's ground floor. Two burly men in shorts and tee shirts were lifting weights. A third was using a treadmill. There was what appeared to be a servants' entrance in the far right corner. It was a small, nondescript door that looked out of place with the rest of the building's architectural finesse.

He laid his case on the ground and opened it. It did not contain a musical instrument. He took out a black device that was about the size of a large-screen smart phone, but twice as thick. There were two short antenna-like projections at the top. He pressed a button on the side and a small, bright green light came on near one of the antennas, indicating the device was operational. He looked at the back of the villa again and saw three CCTV security cameras arcing slowly back and forth. He had known they would be there, along with others, monitoring different fields of view at various points around the villa. It would have been simpler to generate interference if they had been wireless, operating on 900 MHz, 2.4 GHz, or even 5.8 GHz frequency band. But he was prepared for the hardwired versions, too. That was the purpose of the little black device. He pressed a rocker switch on the bottom left side of the device, then another rocker on the bottom right. The first switch caused the device to emit a low frequency signal, 16kHz, that scrambled the signal from the cameras to the monitors inside the villa. The second switch activated another signal that interfered with cell phone operations within a radius of three hundred feet.

He set the device on the ground, knowing the security team inside the villa would react quickly. He pulled two other objects from the case, a 9mm SIG 226 with suppressor and a spare magazine. He closed the case, dropped the magazine into a pocket in his thobe, and attached the suppressor to the SIG. Gripping the SIG in his right hand and the handle of the mysterious case in his left, he stood and ran with astonishing speed across the yard toward the servants' entrance. Expecting it to be locked, he fired a single round into the mechanism as he approached it. He kicked the damaged door open and leaped through the doorway. His brain registered motion in the corner periphery of his left eye. With a movement too fast for the human eye to follow, he snapped off a shot and heard a satisfying groan as the steel jacketed hollow-point slug tore through its victim. He moved through a small antechamber that contained a bank of lockers. He assumed it had been designed as a place for servants to deposit personal items before beginning their shifts. He entered the kitchen area, all stainless steel appliances, marble countertops, and dark wood cabinetry. The flooring consisted of neutral, eighteen-inch squares of ceramic tile.

As part of his research in preparation for this mission, he'd studied the history of the six-bedroom, seven-bathroom house online. He'd found the original sales collateral, as well as more recent details when the place had been on the rental market before being leased to its current occupants.

He crossed the kitchen in two giant steps and paused where it exited into a wide hallway. He heard more than one pair of footsteps rapidly approaching. He spun out of the kitchen in a low crouch and shot two armed men approaching from opposite directions. His detailed research had told him that the usual complement of body-guards was eight. Three were down and three more would be coming from the gym on the opposite side of the house. That left only another two to protect the quarry that he'd tracked to this place.

To his right was the laundry facility. He didn't hear any sounds from that direction, so he stretched out on the floor of the hallway facing in the opposite direction. A moment later two of the men from the gym burst into view, still sweating heavily from their workouts. The intruder shot each of them in the center of the chest. He smiled to himself; at least the third man from the gym was trying to make it chal-lenging. The intruder quickly recrossed the kitchen and the servants' antechamber. He flattened himself against the wall beside the servants' entrance from the yard area. As he did, an arm slowly poked its way through the open doorway. Its hand gripped a Ruger SR9. The killer shot the hand at close range and in less than a second had spun into the doorway and shot the now-wounded bodyguard between the eyes. Six down, two to go.

The downstairs part of the house was silent now, but a cacophony of shouts cascaded down from the second level. The voices were a mixture of Arabic and Pashtu. The intruder's intuition told him the remaining two bodyguards were upstairs with the people who were his real targets. The muscle was merely the gatekeeper, and not very effec-tive at that. Still, attempting to climb the stairs would have been suici-dal. The surviving bodyguards would be armed and waiting. For them, it would be like shooting fish in a barrel.

He slipped back out through the servants' entrance and paused in the shade of the overhanging balcony above. Slowly, he inched out and looked up. He didn't see anyone leaning over the balcony. He listened for a few moments, but he didn't hear any sounds coming from it either. He gripped the handle of the case with his teeth, and dropped the SIG into a pocket of his thobe. With a tremendous leap, he was able to grasp the edge of the balcony floor. An instant later, and with a couple of moves that a world-class gymnast would die to be able to do, he yanked his body up and over the top of the wrought iron railing that enclosed the balcony. He landed silently in a crouch, with the SIG back in his right hand and aimed into the bedroom behind the balcony. The room was empty, as was its adjoining bathroom. He quickly crossed the room to the door that opened into another spacious hallway. There was another bedroom opposite the one he was in. It too was empty and the bathroom door was open. He stole a quick glance down the hallway. Empty. He stepped out and crept slowly toward the center of the house. There was another bedroom to his left. It also was empty.

The hallway opened into a large living area in the center of the second floor. The two remaining gunmen, with their backs to him, were semi-crouched near the top of the stairwell. Each held a weapon in both hands, aimed down the stairs. Behind them, near the center of the room, five other men were staring intensely toward the stairs. They were older than the bodyguards, middle-aged and gray-haired, and dressed in casual western wear. One had lost almost all of his hair, but the remaining strands were long and greasy-looking. The other four had more scalp coverage. Their hair also was long, but bushy. All of them had long, full beards in various shades of gray. Each had a cell phone in hand, now useless because of the scrambling signal the intruder had activated.

The killer slipped silently up behind the five men. Aiming the SIG through a space between two of them, he squeezed off two rounds. The hollow point .9 mm slugs blew through the back of the two body-guards' skulls, scattering brain matter, blood, and bone shards down the stairwell. There was a moment of shock, then the five men spun almost in unison and stared at the intruder. The looks on their faces spoke volumes. They were having trouble getting their minds around what had just happened. The intruder standing before them was an enigma.

He was very muscular, but appeared old and wrinkled. He wore an old, dirty thobe. A white knitted taqiyah covered his head. He had long, gray hair and a beard to match. And sunglasses. And held a battered case of some kind in his left hand. But it was the right hand that drew everyone's attention. It held the SIG, and it was moving slowly, almost indolently back and forth between the five men.

In Pashtu, the man with the gun said, "Sit."

The five men stared at him sullenly, defiantly. The balding one said, "Even with the weapon, you are only one man, and an old one at that. There are five of us, all within a few feet of you. Perhaps you can shoot one of us, maybe even two. But the others will overpower you and kill you with our bare hands. It is you who should sit."

The man with the gun shot the spokesman in the kneecap. The victim shrieked in pain and collapsed backward onto a banquette that ringed the center of the spacious living area. The banquette surrounded some sort of large, abstract, ornamental object that looked like an Arabian Nights version of a tree.

"Next?" said the gunman.

The other four men quickly sat down, each staring in fascination at the muzzle of the SIG.

The gunman, no longer bent and stooped, was a powerfully built six feet two inches tall. He reached up casually and removed a wig. Underneath, his own hair was short and medium brown in color. Next he stripped away the long, gray beard, revealing several days' growth of his own stubble. Its color matched the hair on his head. Then he peeled the rubbery compound from his face that had given it an aged, wrinkled appearance. Finally, he removed the sunglasses. His eyes were the blue of a high alpine glacier, but colder.

The wounded man sat sobbing and clutching his ruined knee with both hands. There wasn't much blood. The slug had drilled through bone and cartilage but had not hit any major blood vessels.

The man sitting to his right was heavyset with a face that looked like a bulldog with a full beard. "Who are you? What do you want with us?"

"Think of me as a representative of the American people."

"The CIA sent you? You are a SEAL? A Delta?"

"Green Beret?" said the man to his right.

The gunman shook his head. "I said 'American people,' not the U.S. government."

The men looked at each other questioningly. Finally, the bulldog said, "There is only one of you?"

"Seems that's all that was needed."

"But we have eight men guarding us. Eight very well trained and capable men."

"You still have eight men. They're just dead, that's all."

The man sitting on the far left of the group said, "You are a fool. Do you not know who we are?"

"I like tests," the gunman said. "Let's see how I do." He looked at the man who had just spoken and said, "Let's start with you. You're Karmal Kundi, former governor of Afghanistan's Helmand province. You were Mullah Omar's right hand man, brokering a deal with the Iranians that secured their support for the Taliban's efforts against the American-led coalition. You also were a major drug trafficker and a strong supporter of al Qaeda."

He turned to the man on Kundi's right. "You're Mullah Nufail Noorzai, a senior Taliban military commander wanted by the United Nations for war crimes, including the murder of thousands of Shiite Muslims. You fought with al Qaeda against the Northern alliance, and later against the Coalition forces."

"You, in the middle," he said, pointing at the wounded man, "the crybaby with the owie on his knee. You're Mullah Marjan Jadoon, former Taliban army chief of staff. You also are wanted by the UN for war crimes including the murder of thousands of Shiites. You have known associations with such Islamic terrorist groups as al Qaeda, Islamic Movement of Uzbekistan, Hezb-e-Islami Gulbuddin, and Harakat-i-Inqilab-i-Islami. You also worked closely with top al Qaeda commanders."

The bulldog was next. The gunman motioned at him with the SIG. "You're Atal Yusaf Khel, the Taliban deputy minister of intelligence. Among other things, you were a keystone in the Taliban's efforts to form alliances with other Islamic terrorist groups to fight against U.S. and Coalition forces."

Turning to the fifth and final man seated on the banquette, the gunman said, "That brings us to you. You are Mehtar Malik, a senior Taliban security official who had powerful connections to Anti-Coalition groups including al Qaeda, the Taliban, the Haqqani Network, and the Hezb-e-Islami Gulbuddin. You met regularly with al Qaeda operatives to coordinate attacks against U.S.-led forces."

He looked at the five men. "Well, how did I do? An A-Plus?"

Kundi said, "I don't understand. Who sent you? Why are you here?"

"I told you, I'm here on behalf of the American people. I'm here to right a wrong."

"What are you talking about?" Malik said. "We are here as the guests of the government of the State of Qatar and its rulers, the Al Thani family. Perhaps you should take this up with them."

Yusaf Khel, the bulldog, eyed the battered case in the gunman's left hand. "What is that? Do you plan to play an instrument for us?" The sarcasm was evident.

The gunman smiled. "Yes, in a manner of speaking. What is in this case isn't exactly a musical instrument, but under the right circumstances it literally can sing."

The five men stared at the case and squinted their eyes in puzzlement.

Sticking the butt of the SIG between his teeth, the gunman opened the case and reached inside. His hand emerged holding a weapon with a curved, slender, twenty-eight inch single-edged blade. It had a circular guard and long grip to accommodate two hands.

He dropped the SIG into the case and closed it.

Holding it up for the men to see, he said, "This is *doragon no chi.* In Japanese that means "Dragon's Blood." It's a *katana,* and was made hundreds of years ago for a samurai lord, a *diamyo*, by a revered swordsmith. The smith is said to have folded it over and hammered out the impurities in the steel more than thirty thousand times." He pointed to an inscription written in gold inlay on the blade in an old style of

Japanese. "This says that, when tested, it cut through five stacked corpses in a single slice. That was by someone far less powerful than I. In my hands, it has cut through eight bodies in a single slice."

Jadoon, eyes glued to the blade and his face a mixture of fear and skepticism, said, "What is your intention?"

"When I identified each of you, I omitted the one thing that you have in common, besides your misbegotten allegiance to the Taliban's murderous seventh century dogma." He paused and fixed each of them, one by one, with an icy stare. "The fool in the White House, who clearly doesn't give a damn what the nation's citizens want, gave each of you a get-out-of-jail card from Gitmo."

"Yes," said Noorzai. "But it was simply a matter of exchanging one prison for another. We are essentially under house arrest here in Qatar. We can't go anywhere. We can't entertain visitors. We can't even make telephone calls. How can that be…what did you call it…a get-out-of-jail card?"

The man with the sword snorted derisively. "That's bullshit. Were you stupid enough to believe you weren't under surveillance? You've become increasingly adept at circumventing the sanctions measures. You've made phone calls to reestablish contacts with the Taliban in Afghanistan. Members of the al-Qaida-affiliated Haqqani militant group have travel to Qatar to meet with you. Even the politically corrupt UN has acknowledged that each of you has violated the no-travel ban."

"Even so, it was a fair exchange!" Kundi said pleadingly. "You got Kevin Johnson in return."

"A coward and deserter in exchange for five of the worst butchers in the Taliban. Some deal. An independent review by the Government Accountability Office clearly said the president broke the law by failing to consult Congress before authorizing your exchange for Johnson. It was an act that never did sit well with the American public, but the candy-asses they elected to Congress were too incompetent to stop it." He paused and gave them a ruthless, frigid smile. "In my country we have a saying—paybacks are a bitch."

Still tightly clutching his wounded knee, Jadoon wailed, "Please, kill the others, but spare me. I will give you valuable information for your government."

"I don't currently have a government. Besides it's too late for you." The swordsman brought the blade up in a blinding flash of highly polished metal, then down through Jadoon. The blow cleanly severed him into two equal halves from the crown of his head to his crotch. For a long, agonizing second, his comrades stared disbelievingly at the gore that, a moment before, had been their companion. Then, all four struggled at once to get to their feet. The sword slashed instantly, from left to right and back again. The blows separated Kundi's and Noorzai's torsos from their lower extremities. The halves tumbled to the floor.

The swordsman leaped nimbly across the rapidly expanding pool of blood flowing from the remains of Jadoon. He flicked the blade at Malik. The victim's head slid off its neck and toppled to the floor as the body collapsed back onto the now-bloody banquette.

Of the five, only Yusaf Khel remained alive. He saw there would be no escape. He stood defiantly, legs wide apart and hands balled into fists on his hips. "I am a warrior of Islam. I do not fear death. In a moment, I shall be in Paradise, enjoying the pleasures of seventy-two virgins."

"You're no warrior. You're a drug-dealing thug and murderer, a disgrace to the peaceful tenets of your professed religion." The swordsman paused and smiled a grim little smile. "And those virgins may be in for a disappointment." The sword flicked and Yusaf Khel's testicles and penis were neatly separated from his body.

Yusaf Khel made a screeching sound and grabbed his injured crotch with both hands. His knees buckled thrusting his head forward. The sword flicked through the air once more. Yusaf Khel's head was separated from his neck.

The swordsman ripped off the old, dirty thobe he'd been wearing and used it to wipe blood splatters off his face and hands and to clean the gory blade. Then he replaced the katana in the case, and removed a white polo shirt, khaki trousers, a pair of tan colored boat shoes, and a Canadian passport. His plan called for him to shave off his natural brown stubble using a razor that belonged to any of the bodyguards. From the looks of their beards, he doubted any of the Taliban Five had much experience with shaving. Next, he'd use one of the cars in the garage downstairs to drive to the marina, where he had arranged in advance for a rental boat. A dust storm had been forecast to hit the area later in the day. That would put a damper on any police activities, assuming the grisly scene was discovered anytime soon. He'd pilot the rented boat the one hundred and thirty-five nautical miles to the King Abdul Aziz Sea Port in Dammam, the capital of Saudi Arabia's Eastern Province and the country's fifth largest city. From the seaport, it was a twenty-kilometer cab ride to the King Fahd International Airport, the largest airport in the world in terms of land area. He already had a ticket on Lufthansa to Frankfurt via Kuwait City. Life was good.

Chapter 39

MIRANSHAH, PAKISTAN

THE AIR WAS thin and crisp. An early winter was settling over the rugged mountains that were strung along the border between Afghanistan and Pakistan. Turan Salam was used to the weather and the mountains. Recently turned seventeen, he had lived in the area his whole life. But the thin air and the cold wouldn't have mattered even if he had been a native of a more temperate climate. He had spent the past several months training in these ancient, jagged peaks. It had been brutal, both physically and emotionally. Several of his campmates had failed the rigors of the program or given up. They had never been seen or heard from again. This message wasn't lost on Turan and his surviving campmates. On the other hand, he thrived on the regimen. His formerly thin body had filled out with twenty pounds of new muscle. Never much of a student in the madrassa, the hands-on training in the tactics and challenges of waging holy war had fully captured his imagination and spirit.

He was particularly excited tonight. The long months of pain and exhaustion were about to be rewarded with an actual mission against the enemies of Islam. It would be Turan's first taste of real combat, but he felt confident in his newfound abilities. His mentor, Bazir Haqqani, was only a few years older than Turan, but already he was a battle hardened veteran and highly regarded field officer in the Holy Army of the Caliphate.

Bazir had pulled Turan aside and explained the nature of that evening's operation.

"Tonight's mission is a raid on a COP operated jointly by the American crusaders and their Afghan lackeys."

Turan looked puzzled. "What is this COP?"

"It means Combat Outpost. The Infidels have many of them. They locate them at places where they can observe our movements along the border. The Infidels call this particular COP 'Spera.'"

"Spera?" Turan said. "I thought that was a town about twelve kilometers beyond the border?"

Bazir smiled and tousled the younger man's hair. "You have been studying the maps, my would-be warrior. That's very good. And, yes, Spera is where you have said. It's the largest community in the immediate area, so the Infidels used its name. But the COP is nearer the tiny village of Tora Tiža, only five hundred meters inside the border."

"The Durand Line," Turan said in reference to the fourteen-hundred-mile long line separating Afghanistan from Pakistan. It cut through the Pashtun tribal areas, politically dividing ethnic Pashtuns, who lived on both sides of the border. It separated the Federally Administered Tribal Areas of Pakistan—FATA, including Turan's home in South Waziristan, from the northeastern and southern provinces of Afghanistan. Spera was in the province of Khost, which abutted both North and South Waziristan.

"I thought the Infidels had pulled back from the border some time ago, leaving control of it to the Afghan Border Police."

"The former COP Spera was closed at the end of the year 2010. But their egos in the face of defeat and the incompetence of the ABP, caused the Americans to build a new COP near Tora Tiža." A thin, mean smile flickered across Bazir's handsome face. "It is the incompetence, corruption, and cowardliness of the ABP that has made the Durand Line one of the most dangerous areas in the world."

Turan had been raised on tales of the endless militant activities and illegal smuggling that occurred in the region. Because of the absence of government control, and the fact that it was legal to carry guns in the region, assault rifles and explosives were a common sight. It was a hotbed for many forms of illegal activities, including the smuggling of weapons and narcotics, as well as many other commodities. The porousness of the border encouraged incursions by militants from Pakistan's FATA areas.

"This area of the accursed Durand Line is not controlled by the ABP or the soldiers of the Western nations," Bazir said with a prideful smile. "It is controlled by my family, the Haqqanis."

Turan knew about the Haqqani Network, a powerful guerrilla insurgent group allied with the Taliban. It was engaged in asymmetric warfare against NATO forces and the government of Afghanistan. Bazir's uncle Maulvi Jalaluddin Haqqani and his son Sirajuddin Haqqani led the group. *Bazir comes by his warrior's bloodline legitimately*, Turan thought.

"The presence of the Infidels and their Afghani apostates is an outrage," Bazir said. "They *will* be made to pay for it."

"Is that why you have brought us here to Miranshah?" Turan said. There was a certain eagerness in his voice.

Bazir nodded. "Yes, it is time for you and the other trainees to prove yourselves worthy of joining our jihad. Simulated fighting is a thing of the past. Now you will be tested in the heat of battle. From this point forward, death will be your constant companion."

Chapter 40
DOHA QATAR

MUKUT HAD temporality lost sight of the old man when he'd crossed Al Buhaira Street and disappeared into the thick landscaping that shielded the West Bay Lagoon community from the rest of Doha. Scurrying through the brush, Mukut again caught sight of his quarry. The old man was kneeling near the edge of the broad lawn that stretched from the woods to the rear of a palatial villa. He watched curiously as the man took some sort of device from the battered case, made some adjustments to it, then set it on the ground beside him. Next he took a firearm from the case. He attached a long extension to it, which Mukut thought was a sound suppressor.

Suddenly, the man sprinted across the lawn. He moved faster than Mukut had ever seen any human move, more like a big jungle cat, a cheetah perhaps. Previously old and stooped, now he was tall and powerful. Was he *shaitan djinni*, a shape shifter possessed of magical powers? The man fired a shot at a small wooden door as he approached it, then kicked it open. Almost immediately, Mukut heard another shot. Despite the effect of the suppressor, the weapon still made a sharp, spitting sound.

Mukut was on what he'd once heard an imam refer to as the horns of a dilemma. On one hand, his survival instincts urged him to run from the scene as fast as he could. On the other, his curiosity was inflamed by the scene unfolding before him. Who *was* this strange man? What was his purpose? Could it possibly present Mukut with an opportunity for enrichment? After a few moments' hesitation, curiosity and greed won out. He stayed in the shadows of the woods and watched.

Mukut heard four more shots fired from the suppressed weapon. Then he saw a burly man wearing running shorts and a singlet top emerge through opened glass sliders and creep toward the same door the now-not-so-old man had entered. The man in shorts held a weapon of his own extended in front of him. He seemed to pause momentarily at the doorway, then carefully stuck the gun inside. Suddenly, the gun and most of the hand that had held it were blown away. Before the man could react, the intruder appeared in the doorway and shot him in the head.

The intruder swept his gaze across the yard and woods beyond. For a few terrorizing moments, Mukut felt as though the man was staring directly at him. His instinct screamed at him to run, but his legs suddenly were too weak to respond. He felt the warm flow of urine soaking his jeans as he squatted in the shadows, wishing he could merge into the ground itself.

After a moment or two, the man with the gun leaned out and peered up at the balcony above. Mukut watched in fearful fascination. The man dropped the weapon into a deep pocket of his tattered thobe, then with the handle of the case clenched in his teeth, leaped straight up and grasped the edge of the balcony. A moment later he yanked himself upward and, grabbing the top rail of the balustrade, vaulted over it. He landed soundlessly on the balcony. Mukut couldn't begin to imagine the agility, and, even more, the strength required to do such a thing. He stayed in the bushes for a few more minutes, watching the balcony. He barely heard the sound of two more shots; much duller sounds, as if they had come from deep inside the house.

It was a magnificent house. Given its location, the owners were wealthy people. Was the gunman here to rob them? Could he possibly carry away all the treasures that the house must contain? No way.

There would be plenty of leftovers for Mukut after the man had left. But then he had another thought. He stared at the cameras sweeping slowly back and forth across the wide lawn. It made sense that there would be a security system, and a very sophisticated one at that. Surely the police were on their way. But he didn't hear any sirens. Perhaps the wisest course of action was to phone the police and keep an eye on the man until they arrived. How could the owners of the house not reward him richly for his services? It seemed like a much better idea than hanging around after the man left, and perhaps being apprehended by the police and charged with these shootings.

He pulled his cell phone from a back pocket of his jeans and pressed the digits of the emergency number. The message on the screen said service was unavailable. This puzzled Mukut. It had given no indication of not functioning properly when he'd used it a few minutes earlier to take a photo of this strange man. Maybe it was the thick canopy of tree branches. Or maybe it was this man's magic. He half-walked, half-crawled back to the edge of the inner belt of landscaping in West Bay Lagoon. It was more than four hundred feet from where he'd been squatting and watching the house. When he was connected to the police, he used the location application on the phone to provide an address along with an excited, half-babbled description of what he was witnessing. When he gave the address, the policeman seemed stunned and made Mukut repeat it twice. He told the police official that the intruder was armed and had shot at least one man.

Within minutes the entire neighborhood was swarming with police officers and members of the Qatar State Security, a branch of the Ministry of Interior that dealt with matters relating to terrorism and espionage. The noise must have alerted the intruder. He rushed out onto the balcony he'd previously scaled. With a tremendous heave, he threw the old case all the way into the woods. It landed within a few meters of Mukut. The man disappeared back into the house and Mukut crawled over to the case. It was old and beat-up, but it was sturdily made and hadn't burst open.

He worked the clasps and opened it and pulled out the bloodstained thobe, flinging it aside. Inside the case was the pistol, silencer, and extra magazine. It also held a sword of some kind. The handle was big enough for two hands to hold it at the same time. The blade was slightly curved. Strange looking figures were inscribed on it in what appeared to Mukut to be gold inlay. He didn't know what it was exactly, but he guessed that it had value. And he knew where he could sell it and the pistol without attracting suspicion to himself. Mukut resealed the case and hauled it back into the woods to a point close to the road. He would go and meet with the police and let them know he was the one who had called. And ask for his reward. Later he would recover the case and take it to Saadi Al-Hamad, a black-market operator who might know what the value of the sword was. With any luck, he might pay Mukut as much as half of that sum.

INSIDE THE BLOODIED VILLA, the killer realized his exfiltration Plan A no longer was feasible. Time for Plan B—the worst-case scenario. He put the sword, the suppressed Sig, the spare magazine, and the soiled thobe in the case and ran out onto the balcony at the rear of the house. Like an Olympic hammer-thrower, he used both hands and all of his considerable strength to fling the case far out into the thick shrubbery behind the villa. He swiftly moved to a clean, open area of floor in the main room near the top of the stairs, and knelt facing in that direction with his hands behind his head.

Chapter 41

TORA TIŽA, AFGHANISTAN

AT ITS BEST, Miranshah had been a rough, dusty outpost in North Waziristan about sixteen kilometers from the border with Afghanistan's Khost province. The town spread along the banks of the Tochi River in a wide valley surrounded by the foothills of the towering Hindu Kush mountains. The narrow, deep valleys along the Durand Line had sheltered tribal fighters for countless centuries. Today, militant Islamists, smugglers, drug runners, and other unsavory types moved through the area with near impunity, as they crossed back and forth between the two countries. Policing it was a task that defied conventional military operations.

It was Miranshah's convenient location close to those sheltering valleys that had led to its becoming a virtual munitions factory and base of operations for militants. Ironically, it also was the administrative headquarters of the North Waziristan Agency in Pakistan's FATA region. It was a combustible mix, and the explosion was inevitable. Today, the all but deserted town was mostly rubble and craters; the aftermath of the violent conflict between the militants and the Pakistani military.

Bazir had gathered his young soldiers in a partially ruined mosque to shelter them from the prying eyes of the Infidels' drones and satellites. To pass time, he asked them questions relating to the history of the area.

"Do any of you know how this wretched town got its name?" Bazir asked.

The young men looked at each other and shrugged. No one spoke.

"It was named after Miran Shah, a Timurid ruler. He was the son of Timur, one of the greatest warriors in history. Timur's battlefield injuries crippled one of his legs. The Infidels call him Timur the Lame or Tamerlane. Tonight, I want you to summon Timur's courage and ferocity in battle."

He paused for effect and looked around the room at his young charges. "You are going to attack an Infidel outpost on the other side of the border. They are well armed and will fight back. But you will ignore the danger and kill them. Every one of them."

Later, when it was dark, a number of severely battered Toyota Hilux pickups drove up to the mosque and the young men scrambled on board. Keeping an eye out for drones, they were driven in a mostly southerly direction for about fifteen kilometers. The road, such as it was, was narrow, unpaved, and bone-jarringly bumpy. A good portion of it was dry riverbed. Eventually the convoy swung toward the west and struggled up rock-strewn creek beds into the mouth of a steep-sided valley. When they finally stopped, Bazir told them they were less than five kilometers from the new U.S. Army COP near Tora Tiža.

The outpost was situated on a high ridgeline about five hundred meters from the border. The U.S. military had chosen the location because it provided a clear view of the Durand Line for several kilometers in either direction. It was staffed by forty U.S. Army Special Forces troops plus an Afghan Army platoon.

It was late in the evening and moonless when the Hilux trucks stopped in the dry creek bed southeast of the COP on the Pakistan side of the border. Bazir split his forces into two groups, taking personal charge of one of them. He placed his uncle, a scarred and grizzled Haqqani warrior named Dawar Masood, in charge of the other group. They had local members of the Haqqani Network guiding them. The guides assured Bazir that the Infidels had not yet set up detection devices on the COP's perimeter. They also advised that no drones had been spotted in the area recently.

Bazir's group, which included Turan, worked its way up a tree-covered slope. They were careful to stay below a jagged ridgeline that split off from the one that harbored the COP. It was an approach that shielded them from the line of sight of the occupants of the outpost. Masood led the other force along a dry creek bed to a point southwest of the COP. Then his men scaled a steep, forested slope to a point on the ridgeline that was behind the targeted outpost.

Bazir settled his men into the deep shadows just beneath the ridgeline's serrated edge. The route taken by Masood's group was longer and would require more time to get into position. Watches had been coordinated before the two groups had split up. Bazir glanced at his. He sheltered its face and triggered the small light on the dial for only an instant. It was time.

He whispered a command to Turan who was next in line behind him. Turan passed it to the next man and so on. Shortly, the rear half of Bazir's force broke off and slipped quickly over the ridgeline. Bazir's group would approach the COP in parallel lines, one on each side of the ridgeline. Masood and his men, similarly arrayed, would come from the opposite direction, catching the occupants of the COP in a deadly crossfire.

Slowly, carefully, the budding HAC warriors crept toward the encampment. It was a particularly dark night, making visibility almost zero. The incessant wind in the ancient and rugged mountains provided additional cover as it rattled tree limbs and whistled eerily through spaces in the large piles of talus that covered the slopes.

Bazir's men had crept to within fifteen meters of the COP's outer perimeter, when they suddenly heard several whooshing sounds. Trails of sparks rose into the dark sky. Seconds later a half dozen flares burst above them.

"Shit!" Bazir screamed in frustration.

"What is happening?" a suddenly confused Turan said.

"They know we're here," Bazir shouted as he began scrambling back in the direction from which they'd come. "Those idiot guides have failed us. The Infidels must have sensors in place after all. Or drones." He waved at Turan and the others. "Come, come! We must get out of here."

At once the night erupted in gunfire as the Americans and their Afghan allies opened up on the now well-illuminated militants. Turan heard the deadly rounds whizzing through the air; some buzzing close to his head like angry hornets, others snapping twigs and branches near him. What moments earlier had seemed so still, so benign now was chaotic. Panic and confusion swept through Bazir's young charges. After a second's hesitation, they scrambled to their feet and fled after Bazir.

As Turan stumbled down the steep escarpment, he saw his good friend Eimal just ahead and to the right. One moment he was whole. In the next, a .50 caliber slug smashed into the back of his neck, effectively decapitating him. On Turan's left, Zemaray, a boy from his own home village near Wana, was hit in the upper right leg. He stumbled and fell, then scrambled painfully to his feet. Two steps later, a slug severed his spine. He fell face first into the ragged scree, unable to move his arms to break the fall.

Propelled by sheer terror, Turan ran even faster toward the denser part of the forest just below. He breathlessly reached its sanctuary when he felt a sharp, stinging pain in his left shoulder. The sudden disorientation caused him to crash headlong into a stout tree trunk. The impact was followed instantly by an all-encompassing blackness as his world went dark.

Chapter 42
BEIJING

ZHENG BAO XUN was oblivious to the limo he was riding in, its driver, and the street scene unfolding beyond the car's deeply tinted glass. He had been poring over the notes and details for the weekly meeting of the Politburo Standing Committee. As the chairperson of the Chinese People's Political Consultative Conference, as well as Minister of Finance of the Peoples Republic, Zheng was the third ranking member of the standing committee. The committee currently consisted of eight members. The chairman was Jiang Qui Xing. He also was President of the People's Republic of China and the General Secretary of the Communist Party of China, the most powerful man in China. Zheng held no illusions that the matters he was studying would be decided in any sort of egalitarian fashion. Regardless what the agenda may prescribe, Jiang would introduce the topic, express his position, and the other members would support it unanimously. Later everyone would agree that the decision had been voluntarily made by consensus. And so it was every week.

While Zheng studied his materials for the meeting, his driver had navigated the traffic on the crowded, fourteen-lane West Chang'an Avenue and pulled the limo to a stop on the north side of the road near Xinhua Gate, or "Gate of New China". It was the most important entrance to the Chinese government compound at Xinhuamen, near the Forbidden City in Beijing. The gate was inscribed with two slogans: "long live the great Communist Party of China" and "long live the invincible Mao Zedong Thought." Behind the entrance was a screen wall bearing the slogan "Serve the People", written in Mao's hand-writing.

The driver came around and opened the door for him. Zheng exited the limo, and with a firm grasp on the handle of his Bosca briefcase, passed by the gate. The fine leather of the briefcase had been hand selected and dyed cognac in color. It was large enough to accommodate his laptop computer and an assortment of files and everyday necessities. He began strolling through the vast gardened area behind the gate as he made his way toward the building where the meeting was to be held. He could have been driven to the meeting site in the government compound of Zhongnanhai, but because of the beautiful weather he had chosen to walk this last short distance.

Zhongnanhai was located in what had been the imperial gardens in the Imperial City located immediately west of the Forbidden City. The site now served as the central headquarters for the Communist Party of China and the State Council (central government) of the People's Republic of China. As a result, the word Zhongnanhai was used frequently as a metonym for the Chinese government similar to the way Brussels was used to indicate the government of the European Union.

The low temperature that morning had been around sixty degrees Fahrenheit and was climbing quickly toward an expected high in the mid-eighties. Humidity was low, making the weather even crisper and more pleasant. The bright greens of the late spring foliage coupled with the delicate aromas of the prolific flowers and blossoms gave an almost magical atmosphere to his surroundings. Zheng felt good. His plans were unfolding as he had intended.

He arrived at the meeting site and took his assigned seat among the other seven members of the committee, including Jiang Qui Xing. It wasn't uncommon for other important officials to be invited to attend the meetings if the topics to be discussed fell within their areas of expert skill or knowledge. Zheng was surprised, however, to see General Liu Chunhua, chairman of the Central Military Commission. There had been no mention of his attending the meeting in the agenda and supporting documents.

Nominally the CMC exercised command and control of the People's Liberation Army, People's Armed Police, and People's Liberation Army militia. Its chairman was titled the commander-in-chief of China's armed forces. In reality, Jiang, as Secretary General of the Communist Party, was the ultimate authority.

Jiang quickly called the meeting to order. Zheng noted that the chairman seemed to be in a particularly jovial mood this morning. Hopefully, no heads would roll, especially Zheng's.

After dispensing with opening formalities, Jiang smiled broadly. "Comrades, I have come upon a great scheme to further the destruction of the economic strength of the West."

Zheng glanced furtively at General Chunhua. His almost famous impassivity cracked for a mere nanosecond when Jiang claimed the ownership of this new "scheme." It was enough. It confirmed what Zheng suspected: Chunhua was the real architect of the plan.

"Please, Comrade Chairman, share this wonderful plan with us. We are most interested in hearing what your superior intellect has devised," said Soong Jiabao, the fourth-ranking member of the Committee as Secretary of the Central Commission for Discipline Inspection. His eagerness to move up as a member of the Standing Committee was well known by all of the other members. To do so, he would have to displace Zheng, the number three member. Soong's incessant ass-kissing was obvious to everyone except, perhaps, Jiang. Zheng scowled and reaffirmed his mental note to have Soong and his entire family executed once he had replaced Jiang.

Jiang nodded graciously at Soong. "Our temporary ally in the Middle East, Nadir Shah, has requested additional heavy weaponry. As we know, his struggle to establish his caliphate is failing. The combined forces facing him are simply too strong."

"But we have been supplying him with sophisticated armaments for some time, Comrade Chairman," Zheng said. "Isn't his problem more a matter of insufficient numbers of soldiers who also are insufficiently trained in the use of the weapons we provide?"

Jiang's smile faded a bit. "Yes, Minister Zheng, I was just about to mention that myself."

"My sincere apologies. I did not mean to interrupt." Sweat began to form on Zheng's brow despite the efficiency of the air-conditioning equipment.

The chairman continued to stare at Zheng for a few more uncomfortable moments. "As I was about to say, it is true that Shah's problem is his strength of force. That is where my brilliant thoughts come into play." He paused for a moment, then continued. The broad smile was back.

"Do you remember, Comrades, when China had the prescience to purchase several small nuclear devices from the Russians, I believe they are commonly referred to as 'suitcase bombs,? '"

Heads bobbed around the table.

"Imagine what would happen in the United States if Shah's operatives detonated a few of them in America."

Now Zheng knew why General Chunhua was present at the meeting. The CMC controlled the sites where China's nuclear weapons were stored. This included Hainan Island and its extensive underground facilities.

Initially there was silence around the table, as each member looked at the others. No one was certain what to say. Sometimes Jiang purposely would offer a stupid statement just to see who would bite, then he would castigate that member in front of the others.

Finally, after carefully weighing the risk-reward aspects, Soong spoke up. "Would it not force the Americans, and by logical extension their Western allies, to reallocate resources from foreign operations to domestic ones?"

"Very good, Comrade Soong. And what effect would that have on their economies?"

This time Zheng wasn't going to let the ass-kisser speak first. "Terrorism of that caliber in the homeland would cripple their economies."

Jiang nodded vigorously in agreement. "As you are an expert in matters of the economy, Comrade Zheng, I am not surprised by your quick response." Jiang paused and looked around the table. "So we are agreed, yes?"

All heads around the table bobbed in unison. Except one. The oldest member in terms of age, Huang Ziyang, quietly said, "This is a very ambitious, but dangerous plan, Comrade Chairman. If the West is able to trace these weapons back to China, there will be a terrible price to be paid."

The smile vanished from Jiang's face, replaced by a dark and angry scowl. "*If* they were to be traced back, yes, that would present a problem, Comrade Huang."

Zheng, and he believed most of the others at the table, agreed with Huang. But he knew that Huang had passed his sixty-eighth birthday and was due to be replaced very soon. Huang had no power. Agreeing with him openly would be a fool's errand.

"I will instruct General Chunhua to select six of these nuclear devices for distribution to Nadir Shah. I also am appointing our very able minister of finance, Comrade Zheng, to see to the delivery. He is quite experienced in seeing that the distribution of weapons to Shah's forces leaves no fingerprints that could be traced back to the People's Republic."

He turned toward General Chunhua. "General you will provide Comrade Zheng with whatever he needs in order to do his job successfully."

The general nodded gravely with a half bow, "Yes, Comrade Chairman. It will be done."

Chapter 43

THE CAMP

BRENDAN WHELAN WAS ANGRY. He knew the brutish killer, his own brother Maksym, wouldn't rest until he had killed Whelan and his entire family, and perhaps anyone who'd had the misfortune to even know Whelan. Levell also was well aware of this, yet he had insisted that Whelan immediately fly to the United States for a meeting. While he had high regard for the abilities of family and friends guarding his wife and sons back in Dingle, Whelan knew that, ultimately, they were no match for Maksym. Whelan wasn't sure how even *he* would fare against Maksym. They did have the same genetic attributes. In theory that made it more of a level playing field. In theory. The potential game changer was Sven Larsen, who was genetically superior like Whelan and Maksym. Together the two of them, he and Larsen, should be more than a match for Maksym. In theory.

Whelan's anger wasn't just based on Levell's calling him away from Ireland at such a dangerous time. It was further stoked by Levell's demand that he bring Larsen with him to America. Whelan would have liked to tell him to shove it, but there was something in Levell's voice —something he couldn't quite identify, something he'd never heard before. He had talked it over with Caitlin. She cared deeply for the Old

Man, as the Dogs affectionately referred to their mentor. Reluctantly, she'd encouraged him to go.

If Levell's voice on the phone had been troubling, his appearance was downright shocking. Whelan had known the old Cold Warrior for more than twenty years. The man had been his mentor, a second father. He had been with the Old Man in a variety of situations, many of them dangerous, even desperate. He had seen Levell in many moods—angry, triumphant, sad, brooding, and, on extremely rare occasions, almost happy. But no matter the circumstances, Whelan had never seen Levell despondent. Whelan wasn't sure what to make of it. He'd doubted that anything had ever gotten the Old Man down. Not even Levell's near-death experience as a marine in the jungles of Vietnam, or the incident that had robbed him of the use of his legs.

Levell had summoned Whelan and Larsen to this familiar setting in the heavily forested mountains of western North Carolina. The drafty old cottage was familiar. It had been home to Whelan, Larsen, and the four other surviving members of the Sleeping Dogs during their training exercises. It had been where Levell and other members of the SAS—the Society of Adam Smith—had reunited the Dogs after almost twenty years of hiding from a Presidential Decision Directive calling for their termination on sight with extreme prejudice. Levell had carefully selected this location for its remoteness and rugged environment. Determining who owned the property would require a lifetime of effort by a skilled title searcher. It was another masterful coup, compliments of the staggering wealth and influence of the Mueller brothers, SAS's founders and principal benefactors.

The dwelling was made of fieldstones mortared together decades earlier. The sagging trusses supported a roof of cedar shake shingles that were warped with age and darkened by the accumulation of mold. The interior was chilly and damp. There was a faint but distinctive odor of mildew. The cottage squatted high on a slope in the midst of a thick old-growth forest adjacent to the Pisgah National Forest, not far from the town of Brevard. Much of the sunlight was blocked by an umbrella of tall Fraser firs and red spruces, trees that only grew above the four-thousand-foot mark in the Southern Appalachians. It created a dark, cave-like atmosphere. A few small, cracked, grime encrusted windows filtered out most of the sparse light that managed to trickle through the thick canopy of branches. Although officially referred to as "the Cabin," Whelan and the other Dogs had redubbed the place "the Cavern." Rafe Almeida had referred to it as "Hotel California." He said the place reminded him of a line in an Eagles song: "You can check out anytime you like/But you can never leave." The Cabin was part of a larger facility known simply as "the Camp."

When Whelan and Larsen entered, Levell was sitting in a simple wooden chair at a battered and scarred table that had been squeezed into the cramped kitchen. Whelan assumed that Nando, Levell's personal assistant, driver, and bodyguard, had assisted the Old Man from his wheelchair to the seat at the table. Although he didn't see Nando, he sensed the Brazilian capoeira expert was close at hand. Levell didn't hire incompetents under any circumstances.

There was a cup of coffee in front of Levell that had long grown cold. It matched the expression on the Old Man's face. Whelan struggled to find the word that described it: "despairing," "forlorn," "hopeless," "depressed," "disheartened," "dispirited"? Then it came to him: "funereal." He glanced at Larsen, who simply shrugged.

Without looking up, Levell made a small motion toward the other chairs at the table. The two men sat down, Larsen carefully, as though he didn't trust the rickety chair to accommodate his muscular bulk.

"You look..." Whelan searched for the right word, "unsettled. Something wrong, Cliff?"

Ordinarily the essence of dynamism, the Old Man continued to stare at the tabletop for several long seconds. There was an uncharacteristic three-day stubble on his cheeks, and his hair was unkempt. The two newcomers had never known Levell to be anything but a spit and polish ex-Jarhead. There was a slight tremor in the hand that was resting on the table.

At last he looked up and locked eyes briefly with each man. "It's all just a fucking waste of time."

The other two men exchanged glances again. "I think you started in the middle of a sentence, Cliff. What's a waste of time?" Whelan said.

Rage flared in Levell's clear blue eyes. "This is!" He waved his arms angrily for a moment. "Trying to save this country's useless ass from the stupidity of its own people."

Whelan was shocked. Levell had created the SAS to form a shadow government of patriots with wealth and/or positions in high places for the purpose of shepherding his beloved America through the most dangerous period in its history. The goal was to fight its evermore powerful and prolific enemies, and hold together existing alliances until the American electorate came to its collective senses and placed responsible, competent people in the highest offices in the land. Now, if Whelan had heard him right, Levell was giving up.

"I don't understand, Cliff. Are you saying that you're throwing in the towel, that the SAS is declaring defeat?"

Levell stared at the tabletop again and slowly shook his head back and forth. "I don't know what the hell I'm saying. I know I summoned you two here from Ireland, knowing full well that your family, Brendan, is in danger because of that fuck Maksym. But I did that when I was still delusional enough to think getting you to put the unit back together could make a difference."

Larsen stiffened visible in his seat and said icily, "I don't get *summoned*. I'm not your damn errand boy."

"Okay, you sensitive bastard," Levell growled between clenched teeth. "I *asked* you to come. It was because I was afraid that if I left you behind without Brendan keeping an eye on you, you'd cause more trouble than any good you might do."

"And I'm not interested in being a part of the Dogs anymore," Larsen said, his voice rising. "My involvement got my family killed. All I want is to slowly and agonizingly bleed the life out of Maksym."

Whelan raised his hand and made a tamping motion. "Calm down, dammit. Let's not compound the issues—until we find out what they are—with unnecessary antagonism." He turned toward Levell. "What the hell is going on? Why the apparent change of heart?"

"It's the reality that this country's too far into the weeds. The course is clear; it's too late to alter it."

Whelan stared at Levell for a few moments while he tried to digest what the old Cold Warrior was saying. "I've never known you to be negative about anything, Cliff. What makes you think SAS is losing the fight?"

Levell sighed. "The goddamn president's got dictatorial powers, and he's using them to weaken the nation's military and intelligence abilities. Congress is totally ineffective, a bunch of self-serving bastards. For reasons of job security and allegiance to the pro-left power structure, government entities like the DOJ, the IRS, ATF, DHS, the FBI and others aren't making any effort to counter this course. Law enforcement is on the run because the leftists in the media endlessly portray them as jackbooted racists and worse. Street mobs of all kinds grow more prevalent and more dangerous by the day. Students are now running the colleges, like inmates running asylums. The über rich gladly contribute a substantial part of their resources to the president's party to preserve the status quo because it enables their wealth to escalate far beyond reason. The middle class—the foundation of a free and capitalist society—is shrinking into oblivion. Our staunchest allies have been thrown under the bus. And on and on it goes." He looked at the two men and said, "We are looking at the imposition on mankind of another Dark Ages—a thousand years of misery, deprivation, and suffering."

Larsen said, "You know I've been a loyal soldier for years, but I never liked your politics. I think the president's party has done some pretty good things for this country. They gave us health care. They've kept the country out of wars. They've focused on important shit like climate change. And they've stopped people like you from spying on American citizens."

If looks could kill, the heat emanating from Levell's glare would have crisped Larsen. "You're a fucking moron, Larsen!"

"Whoa!" Whelan said. Although he couldn't actually see him, he could sense Nando had moved closer to the small room. "Let's try approaching this from a different perspective."

Neither Levell nor Larsen would be the first to break eye contact. It was a macho thing.

"Look at me, both of you!" Whelan growled. It did the trick. Both heads turned toward him.

"As I see it, Cliff, the SAS, though well-intentioned, may have been taking the wrong approach to the problem. You've been pursuing a multitude of tactics, but maybe what is needed is a strategy."

"What are you suggesting?" Levell said suspiciously.

Whelan leaned back in his chair, hoping it would ease the tension. "Think about how Fairchilde and his AGU cronies have gotten where they are today. They started with a single goal—establish and control a one-world government. To accomplish this, they developed an overarching strategy—destroy the United States, the one power that could deny them what they covet. Tactics entered the picture only at the third level, and they're designed to weaken America until it's unable to defend itself."

Levell nodded slowly but didn't speak.

Instead, it was Larsen. "What are these AGU tactics you're talking about?"

"They come in two flavors, domestic and foreign," Whelan said. "But first, AGU had to gain control of one of the two major political parties in the U.S. They accomplished that decades ago. That enabled AGU to further its agenda of destruction from within."

The edges of Larsen's mouth tightened, and his eyes narrowed into a semi-squint. "How is this 'destruction from within' supposed to work?"

"First, you remake the party's power structure so it consists primarily of those on board with the goal. Then you fund leftist candidates for public office, from the White House on down. These generally are weaklings who are afraid of their own shadows and think a big government is necessary to keep the smarter, stronger, more ambitious types in business and industry at bay. But there also are ideologues who believe most of us can't make good decisions and need to have a ruling elite of intellectually superior people—them—to do it for us."

Larsen stared at Whelan. There was an angry look in his eyes. "So you're saying you don't like people who vote for the other party."

"Yeah."

"You still haven't explained how that party is destroying America."

"Maybe because you interrupted me." Whelan sat forward in his chair, leaning toward Larsen menacingly.

The other man didn't say anything; he just continued to glare at Whelan.

"These leftist candidates follow party protocol. They favor amnesty for illegal aliens and open borders that invite countless more. In return, these aliens show their gratitude by supporting the leftists. The bigger these so-called progressives grow the government, the more regulations are generated that strangle small businesses, which are the lifeblood of the middle class. Only societies based on free enterprise generate the opportunities that create a large middle class, and that middle class prevents totalitarian regimes, like socialism and communism, from developing."

Larsen's glare softened slightly as he thought about Whelan's words.

"It gets worse. Sustaining this enormous, unwieldy, inefficient government always leads to greater and greater deficit spending. This requires an ever-expanding debt burden. And that, in turn, weakens the currency, creating inflation. That eventually leads to the collapse of the currency and economic chaos. But this current administration goes way beyond that, pitting its own citizens against each other on the bases of race, gender, religion, ethnicity, income, political views, and a lot more."

The angry look had disappeared completely from Larsen's face. It was replaced by an expression that mixed concern with confusion. "I'm not saying I agree with you; I just never thought of it that way is all."

"That's just the half of it," Levell said in his familiar raspy growl. "Tell him about the foreign aspects of AGU's and this administration's actions."

Whelan turned back to Larsen. "Avoiding war is a fool's errand. Calling it 'leading from behind' is merely an effort to sanitize the lunacy. This country's proliferating enemies draw encouragement and confidence from our underreacting to threats." He glanced at Levell.

"Cliff mentioned how the administration has neutered the intelligence community, leaving us unable to gather the SIGINT and HUMINT (signal intelligence and human intelligence) necessary to anticipate terrorist activities. He also mentioned gutting the military, which leads to an underfunded and undermanned military presence in the face of increasing global threats."

Whelan looked at Larsen. He could almost hear the wheels turning in the other man's head.

"Whelan didn't mention that this administration, dancing to AGU's tune, has insulted, admonished, and alienated our traditional allies. Other than the Israelis and Kurds, most of them are pussies anyway. Now those one-time allies are scurrying to align themselves with our enemies in an effort to save their own sorry asses." Levell shook his head in contempt.

Except for the creaking of the aged logs and the wind whistling through cracks in the ancient mortar, the room was still for several moments.

Finally, Larsen put his hands behind his head, leaned back in his chair, and stretched. When he straightened, he turned to Whelan. "You told Cliff that maybe the problem was SAS's strategy, that maybe they needed a change in tactics. What did you have in mind?"

"The original SAS called for the formation of a shadow government to do two things until this country elects a government that's responsive and responsible. First— form strategic alliances with other countries to share intel and try to hold the line against aggression and terrorism that are the natural byproducts of the current administration's ideology and incompetence. The second—pending the return of the U.S.'s strengthened military—is to fight brush wars using these allies and, where the situation dictates it, the Dogs." He looked at Levell.

The Old Man nodded.

"If you recall, Sven, we were all in Malta a while back while Cliff tried to put together an effective coalition to go after that fucking caliphate in the Middle East. Even with the formation of a military alliance by Sunni nations, it doesn't look like that's working out. None of them has the military capability or, more importantly, the desire to put their undertrained troops in all-out combat."

"So you've got a better idea," Larsen said.

"Better? Maybe. It's more direct and doesn't rely as much on the active cooperation of Cliff's erstwhile allies."

"It wasn't such a bad idea," Levell said. "But the entry of the Russians into the vacuum that was created in the Middle East by the current administration has totally altered the situation. The Iranians got an ombudsman for their designs on the geopolitics of the area. To compound matters, the fucking Turks are warring against the Kurds more than they are the caliphate. That's a disaster in the making. The Kurds, along with the Israelis, are the finest fighting force in that part of the world. Like the Israelis, they are fighters first and farmers, shop-keepers, business professionals, and teachers second." Levell paused and then added, "I'll give that arrogant, weak-kneed, know-it-all bastard of a president credit—much of the struggle *is* an Islamic war in the Middle East; it should be *their* troops in combat, not ours."

"I agree with that part about it not being our troops who should be involved," Larsen said.

He turned to Levell. "SAS has amazing resources. Why not just put them behind your presidential candidate and regain control of the government?"

"SAS isn't backing or assisting any candidate. It's crucial for this country's future that Americans realize what's at stake and make the right choice. What we want for the election is a level playing field, but it's necessary that our enemies be held at bay until—hopefully—a strong, rational candidate is elected, one who can lead the nation away from AGU's influence and restore America's might."

Whelan said, "What if the electorate takes the path of least resis-tance, as usual?"

"You mean the path of greatest entitlement? That's the likely outcome, especially given that a presidential election is like a casting call for charlatans. In that case, regime change by force may become necessary. But once that path is trod, history shows the odds are indeed slim that those who take it will ever walk it back," Levell said.

"What's the alternative you mentioned, Whelan?" Larsen said.

"Yeah, I'm listening too," Levell said. "The irony isn't lost on me —an Irishman being the one to propose a strategy for preserving democracy and personal freedoms…in other words, civilization."

"Irony?" Larsen said.

"Yeah. It was Ireland's patron saint, Patrick, who was responsible for the preservation of civilization during the Dark Ages; otherwise, it would have been snuffed out. Because of his efforts, literacy and knowledge flourished in Ireland while the light of learning went out in the rest of Europe, as it was overrun by hordes of barbarians who destroyed libraries, universities, and monasteries. Books, scrolls, and other recordings of the evolution of civilization were lost forever. But because of the Irish monks and scribes on the remote Dingle Peninsula, the flame of human accomplishment continued to flicker. They laboriously copied ancient manuscripts from Greece and Rome, both pagan and Christian."

He looked at Larsen. "Now do you see the irony? Apparently it falls to the Irish to save our collective asses in times of global holocaust."

Larsen shrugged. "I don't give a shit who saves it, as long as it gets saved." He turned toward Whelan. "What's your plan?"

"It's simple. Thanks to SAS's intelligence operations, we know there are a relatively few key individuals in the world who are behind all the terrorism and aggression. Why not do the politically incorrect thing and just assassinate them? It takes them out of the game and sends a clear message to others who might think about trying to replace them."

Larsen crossed his massive arms and, with a sulky look, said, "And of course it's us who has to do the killing. It's always us."

The chill in Whelan's eyes almost lowered the temperature in the room. "It's beyond the realm of possibility for Norms. They'd just fuck it up and make things worse."

There was a long period of silence. Finally, Larsen sighed, but it sounded more like a long grunt from a water buffalo. He said, "So we do this instead of killing Maksym."

"No," Whelan said, and smiled a cold, mirthless smile. "*First*, we kill Maksym." He looked over at the disheveled Levell, who was slumped in his chair. The Old Man looked worn out, maybe even frail. Concerned, Whelan said, "What is it, Cliff? What's the problem?"

Now it was Levell's turn to take a deep breath and utter a long sigh. "I owe you the Maksym kill. Both of you. And I will see that you get the opportunity to collect."

"Why do I sense a 'but' in there, Cliff?" Whelan said.

"Before we constitute the Dogs as an assassins' league, as much as that appeals to me, there's something more pressing."

Larsen and Whelan glanced at each other.

"More important than eliminating the megalomaniacs who want to destroy free societies?" Whelan said.

"More important than killing Maksym?" Larsen said, sitting up in his chair and leaning toward Levell.

"Killing the leaders of Russia, China, Iran, and their ilk won't do much good if there's no America left. There's a preeminent threat to the homeland. It may already be too late, but we've got to try to stop it. Everything else will have to wait."

Whelan and Larsen looked at each other and then back at Levell.

"What is this threat?" Whelan said.

Levell cleared his throat. It didn't improve the raspiness of his voice. Absentmindedly, he took a sip of the cold coffee. His eyes opened in shock and, without hesitation, he quickly spit it back in the cup. With a grimace, he shoved the cup an arm's length away. "The threat is China."

"More so than Muslim terrorists?" Larsen said.

"Who the hell do you think is backing those bastards?"

"You said 'preeminent threat.' What does that mean in terms of immediacy?" Whelan said.

"Yeah, and what the hell is it they're planning to do that's any worse than all the shit they're already doing?" Larsen said.

"Considering who our members are, SAS's intelligence capabilities are better than those of most nations. It's been an open secret for decades that the USSR manufactured something like one hundred thirty-two so-called suitcase nukes. They called them RA-115s. Since the evil empire crumbled, only forty-eight have been accounted for."

Whelan said, "So that means eighty-four are still missing."

Levell nodded.

"The Cold War was a long time ago. Are these RA-115s still usable?"

"Yes. They need to be kept wired to a source of electricity. But even if that fails, they have battery backup."

"Got any idea where they are?" Larsen said.

Levell stared at the Man With No Neck for several long moments. "You think if I knew where the fuck they were, they'd still be missing? What the fuck's the matter with you?"

"I think Sven was asking do we have any tangible reason to believe any of them may be in the hands of our current enemies," Whelan said.

Levell seemed to be calmer. "We learned very recently from a reliable source that many of them were acquired by the Chinese after the USSR collapsed. Russia needed the money so badly it was willing to risk further weaponizing a potential rival on the world stage. Of those, maybe as many as a half dozen, have been provided to HAC."

Whelan whistled. "Damn, that's definitely a 'preeminent threat.'" He sat back in his chair and looked over at Larsen for a moment. Turning back to Levell, he said, "Do you have intel on the location of these RA-115s?"

"Yes, they're being smuggled into the USA."

Whelan and Larsen exchanged glances again.

"Any idea when?" Whelan said.

Levell nodded his head up and down slowly. "Yes. As we speak."

Chapter 44
GWADAR, PAKISTAN

THE SUCCESS of Zheng's meteoric rise through the ranks of the Communist Party and China's governing class was based largely on his dogmatic allegiance to placing his trust in no one. But, he occasionally had to admit to himself, there were times when he couldn't be in multiple places at once, and was forced to rely on others. This was one of those times.

Jiang had been very clear that Zheng would have paramount responsibility for the success in both the delivery of the nuclear devices to HAC and the absence of any evidence linking the nukes to China. Zheng had made it a point to be present when the six individual devices had been removed from storage near the People's Liberation Army Navy's Yulin Naval Base on the southernmost coast of Hainan Island. He'd arranged to have them carefully disguised and shipped to Pakistan with a cargo of supplies and materials aboard a PIA plane. PIA was the air freight division of Pakistan International Airlines. He even accompanied the plane to its destination in the burgeoning seaport of Gwadar.

He was pleased to find that Maksym's arrival had preceded his own. This was where the reliance part came into play. While the transfer from the plane was taking place, the two men sought respite from the dry heat of Gwadar's desert climate in the airport's VIP lounge. Zheng sipped tea made with water he specifically had brought with him from China. He'd heard too many bad things about what happened to travelers who drank the local waters. Maksym drank ice water, unconcerned that any microbe could have power over someone like him.

"Why was this place chosen?"

Zheng set the teacup on a small table in front of his chair. "You disapprove?"

Maksym shook his large head. "Don't presume to know what I'm thinking." It came out as a low, deep growl. "Pakistan is a large place. So why here?"

"There are a couple of good reasons. First, it provides a good cover because of CPEC."

"CPEC?"

"The China-Pakistan Economic Corridor. It's a fifty-one billion dollar collection of projects intended to improve Pakistan's infrastructure, as well as deepen the trade relations between the two nations."

Maksym snorted derisively. "I'd hoped you knew better than to try to sell that bullshit to me. It's really a part of China's One Belt, One Road initiative. Basically, it's an attempt to reestablish the old Silk Road."

"Yes, it's central to cultural interaction through Eurasia."

"Spare me the Chicom bullshit, Zheng. It's part of China's ambitious strategy to exercise dominion over the entire Asian continent and beyond."

Zheng smiled coyly. "And if in the process it enhances the quality of life and economic prospects for billions of people, what harm is there? It's essentially what the Americans attempted to do with their Tran-Pacific Partnership."

Maksym stood and walked over to bar and got a refill of ice water. When he returned, he said, "So the nukes are being transferred to a fishing scow in the harbor. At that point, I babysit them all the way to their final destination, yes?"

"Exactly. Who better to 'babysit,' as you call it, than you?" Zheng smiled benignly. "You see, my friend, I place a great deal of faith in your unique abilities."

"You don't trust a fucking soul. But you're right; there is no one better suited for this task, given its importance." He fixed the small Chinese man with a hard gaze. "And I expect to be compensated accordingly."

"What reason did you give our mutual friend Harland Fairchilde for your absence?"

"The same as usually. Given what he pays me, I tell him I'm looking at global investment opportunities."

"And he doesn't ask why you don't consult with him on that, considering he runs one of the largest investment houses in the world?"

"Of course he does. He even gets pissy about it."

"How do you handle that?"

Maksym leaned his mass forward and stared balefully into Zheng's eyes. "I look at him the way I'm looking at you."

The other man unconsciously pushed back against the cushions of his chair. "Yes, I'm sure that's quite effective," he said hastily. To change the subject, he said, "Once I've seen the merchandise safely stowed aboard the scow, my personal involvement is finished. I am relying on you to assure its safe delivery to the ultimate destination."

"I'll see that it's done."

There were several moments of silence before Maksym said, "The next stop, Chābahār, is about two hundred or so nautical miles away. How long am I going to be stuck on that stinking boat?"

"It travels at about twelve knots, so it should take about eighteen hours. I trust you are looking forward to your sea cruise." A trace of a smile flickered across Zheng's face.

Maksym ignored the comment. "Chābahār is in Iran. Why didn't you just have the Pakistanis fly the goods directly there?"

"The more players that we can insert between China and the ultimate destination, the better. Chābahār is not only a port city, it also has a twelve-thousand-foot runway. And Iran Air Cargo, a subsidiary of the nation's flag carrier, flies regularly from there to South America.

Ostensibly the plane will be carrying Iranian goods for marketing in Venezuela."

"What kind of plane?"

"Airbus A300. Is that suitable for your needs?" Zheng regretted making the snide remark almost before it left his mouth.

Maksym's huge right hand snaked out and grabbed the Chinese man by his pencil neck. He yanked him forward until their noses were touching. It took all of Zheng's resolve and effort not to lose sphincter control.

"The price for this mission just doubled, you wise-assed little slope." He flung Zheng back in his seat with enough force that it nearly flipped his heavy chair over backward.

Zheng glanced hastily around the lounge. Fortunately, it was nearly empty. He rubbed his throat. When his voice came out, it was raspy, like he had a case of laryngitis. "That was foolish of me. I apologize." He quickly added, "The plane doesn't have sufficient range to make it all the way to Venezuela without refueling."

"Yeah? Where is that going to happen?"

"The FBO in Murtala Muhammed International Airport in Lagos, Nigeria."

"Africa's a big place. Why there?"

"It's approximately halfway. In addition, we have good relations with Nigeria. China is investing more than eight billion dollars in a railway connecting Lagos with Kano." Zheng smiled. "It also employs eleven thousand Chinese workers. We also are building a massive hydroelectric dam in the Mambilla plateau. These efforts buy a great deal of cooperation in matters such as moving goods though the country without inspections."

"The next stop is Venezuela?"

"Yes, the Arturo Michelena International Airport in Valencia. We have an excellent relationship with the Marxist wannabes running the current government in Venezuela."

"Where the fuck is Valencia?"

"West of Caracas."

"Then what?"

"The specific merchandise will be transferred to a smaller aircraft chartered by an Iran-affiliated group that is a part of Hezbollah."

"Mexico's the final destination?"

"Yes, General Roberto Fierro Villalobos International Airport near Chihuahua, Mexico."

"And my job is done at that point."

Zheng hesitated momentarily. "Very nearly. Hezbollah will store five of the devices in an old warehouse on the northern outskirts of Chihuahua. The Iranis have agreed that Hezbollah will not release any of the others until China has given its blessing."

"You want to see how effectively the ragheads use the first one."

"Exactly."

"And that first one?"

"Hezbollah will deliver it to representatives of HAC who will truck it north to HAC's encampment near a village called San Luis. I want you to make certain it arrives at the encampment. Then your involvement is at an end."

Maksym rubbed his stubbled chin thoughtfully. "Seems like a hell of a complicated plan just to deliver six nukes to a terrorist group. Why didn't you just turn them over to HAC anywhere along the way?"

"Because I don't trust Nadir Shah and his people to be able to pull it off. They're psychopaths, all emotion and fury and no brains."

"And yet you expect them to transport a nuclear device across Mexico's border with the United States, infiltrate the target area undetected, and detonate the bomb successfully?"

Zheng smiled and nodded. "That is why we are providing them with a single device at first. If they prove they are capable, we will release the remaining five to them."

"What's their initial target?"

"That's part of this test. We've left that entirely up to them." He shrugged. "We'll see how effectively they use it."

Maksym looked off into the distance beyond Zheng's shoulder. A wisp of a smile played at the corners of his mouth. "I hope those ragheads are successful." He hesitated a moment then said, "With any luck, their efforts won't kill the Sleeping Dogs, just draw them out en masse so *I* can kill them."

"To paraphrase the German poet Goethe, 'beware of what you wish for,'" Zheng said.

Maksym gave him a puzzled look. "What's that supposed to mean?"

With an inscrutable smile, Zheng said, "The Chinese New Year will be celebrated soon. It is a Yang year, meaning it is good for the creature being celebrated. This time it's the Year of the Dog."

———————

DEAR READER,

If you enjoyed reading *Year of the Dog*, please post a favorable review on Amazon.com, Apple Books, Barnes&Noble/Nook, Goodreads, Kobo or Google Play. Reviews not only help writers succeed at their craft but also provide valuable information for prospective readers. Thank you.

John Wayne Falbey

Special Preview
THE DOGS OF WAR, A SLEEPING DOGS THRILLER

THEY'RE HERE. In America. Thousands of Islamic terrorists committed to a rabid jihad that only ends when they've butchered the last man, woman, and child, or have been blown off the face of the earth themselves. With an incompetent—or worse yet, sympathetic government pretending the threat doesn't exist or is "being contained," the odds of western civilization being snuffed out are growing stronger every day.

Time to prevent this horror is growing ever shorter, as the jihadis rapidly expand their capabilities and build their presence in America and other free world countries by building cells, stockpiling weapons, assembling explosives, and identifying soft targets. In addition, they're targeting police and first responder facilities, military installations, and electrical and communications grids. Meanwhile, the Chinese are solidifying their dominion throughout Asia, and setting their sights on the rest of the globe. The Russian president is intensifying his threat against the free peoples of Europe and beyond. Cyberwarfare is ramping up from Beijing and Moscow to Pyongyang, Tehran, Havana and elsewhere. And AGU—the Alliance for Global Unity is orchestrating it all.

The best hope for survival is the deadliest hunter-killer team the world has ever known—the Sleeping Dogs. But how to reassemble them? Cliff Levell and SAS—the Society of Adam Smith, AGU's counterpart, assigns Brendan Whelan the task of reassembling the men in his old unit. Three are being held in maximum-security prisons, one is battling alcoholism, and another is maniacally obsessed with avenging the murder of his wife and sons. But Levell has a plan—and a prospective new member of the Dogs to be recruited in Australia. Is there enough time?

Other Books by John Wayne Falbey

THE SLEEPING DOGS SERIES: The Far Left has undermined the America of freedom and opportunity as we knew it. Their goal is to destroy our democratic, capitalist system by eradicating the middle class. In its place, they are establishing a New World Order based on radical socialism that consists of them as the elite and absolute rulers over an enormous mass of poor and struggling souls who have no freedom of speech, expression, even thought. But a small group of patriots well-placed in politics, industry, and the military fight back. They bring back a forgotten band of exceptional warriors who purposely have been in hiding for almost twenty years—the Sleeping Dogs special operations unit. The Far Left is about to find out why, as Chaucer noted so long ago, it's a bad idea to wake a sleeping dog.

Sleeping Dogs: The Awakening, a Thriller
Endangered Species, a Sleeping Dogs Thriller
The Year of the Dog, a Sleeping Dogs Thriller
The Dogs of War, a Sleeping Dogs Thriller
A Deadlier Breed, a Sleeping Dogs Thriller
The Devil's Litter, a Sleeping Dogs Thriller
The People's Republic of America, a Sleeping Dogs Thriller

The Quixotics: Three disillusioned special ops veterans of the Vietnam War run guns to anti-Castro forces in Cuba. And find more than they bargained for.

The Taxman Cometh: A rogue IRS agent leads a raid on the wrong house and destroys Finn O'Casey's world. A sympathetic neighbor who is also the leader of organized crime is not who he seems. He and the IRS agent thought O'Casey was a mild-mannered accountant. They thought wrong. O'Casey, a former member of an elite special operations unit, goes dark and joins his warrior comrades to wreak vengeance. The moral: *Be careful who you choose as a victim.*

ALL BOOKS ARE AVAILABLE in digital versions at Amazon/Kindle, Apple Books, Barnes & Noble/Nook, Google Play, Smashwords, and all online booksellers. Available in print versions at Amazon, Barnes & Noble, and your favorite bookstore.

A Note From The Author

MY PERSONAL PHILOSOPHY as a writer of fiction, a teller of tales, is that my first obligation to my readers is to entertain them. A second important duty is to be authentic. In fantasy or science fiction, the author has free rein to shoot from the hip. But with fiction that is based on the world we live in today, places and objects should be accurately described and depicted. This is why I exercise a ratio of 4:1—research to writing. If I describe a weapon, vehicle, or any other object, I want readers who are familiar with them to be satisfied that I nailed the description. Likewise, with locations, I want my readers who have visited those locales to think "that's exactly how I remember it."

The third responsibility of the fiction writer is to educate the reader. Don't glaze their eyes over, but regale them with facts and information that help broaden their knowledge, all within the context of the storylines. One of my undergraduate majors was History. Most people seem to loathe taking history courses because of all the names, dates, and places that have to be memorized for exam purposes. But to me it was a fascinating panorama playing out chronologically on a global stage. I could see the "players" and places in my imagination. That thirst for knowledge about the "world out there" remains as strong as ever. Consequently, when I write, I research to learn about the people and the places that are woven into the storylines. When I read other writers' works, I like to be educated as well as entertained. I try to do the same things in my books.

This novel is a work of fiction and isn't intended to proselytize, praise, or condemn any specific political, religious, economic, or social philosophy. It's just a story intended to entertain. It is fabricated, however, on events occurring in the U.S. and globally, and splashed across today's headlines. It tells the story from the perspectives of various players. Likewise, any resemblance to persons living or dead is purely coincidental. What is not entirely fictional, however, is the theory of genetics explored in the book. It's based on considerable research, but necessarily includes a certain amount of speculation. It is a fact that scientists have determined that those with Western European bloodlines have some Neanderthal DNA. The European Early Modern Humans, or EEMH, from whom all those of European ancestry are descended, interbred with the Neanderthal. These early Homo sapiens ancestors were as large as humans today, and they were more powerful and physically robust. Intriguingly, their brains were one-eighth larger than modern man's. Sound like Whelan and his colleagues?

Also, factually speaking, the tidal wave of illegal immigrants pouring across our border with Mexico does include cadres of well-trained, dedicated jihadis. They have spread across our country in cells. You shouldn't have to guess what their purpose is. Scare tactics on my part? No, for example, the details of this situation, as discussed in Chapter 15, are based on in-depth research not speculation.

Acknowledgments

Throughout school, my English and Language Arts teachers uniformly encouraged me to write. But, like John Lennon famously said about life, I was "busy doing other things." Now, after careers in law, real estate development, and academia (what was I thinking?), I enjoy writing, and work continuously to become better at my craft. But the story isn't about me. There are many people to whom I am especially grateful. Not the least of whom are my readers. I write for you.

A great many people have contributed to the experiences that have shaped me as an individual, and developed the perspectives that influence my writing. I'm grateful to each of them, even the ones who were involved in the not so pleasant experiences. Each of us, after all, is the product of the sum total of our life experiences—good and not so good.

Without doubt, the most important person in my life is my wife, "Annie". She has been my most ardent supporter in this effort. She is the critic, whose opinion I value above all others.

Our son Ryan, an articulate, intelligent young man, has spent many hours proofreading my efforts and offering valuable comments and suggestions, including cover art, layout, and how to maximize the use of social media.

My dad played a major role in my desire to write (as well as my being an Irishman). He encouraged my thirst for adventure stories as a youngster. He also gifted me with an Irishman's appreciation of humor.

At a very early age, my mother taught me to read and took me to the local library, where I was introduced to a vast treasure trove of adventure. She also instilled in me toughness in the face of challenges, and a refusal to settle for second best.

I owe a special thanks to the members of my writers' group—Howard Giordano, Jean Harrington, Jeff Bruce, and Karna Bodman—gifted and oft-published writers every one. In addition to writing, they each are a unique and wonderful combination of editor and beta reader.

My thanks also to Tatiana Villa at Vila Design for her creativity and talent in designing the cover of the book.

Finally, no writer springs—Athena-like—fully formed into the world, and deserving of a place on the best-seller lists. Editors are a necessary intermediary. The Sleeping Dogs series has greatly bene-fitted from the efforts of Caitlin Alexander, Martine Bellen, and Andrea Robb.

Last but not least, my deepest gratitude to the men and women of the United States military and our law enforcement agencies. Your sacrifices keep us safe.

About the Author

John Wayne Falbey writes thrillers set in the contemporary world of international espionage and geopolitical intrigue. His debut novel, *Sleeping Dogs: The Awakening*, has become an international bestseller. Wayne is a native Floridian, transactional attorney, real estate investor and developer, and reformed academic. His wife likes to say, "Wayne has more degrees than a thermometer (four)," including a law degree and a doctorate in business.

IN ADDITION TO PRACTICING LAW and developing real estate, he spent five years in academia, creating and chairing a Master of Science program in real estate development at a graduate school of business in Florida. But writing has always been his first choice.

The author and his Muse

Connect Online

I hope you enjoyed reading *The Year of the Dog* as much as I enjoyed writing it. I invite you to connect with me at:

<u>www.falbeybooks.com</u>

where you can sign up for my occasional newsletter announcing publication dates, signings and appearances, previews of my next novel, and other matters relating to my Sleeping Dogs thrillers and other novels. I also invite you to connect with me through any of the social media below and look forward to hearing from you.

falbeybooks.com
https://www.facebook.com/wayne.falbey
instagram.com/falbeybooks/
falbey@sleepingdogs.biz

www.ingramcontent.com/pod-product-compliance
Lightning Source LLC
Chambersburg PA
CBHW020322040726

47494CB00026B/968